SILENT

PERFECTLY IMPERFECT SERIES

Lies

NEVA ALTAJ

Editing by Susan Stradiotto and Andie Edwards of Beyond The Proof
(www.susanstradiotto.com)
(www.beyondtheproof.ca)

Proofreading by Yvette Rebello (yreditor.com)

Manuscript critique by Anka Lesko (www.amlediting.com)

Sensitivity read by Milica (Instagram @milicasbookshelf)

Stylistic editing by Anna Corbeaux
(www.corbeauxeditorialservices.com)

Cover design by Deranged Doctor
(www.derangeddoctordesign.com)

Perfectly Imperfect
Reading Order & Tropes

1. Painted Scars (Nina & Roman)

Tropes: disabled hero, fake marriage, age gap, opposites attract, possessive/jealous hero

2. Broken Whispers (Bianca & Mikhail)

Tropes: scarred/disabled hero, mute heroine, arranged marriage, age gap, beauty and the beast, OTT possessive/jealous hero

3. Hidden Truths (Angelina & Sergei)

Tropes: age gap, broken hero, only she can calm him down, who did this to you

4. Ruined Secrets (Isabella & Luca)

Tropes: arranged marriage, age gap, OTT possessive/jealous hero, amnesia

5. Stolen Touches (Milene & Salvatore)

Tropes: arranged marriage, disabled hero, age gap, emotionless hero, OTT possessive/jealous hero

6. Fractured Souls (Asya & Pavel)

Tropes: he helps her heal, age gap, who did this to you, possessive/jealous hero, he thinks he's not good enough for her

7. Burned Dreams (Ravenna & Alessandro)

Tropes: bodyguard, forbidden love, revenge, enemies to lovers, age gap, who did this to you, possessive/jealous hero

8. Silent Lies (Sienna & Drago)

Tropes: deaf hero, arranged marriage, age gap, grumpy-sunshine, opposites attract, super OTT possessive/jealous hero

9. Darkest Sins (Nera & Kai)

Tropes: grumpy-sunshine, opposites attract, age-gap, stalker hero, only she can calm him down

Author's Note

One of the main characters in this novel suffers from high-frequency hearing loss. When listening to people speak, a person with this condition may struggle to hear certain consonants such as S, H, or F, which are spoken at a higher pitch. As a result, speech may sound muffled, especially when using the telephone, watching television, or when emersed in noisy environments. People with this type of hearing loss often say they feel like they can *hear* the sound of speech, but do not *understand* the actual words being spoken. They may also find it harder to hear women's and children's voices, as well as other high-pitched sounds (for example, birds singing, beeping of electronic devices). In addition, people with high-frequency hearing loss are often more sensitive to loud noises than people without the condition. Exposure to loud sounds can frequently cause discomfort or pain.

Trigger Warning

Please be aware that this book contains content some readers may find disturbing, such as mentions of an immediate family member's death, as well as graphic descriptions of violence, torture, and gore.

SILENT

PERFECTLY IMPERFECT SERIES

Lies

prologue

Twenty years ago, Serbia
(Drago, 17 years old)

"IT'S THE BLONDE ONE, YOU IDIOT," I MUMBLE AND reach for the bottle of beer on the coffee table.

I don't know why I keep watching these predictable thrillers. Maybe they keep my mind off the shit I don't want to think about. Like, how I need to tell my old man that I failed the third year of secondary school. Again. Or how my mom will lose it in the morning when she realizes I crashed my bike. It's not like I can hide the fact that both my right arm and cheek are scraped raw. It would have been nice if the road rash at least erased the ink fucking Adam screwed up on again. I never should have let him practice on me. It'll take two months for the crap he tattooed on my forearm to heal enough to be covered up. And, hopefully, with something that doesn't fucking sucks. This shit looks more like a donkey than the reaper I told him to do.

Taking another swig from the bottle, I look over at the clock beside the TV. Three in the morning. I should go upstairs and sleep. I promised the girls I would take them to the zoo tomorrow. Dina will probably freak out and cry when she sees my face. Tara will just try to poke the mangled flesh.

I turn off the TV and toss the remote onto the coffee table. I'm halfway across the room when I'm thrown back against the far wall as an earsplitting boom engulfs me. Pain explodes through my right side.

Everything goes black.

My eyes snap open, but I can't make anything out at first. My vision is blurry. There is a sharp pain at the back of my head and on my side. It takes me a moment to realize I'm sprawled on the floor, but when I try to sit up, another jolt of pain shoots through my right shoulder and down my arm. I grit my teeth and press my left hand on the wall, somehow managing to stand. A wave of dizziness hits me and I pause, trying to make the room stop spinning around me. My vision clears a little, but I can still barely see shit. The air is murky, and the only source of light streams in behind me. Something wet slides down the side of my neck, just below my ear. I swipe it away and see blood on my fingers. What the fuck?

I'm still facing the wall, trying to get my bearings when the smell of smoke invades my nostrils. Slowly, I turn around and immediately take an involuntary step back. On the opposite side of the house, beyond the living room and the stairs leading to the upstairs bedrooms, the door to my parents' room hangs askew on its hinges. Part of the outside wall is missing, and the glow from the streetlight illuminates debris piled on the bed and all around the floor. Dust hangs in the air.

"Mom! Dad!" I vault over the overturned furniture, but I can't hear my own voice. I can't hear anything.

My eyes are glued to the fragmented wall piled atop the bed where my parents were sleeping as I try to move the couch out of the way with my one functional arm. The other is useless and numb. I think my shoulder dislocated when the blast threw me against the wall.

The space is filling up with smoke, and it's getting harder to breathe, but I don't see fire anywhere. Frantically, I turn around and catch sight of an orange glow beyond the kitchen threshold. Fear grips me as I shift my gaze to the upper floor, to the door closest to the landing. My sisters' bedroom. My eyes dart between the upstairs door and the wreckage of my parents' room, while my heart beats like crazy. Should I go help Mom and Dad first, or get the girls? An acid taste fills my throat as I take in the magnitude of the destruction on the ground floor. There is no way anyone could have survived that. With one last look at my parents' room, I push down the bile, hurdle the ruined couch and run for the stairs.

When I reach the top step, I'm seized in a fit of coughing. I bury my nose and mouth in the crook of my arm, trying to keep the smoke out of my throat and lungs, and kick the door open.

"Tara!" I shout as I stumble and grab my crying sister off the bed to my left. I shift her to my hip, then turn to find Dina, Tara's twin, standing in the corner of the room. Her eyes are wide and panicked, staring at me. I try reaching for her, but I can't make my right arm move.

"Take my hand. We need to get out," I yell, still unable to hear my words.

Dina shakes her head and plasters her back to the wall. Tara is wailing and thrashing in my hold.

"Fucking now, Dina!" I roar and fall into another coughing fit. "Fuck!" I wheeze.

I try moving my right arm again and fail. The smoke is getting thicker. We have to get out of here, but I can't carry both of my sisters with one arm. Fear and helplessness are suffocating me more than the smoke itself. I'll have to take them out one by one. I need to pick. How the fuck can I choose which sister to save first?

Tara is hysterical, and I've already got her. She'll have to be first.

"I'm taking Tara outside, and I'm coming right back," I yell, looking at Dina's frightened face. She seems so much younger than her four years when she's scared. "Just two minutes, Dina sugar. Don't move."

Throwing a pleading glance at her to make her understand, I turn around and run out of the room.

I don't know how I'm managing to descend the stairs. The smoke stings my eyes, making it almost unbearable to look where I'm going, and I trip several times before I reach the front door.

Outside, neighbors stand in our driveway, gaping at the house. There are flickering red lights visible down the street, getting closer. It's probably the fire department or an ambulance. They will be here any moment, but I can't wait. I thrust crying Tara into the arms of the closest man and dash back into the burning house.

The smoke is so thick that I'm forced to half run, half crawl across the living room. My eyes water and my lungs scream for air. I reach the stairs just as the edge of the rug closest to the kitchen catches on fire. The flames are spreading fast and moving toward the stairway.

I finally make it back up to the girls' bedroom, my eyes straining to see my sister. She's not where I left her, so I lunge toward the bed. Dina is bundled up, hiding under the covers.

"I'm here, sugar." I throw the duvet to the side, grab Dina around her waist, and lift her onto my hip.

Going back toward the front door is out of the question. There's too much smoke. I could try to get us out through the window—it's not too high—but Dad bolted it shut last month because Tara kept opening it, and he was afraid she'd fall out. We have to reach my room at the other end of the hall and use the balcony there.

"Hold on to me!" I can't assess how loud I'm speaking, so I shout just in case. "We're getting out!"

Dina wraps her arms around my neck, clinging to me as her small body trembles in my arms. I step into the hallway, then quickly retreat. The fire has spread upstairs and the heat is cutting off the path to my room. Down the stairs is the only way out.

"It's going to be okay." I place a kiss on my sister's hair. My heart beats so fast it feels like it will burst out of my chest. "It's going to be okay."

Tightening my hold on her, I take a deep breath and step into the hallway again.

I glance over the railing to the lower level of the house where the flames are licking at the kitchen cupboards and crawling up the curtains. The fire has spread to the stairs, its tendrils are reaching between the balusters. I can't decide what's worse: the heat or the smoke. Holding my breath, I sprint down the stairs as fast as I can. The front door is gaping open, and the fire truck has pulled to a stop, firemen pouring out of it. I'm halfway to the entrance when another explosion erupts to my right, the blast throwing me and Dina onto the floor.

It's so hot that it feels like my skin is melting. My sister is lying sprawled a few feet away, wheezing and fighting for breath. I crawl over and pull her to me, then wrap my body around hers to shield her from the flames.

"It's okay, baby. Help is coming," I say next to her ear, just before the darkness swallows me.

Sienna

Fifteen years ago, New York
(Sienna, 5 years old)

I throw myself onto the couch, cross my arms, and huff. "You promised, Mama! It's Luna's sixth birthday party! I'm her best friend. We have to go."

Mama sighs and sits next to me. "I'm so sorry, Sienna. The boss scheduled both me and your dad for this Saturday."

"You and Papa always work." I scowl, pouting my lips.

"Sienna, honey, you know that's not true." She rubs my arm.

I jerk away from her, mumbling, "If you love me, you'll take us. You promised! Papa says keeping promises is the most important thing in the *whole* world."

Mama throws a look at my father, who's standing by the bookshelf. "Edoardo and Sara are working at the casino tonight. Maybe we could ask them to switch? We could work tonight, and they can cover for us on Saturday."

I look up at Papa with wide eyes. *Please say yes!*

"Arturo? Can you take them?" Papa throws over his shoulder to my brother who's sitting in the recliner by the window, fumbling with his phone.

"Nope. I have to work on Saturday," he shakes his head. "But I can watch the pests tonight."

I snort. Arturo has been so busy and serious since he started working for the don.

My father lets out a sigh and pins me with his gaze. "Is it really so important that we both must go? I can try to arrange something so Mama can take you."

"Yes, it's important. Asya!" I wait until my sister looks up from whatever she's drawing at the coffee table, then yell, "Say something!"

She just shrugs.

"See, Asya wants you both to go, too. Please, Papa. We never get to go anywhere together. There'll be clowns! I will never ask for anything ever again."

Papa pushes away from the bookshelf. "Oh, all right. I'm going to call Edoardo."

I squeal in delight and jump into his arms. "Yes! Thank you!"

"As if I could say no to you, baby girl. I love you too much." He places a kiss on the top of my head. "Off to the kitchen, you two. Arturo will get your dinner since Mama and I have to get ready for work."

The doorbell pulls me out of my sleep. I squint at the darkness. Did I dream it?

The bell rings again.

I slide off my bed and tiptoe toward the balcony to look down at the front porch. Two men in suits are speaking to Arturo. Their voices are muffled, so I can't hear what they are saying, nor can I see my brother's face from this angle, but his body suddenly goes ramrod straight. He buries his hands in his hair, tugging on it, then turns toward the open front door and smashes his fist into it. The men say something else and leave, getting into a black car parked on our driveway. When I look back down, Arturo is sitting on the top step, gripping his hair with his bloody hand.

I run back to my bed and get under the blanket, but I'm not sleepy. Who were those men, and why was my brother acting that way? Arturo never hits anything.

I'm staring at the ceiling when I hear someone climbing the stairs and crossing the hallway. A moment later, the sound of our bedroom door opening fills the silence of the night. I sit up in bed and find Arturo standing at the threshold, gripping the doorframe.

"Let's wake Asya up," he says. "I need to tell you both something."

His voice sounds strange. It's not teasing like it usually is when he talks to Asya and me.

After flicking the light switch by the door, Arturo takes a seat on the side of my sister's bed. He looks different from when he tucked us in earlier. His face is pale, and there are dark circles under his eyes. Arturo isn't typically a cheerful person. Papa always says that my brother is too old for his years, whatever that means, but he's always strong. Now, he just looks sad. Lightly, he shakes Asya's shoulder until she sits up in bed, then he taps the spot on his other side.

I go and sit next to him, keeping my gaze glued to his the entire time. A lump formed in my throat when I saw him hit the door outside, but now, I feel like I'm going to throw up. He's going to tell us something bad.

"Something happened tonight. At the casino." He takes my hand into one of his and Asya's in the other, but he doesn't look at either of us. "I need you two to be brave."

"What happened?" Asya asks through her yawn. "Where's Mama?"

"There was . . . a shooting." He squeezes our hands. "A lot of people got hurt."

I yank my hand out of his. We never talk about shootings or guns in our house. Papa doesn't allow it.

"Where are Mama and Pap—?" I sob.

Arturo wraps his arm around me, pulling me to him. I can hear Asya crying as she snuggles into his other side.

"They are gone," Arturo chokes out. "Mama and Papa are gone."

"You are lying! Why are you lying?" I cry out as tears pour down my face, but I know he's not. Arturo never lies.

CHAPTER
one

 Sienna

Present

I APPROACH THE BIG ORNATE DOOR AND KNOCK TWICE.
"Enter," a male voice says from the other side.

I walk inside the office belonging to the boss of the New York Cosa Nostra Family, my green heels clicking on the polished floor as I approach.

"You wanted to see me, Don Ajello," I say in my sweetest voice.

Salvatore Ajello's eyes drift from my grass-green dress to the top of my head and stop on my bun. Feathers are sticking out of it, the same color as my dress. It took me months to find the exact shade.

"Have a seat, Sienna." He nods at the chair opposite him.

I drop into the chair and smooth out my dress, wondering why he called me. It's not every day that someone as meaningless as me, as far as the Cosa Nostra hierarchy is concerned, gets invited to a private meeting with the don.

Ajello leans back and regards me. There's something

disturbing in his gaze, and it makes me feel like I'm being dissected.

"Your sister got married a while back," he says. "You two were very close."

"We *are* close, yes."

"But she's in Chicago now. It must be hard for you."

"Asya loves it there, and I'm happy for her." I grin, trying to keep my voice casual. He really knows how to pick the nerve to poke.

"It's important to make sure one's family is happy. And what about Arturo?"

I narrow my eyes at him. Is there a point to this conversation? "What about him?"

"Your brother is thirty-six, Sienna. He'll probably marry soon. Have his own family. What will you do when that happens? Will you stay with him and be a third wheel?"

Every word he says buries itself like a dagger into my chest. I already feel bad for spending my days doing nothing but hanging out with my friends or reading while Arturo works the entire time. Months ago, I promised myself I'd find a business program to attend so I could finally start doing something with my life, but I still haven't done anything about it.

"I would never stand in the way of my brother's happiness," I say. "When that happens, I'll probably move out. Find a job."

"Why didn't you go to college? Is that still in your plans?"

"I'm not college material, Don Ajello."

"No? And yet, you speak several languages. Arturo told me you learned them all on your own."

"Yes. Italian. English, obviously. Spanish and Portuguese. And I have some knowledge of Russian and Japanese." Does he need a translator for something?

"How long would it take you to learn a new language?" he asks.

"Um, well. It depends. Just speaking or writing as well?"

"Good enough that you can understand what's being said. No writing."

I think about it for a moment. "Three months. Maybe four. Depending on the language."

Ajello nods while his piercing eyes bore into mine. "Perfect. Let's arrange the wedding, then."

"Oh? And who's getting married?"

"You are, Sienna."

I blink twice, wondering if I heard him correctly. Ajello is sitting back, relaxed in his chair. His arms are crossed over his chest as he regards me.

"You wouldn't want to end up alone, would you?" he says with his head tilted to the side.

This bastard. It's as if he can see inside my soul, find the worst of the fears that fester there, and pull them out against my will.

My fingers tighten on the skirt of my dress. "No."

"Then a marriage is a perfect solution."

"Yes, it would seem so." I make myself smile.

"I'm glad we agree on this. I already have someone in mind for you. For the past few years, I've been trying to plant someone inside his organization. This is a great opportunity."

"You need me to spy on my future husband?"

"Yes. You'll be doing a huge service to the Family."

"He's not from Cosa Nostra?"

"No. He's a business associate." Ajello cocks his head. "Your brother won't be happy when I tell him. I need you to convince Arturo that you're okay with this marriage."

"What if he doesn't believe me?"

"Arturo is my underboss. I would even go so far as to call him . . . a friend. I don't have many friends, Sienna, so I'd prefer not to have to kill him for disagreeing with my plans. Make sure he believes you."

"I'll try my best." I force another smile. "Is that all?"

Ajello raises an eyebrow. "You didn't ask who you'll be marrying."

"I guess it doesn't matter."

"Perfect. I'll make the arrangements. You can go."

He stops me as I'm heading toward the door.

"One more thing, Sienna."

I turn around. "Yes?"

"Start learning Serbian. You have three months."

When I exit Ajello's building, I stand in the middle of the sidewalk as people rush by. Parts of various conversations reach me. Laughter. An angry mother calling for her child. The noise washes over me, and it's like I entered a beehive, its walls closing in on me. I want to leave, but I can't make my legs move. Someone bumps me with their elbow, making me stumble to the side, but I'm still stunned and barely register the impact.

Am I really going to marry a man I've never met? I could refuse, but in Cosa Nostra, the don's word is the law, and going against his orders is akin to treason. I could tell Arturo the truth, and he might be able to convince Ajello to drop the idea. My brother saved his life about a decade ago, so I highly doubt the don would actually kill him. But the thing is, Ajello is right. My brother did put his life on hold when our parents were killed. I need to leave.

A shudder passes through my body just thinking about it.

I've never lived alone, and I don't think I can handle it. It's already too lonely with Asya gone and Arturo being away so much for work, so I usually spend time during the day hanging out at Luna's. But the nights are hard.

After what happened when Asya was kidnapped, I promised my brother that I would never take sleeping pills again.

12

But I have considered it. Not to hurt myself; I just can't sleep in an empty house.

If I ask Arturo to stay home more, I'm sure he'll say yes, but I would never do that. He has enough of his own shit to deal with and doesn't need my crap on top of it. My brother's social life has been nonexistent for fifteen years. Outside of work, his sole focus has been on raising Asya and me. He hasn't even brought a woman to our house, ever, and I'm afraid he won't as long as I'm there. It's as if somewhere down the line, he forgot that he's not our parent. I'm not a child anymore and I can't let this continue. Arturo needs to live his own life.

But the mere idea of living alone, with no one to talk to, is sending me into a full-blown panic. I can't do that. I can never do that. If marrying a stranger is the only way not to end up on my own, I'm going to take it. I just need to convince Arturo that it was my idea. He would never allow me to be married off simply because the don ordered it.

"Ms. DeVille."

I look to the right and see my driver standing by the car, holding the door open for me. I cross the distance in silence and slide in the back.

"Is everything okay, Ms. DeVille?" the driver asks as he gets behind the wheel.

"Of course." I give him a beaming smile. "Head to the mall, please. I hear there are some big sales today."

As the car pulls onto the street, I fish the phone out of my purse and dial my brother. It rings several times and goes to voicemail. He's probably in a meeting again.

"Hey, Arturo," I chirp after the beep. "I know you're busy, but I wanted to tell you the news. After Asya got married, it got me thinking about my life, so I went to see the don this morning and asked him if he could arrange a marriage for me. He said yes!" I giggle. "I hope it'll be a lawyer. Or some CEO. Anyway, just wanted to let you know. I'm heading to the mall right now. There's this amazing multicolored chiffon dress I saw online. It's pleated and the shades just blend together so beautifully! It looks like it was made just for me. Love you!"

I throw the phone back into my purse, quickly brush a stray tear off my cheek, and focus my gaze on the street beyond the window.

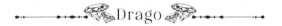

Drago

I observe the man sitting in a puddle of blood at my feet. The left side of his face is so swollen, it looks like it'll burst any second. I grab him around the neck and lift, pressing his back to the wall.

"So, you just happened to blurt out sensitive info while our competition was present?" I ask.

The man whines and wraps his hands around my wrist, trying to free himself. I slam him against the wall and lean close to his face.

"Do you know what I do to traitors, Henry?"

The man's eyes go wide as saucers and he shivers. A moment later, the stench of urine fills the air.

"I see that you do." I smile and reach for the knife lying on the nearby table.

When I press the tip of the blade to Henry's abdomen, right above his navel, he starts thrashing around, so I put more force into my hold. His face gets redder as he fights for air. Keeping my grip on his neck, I drag the knife straight up, slowly. Blood trickles down Henry's naked torso as he screams in agony. When I reach his collarbone, I move the tip of the knife below his left nipple and repeat my efforts, only, this time, slicing horizontally toward his right side. The man chokes a few more times and his body goes limp. His glazed-over eyes stare blankly at me. I finish the shape I'm carving into his front, clean the blade on the leg of his pants, and let his body fall to the floor.

"Bolt him to the wall," I say to the two men standing off to the side and then I turn toward Filip—my second-in-command—who's lounging on the couch. "What did Ajello want?"

"He wants to meet," Filip says. "He has a business proposition for you."

I grab the kitchen towel off the counter and wipe the blood off my hands. "Call him back. Tell him he can shove his proposition up his ass. We're done doing business with Cosa Nostra, as I've already told Arturo countless times."

"Now's not the time to ruffle the don's feathers, Drago." Filip leans forward. "Especially with the new plan we've set in place. Bogdan will retaliate the moment he finds out you've decided to push him out of the arms business. We can't take on the Romanians and the Italians at the same time."

"I doubt that Ajello would give a fuck about our plans. He doesn't work with Bogdan anymore, so I don't see why he would butt into our business. As for his feathers, I wouldn't worry too much about them."

"Everything that happens in New York is Ajello's business. If he thinks the war between us and the Romanians might have even the slightest impact on his projects, he'll do something about it. I actually find it interesting that he picked this exact moment to try reestablishing a collaboration between us."

"You think he found out about the arms deal we're negotiating?"

"He probably knows we're into something, but I don't think he's aware of the details. Then again, you never know with Salvatore Ajello."

"Fucking perfect." I throw the bloody rag on the table.

"Call Ajello. Tell him I'll be out of town for the next couple of months, but I'll think about his request. We can talk when I get back."

"And will you? Think about it?"

I grab my jacket and helmet off the chair and head toward the front door. "No."

Chapter

Two

Sienna

Two months later

I'M LYING ON MY BED, PLAYING A DISNEY MOVIE THAT'S been dubbed in Serbian on my laptop when an email notification shows up at the bottom of the screen. It's probably a newsletter from one of my fashion magazines. I close the pop-up window and continue watching.

I prefer learning languages at my own pace, but since I'm on a deadline, I signed up for an online course, as well. It took me five weeks of daily sessions with a virtual tutor to cover the basics. The Serbian language is very similar to Russian, which I understand on an intermediate level, and that helped somewhat. Thank God I only need to be proficient in speaking it and don't have to know how to write it, because that would take me months. For the past three weeks, I've been focusing on listening. I started with Serbian movies and shows, but there's a lot of slang in those, so they can be hard to follow. I found a Serbian channel online last week, but it's mostly news and politics. It was so boring that I fell asleep watching it yesterday.

Today, I've decided to try something else. *The Little Mermaid* seemed like a nice choice.

The ringing phone on my nightstand pulls my attention. It's the don.

"Don Ajello. What can I—"

"Did you see the email I sent you?"

"Just a second." I exit the movie and flip over to the email tab. There's a message in my inbox, but there is no text, just some attachments. I open the first one. It's a slightly blurry photo of a man entering a building. Only a part of his profile is visible. He's dressed in a leather jacket and dark jeans. I zoom in on the image, trying to make out something more than the man's dark hair and short stubble that is only just visible, but the thing is too grainy.

"Um, okay," I say. "And this is . . .?"

"That's your future husband. Drago Popov. The head of the Serbian crime organization."

"Oh . . . so he's not a lawyer."

"No, Sienna. He's most certainly not a lawyer. For years, Popov's moved more than half of our drugs to Europe, but after the attack on his club by Rocco Pisanno two years ago, Popov cut all ties with Cosa Nostra. Since then, the distributors we've used have been neither as fast nor as reliable as Popov. I want him back in the picture."

"Okay," I mumble. "So, I'm . . . an incentive to seal the deal? You don't need me to spy on him?"

"Of course I do. That's the main reason why I've chosen you for this marriage." The sound of shuffled papers comes across the line. "Most of the underground deals that are made in this city are negotiated at Popov's club, Naos. It's considered neutral territory, suitable for meetings concerning sensitive matters. I need someone reliable on the inside who can gather information on Popov's business and pass it on to me. How's your Serbian now?"

"Well, I can watch *The Little Mermaid* without subtitles." I smile.

"A little what?"

"Mermaid. The movie." He's never heard of *The Little Mermaid*? "Unless a person is speaking too fast or using too much slang, I can understand most of it."

"Good. We'll be moving forward with the wedding sooner than anticipated."

"What? Why?"

"Popov closed a big deal last week, but no one knows what it is. I need to know about it, and I want to know now."

Wow. Controlling much?

"I'm heading to meet him," he continues, "to let him know about the arrangement."

"He doesn't know? What if he says no?"

"Then he's going to die," Ajello barks. "Nino will come to get you at ten. He'll be taking you to Naos."

"Peachy. I'll take Luna with me. And what—"

The line goes dead. I glance at the phone screen. It took me some time to adjust to the way Salvatore Ajello handles phone calls.

I shake my head and focus on the email again, going through the rest of the images, but they seem to be more of the same. Most are out of focus, probably taken with a phone camera in low light or while in motion. There's only one clear photo. It shows Popov standing in a hotel lobby, maybe, his arm wrapped around the waist of a blond haired woman. He's turned away from the camera, so his face is still not visible. At his side, the woman is focused on him. She looks like a movie star, dressed in a tight white dress, platinum blonde hair falling straight down her back nearly to her waist.

If that's his type, he's going to be rather disappointed. That woman has almost a foot on me. I also recently cut my hair, so it barely reaches the middle of my back, and I've never dyed it.

I rather like its dark-brown hue, as plain as it is. It works better with my wardrobe anyway. I check the photos one more time in case I missed one where I could see his face, but nope. I guess I'll have to wait for tonight to find out what my future husband looks like.

I grab my phone again and dial my best friend.

"Luna bella," I chirp. "Do you feel like dancing tonight?"

Drago

I pick up my whiskey and lean back, contemplating the man sitting across from me in my booth.

During the years that I've cooperated with the Italians, I interacted with Arturo, Ajello's underboss. Until the shitshow orchestrated by Rocco Pisano sent our working relationship straight to hell. It was good money, but I have no intention of dealing with the people who turned on me. I thought I was very clear in my message to Arturo—we're done. It looks like I need to repeat myself to the don as well.

"I'm not interested in renewing our collaboration, Ajello."

"Do you have another prospective business in your plans? Because I know for sure no one can supply the quantity and quality you used to get from us."

"The thing is, I don't need your drugs. My commerce in diamonds brings in triple the amount moving cocaine ever did." I shrug.

"It's not about the money. There's too much bad blood between us, Mr. Popov. I can't let you operate in my city unless the feud between our Families is settled."

"Settled?" I take a sip of my drink and regard him. "And how do you plan we do that?"

"Marriage. Specifically, between you and a Cosa Nostra woman."

Did he forget that his capo shot at me and my men while we were conducting a business meeting, and then sent his mercenaries to attack my club? It doesn't matter that those mercenaries weren't members of Cosa Nostra. Or that my men killed all three of them. It doesn't even matter that Rocco Pisano is dead.

"We lost a man in that clusterfuck two years ago. It's not something that can be settled by me marrying a cousin of one of your soldiers, Ajello."

The don places his arms on the back of the sofa, observing me with a calculated look in his eyes. "I'm offering Arturo DeVille's sister for the matrimony."

I tilt my head to the side, considering. A marriage to the sister of the Cosa Nostra underboss is a very lucrative business opportunity. In fact, it seems too good to be true.

"And what is Arturo's view on that idea?" I ask.

"I'll make sure he sees the benefits."

"So, he's against it. What about his sister? Doesn't she have aspirations to marry within the Family?"

"Sienna is a free spirit. She said she's open to new experiences."

"Is she now?" I take another sip of my drink, wondering what's behind this proposition. Because something certainly is. "How old is she?"

"Just turned twenty."

I raise an eyebrow. "Are you screwing with me, Ajello?"

"I'm not . . . *screwing* with you, Mr. Popov. Do you have a specific age requirement for a woman you'd marry?"

"You could say so." I can't help but shake my head. Italians and their arranged marriages.

"Sienna and her friend will be coming here tonight with

my chief of security. Make sure they're let in." Salvatore Ajello stands. "Let me know your decision by morning."

I watch the Cosa Nostra don leave, wondering if I should tell him right away that I have no intention of marrying a woman nearly half my age. Good business opportunity or not.

Filip takes the seat that Ajello just vacated and motions with his head toward the club's exit. "What did the Italian want?"

"To settle the feud between us. He wants us back handling the distribution of his drugs. And he offered Arturo DeVille's sister to me in marriage to close the deal."

Filip's eyes widen. "You're going to accept?"

"No."

"Why not? The drug supply is seriously low, and Ajello has the best product. Also, the familial connection to the Cosa Nostra will give us a much better negotiation position with the Russian Bratva."

"The girl is twenty. I'm not marrying a spoiled, barely out of her teens, Cosa Nostra princess."

The sounds of whatever pop hit fill the room from the overhead speakers. The music isn't loud because the volume won't be turned up until the club opens its doors for the night. However, it's still enough to mess with my already bad hearing, so I have to focus on Filip's mouth and read his lips.

". . . and who the fuck cares?" he says. "Bring the girl home, give her a credit card, and tell her there's no limit. She'll spend her days on shopping sprees and visits to beauty salons. With your work schedule, you'll probably hardly ever see her."

"I would rather never see her." I shake my head. "Do you recall Tara at twenty? The screaming matches? How she locked herself in her room when I wouldn't give her the money for a new car until she earned it? I'm too old to go through all that crap again, with a *wife*."

"Sacrifices must be made for the sake of business." Filip

leans forward. "Italians take family ties very seriously, Drago. A marriage to Arturo's sister will ensure Cosa Nostra won't meddle in our arms business. You shouldn't let this opportunity pass."

I squeeze the bridge of my nose. Am I seriously considering marrying a girl young enough to be my daughter? Our gemstone business and other side ventures already generate significant income. With the arms deal in the picture as well, we'll be damn close to having more money than we can launder through the club. Dipping back into drug transport will only cause more complications. But Filip is right. I can't let this opportunity pass, and it has nothing to do with the money. Work has been the only thing that keeps me going. The more there is, the easier it's to get through the day. Saying "no" to a prospective opportunity is out of the question.

"All right." I sigh. "The girl is coming here tonight with a friend. Nino Gambini will be with them. Tell the men at the door to let them in and make sure they're seated over there." I point at the booth on the opposite side of the room. The one in my direct line of sight.

Filip follows the direction of my finger, then clears his throat. "We have some IT mogul coming in. He booked that booth four months in advance."

"Find him another," I say and wave to the waiter. "I want to check this girl out before I decide if she's worth the trouble."

CHAPTER Three

"Wow." My gaze sweeps the circular room as I take in the amazing sight before me.

The semi-private booths nearly surround the dance floor at the center of the luxurious space. Frosted glass walls set within intricate iron frames separate each booth. The inner sanctum consists of a cozy seating area, including a leather sofa and two matching armchairs around a low, glass-top table. Just to the side of each glass divider, dressed in a pristine white shirt and black pants, stands a server who is ready to fulfill whatever order is made of them at even the slightest wave from the patrons occupying their assigned booths. On the far side of the room is a huge half-round bar with several bartenders tending to the customers gathered along its length. A dozen or so couples are on the dance floor, swaying to a slow tune.

The thing I find strange is that there are fewer than a hundred people here. I don't frequent clubs often because, until last year, Arturo only let me visit places run by Cosa Nostra members, and none of them owned an actual club. My brother has only recently released his reins on me, and only because

I told him I was going to fucking flip if he continued his heli-copter parenting.

"I thought it would be bigger," I mumble.

"With a price tag of fifteen grand per booth a night, you can't expect to have hundreds of people," Nino says as he ush-ers Luna and me after the host who leads us to the last booth on the left-hand side. The only one that's vacant at the moment.

As we walk, I cast another look around the space and run through some quick calculations in my head. Twelve booths, fifteen grand each. That's one hundred and eighty thousand per night. If they are open five nights a week, fifty-two weeks a year, it comes to forty-six point eight million a year. Holy cow!

"So, you're on a mission? Dazzle and leave no man behind kind of thing?" Luna nods at my outfit and laughs, distracting me from my math.

"What? I thought this was tame." I shrug and take a seat on the plush white sofa. Nino lowers himself to the armchair on the left while Luna sits next to me.

"That's a few thousand gold sequins too many to be con-sidered tame, Sienna," she says with a snort. "At least it's not fluorescent green, or something like that."

"I would never put on a green jumpsuit. It would make me look like a grasshopper."

"Thank God for small favors." Luna rolls her eyes.

"But I did get a yellow faux fur jacket last week." I grin just thinking about it. "It's a showstopper."

She arches an eloquent eyebrow at me. "Don't you dare to come anywhere with me while wearing that thing. I still cringe at the thought of you turning up at Valeria's birthday party in that red feathered dress."

"Life's too short to wear boring clothes." I laugh and lean back to observe the crowd.

Luna doesn't understand. No one does. People see my crazy outfits and wide smiles and assume that I must be a super happy person without even the tiniest trouble in the world. And I always make sure to assure them of their convictions.

When my parents died, I didn't want to talk to anyone, but everyone kept asking if I was okay. Arturo. Our aunt, who came to stay with us for a short time afterward. The neighbors. Even Asya. I wasn't okay. How could I be all right when I woke up every morning knowing that it was my fault our mom and dad had died? If I hadn't insisted on them taking us to the party, they wouldn't have gone to work that night. And every time someone asked how I was doing, they reminded me of that fact. I just wanted to be left alone, but everyone kept prodding me until I couldn't take it anymore. So I started pretending that I was okay. I joked and laughed and acted as if everything was fucking perfect. And people finally stopped asking questions.

Over the years, I somehow slid into that persona I created. I shoved aside the things that troubled me, burying them deep inside, never letting them come out. Problems. Fears. Insecurities. Everything got nicely tucked away. If I don't think about the problems, they disappear. I liked that much better than the alternative, but since my sister left to live in Chicago with her husband, I've been feeling so . . . lost. Like a passenger who got left behind, standing alone on an abandoned train platform, watching the last train disappear beyond the horizon.

I don't understand why I feel that way. My brother and sister love me, I know that. They would do anything for me. And still, I never could make myself open up to them because of an irrational fear that they would stop loving me if they realized I'm not all sunshine and rainbows.

"Hey!" Luna nudges me with her elbow. "You okay?"

I blink away my thoughts and laugh. "Of course. Why wouldn't I be? Oh, have I told you about the new story I'm writing?"

"The one about the mail-order bride?"

"Nope. I'm in a shifter romance phase currently. Listen . . ."

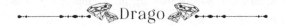Drago

I watch the trio in the booth directly across from mine. The don's chief of security, Nino, sits with his arm thrown over the armchair's back, looking bored as hell. I've met him a few times, but we never talked long enough for me to develop a specific impression. My eyes shift, stopping at the two girls sitting on the sofa in front of Nino, snickering. One of them is wearing a black cocktail dress and has her blonde hair loose, every single strand smooth and in its place. Sophisticated. Classy. That's probably the underboss's sister. She definitely looks the part. I should be focusing on her, but my eyes are drawn toward the girl on the blonde's right.

I noticed her the moment she entered the club, as did the rest of the crowd, men in particular. It's hard to miss a woman wearing a shimmering gold jumpsuit that catches the light every time she moves. It molds to her perfect little body and ties around the neck, leaving her back and shoulders bare. It's ridiculous and absolutely inappropriate for the strict dress code at Naos. If she wasn't with Arturo's sister, my men at the entrance wouldn't have let her in.

I move my gaze from the deep V-neck on the front of the golden monstrosity to her pixie-like face. Sharp cheekbones. A tiny pert nose. Delectable mouth, currently widened into a smile as she says something next to her friend's ear. I'm too far away to read her lips, so I leave my booth and cross behind the bar, passing the bartenders busy pouring drinks. There's a particular spot in the shadows I like, just next to the big pillar that hides the electrical wires within. I lean my shoulder on the wall and focus on the sparkling girl's lips.

"They are fated mates, but he rejects her for another woman.

She decides to run away from the pack. However, she can't shift into her wolf form, so . . ."

I raise an eyebrow. Pack? Shift into a wolf? Even with dimmed lighting in the club, the booth is amply illuminated by the lamp next to the sofa, so I'm pretty sure I've read her lips accurately. The sparkling girl reaches to sweep away a strand of dark-brown hair that's fallen onto her face and tucks it behind her ear. The mass of her locks is weaved into two messy French braids, starting at the crown and running down the sides of her head. Each braid is decorated with what looks like a series of small gold rings. With all the women around in gowns or cocktail dresses, their hair in perfect classy styles, she looks completely out of place. Maybe that's the reason why I can't stop looking at her.

A hand taps me on the shoulder. I turn around to find Filip standing behind me, looking in the same direction I was. "So? What do you think? Not exactly your type."

I throw a quick glance at the girl in the black dress. "Why? I like blondes."

Filip furrows his brows, a grimace taking over his face. "Not the blonde one, Drago. The chick in a gold onesie thing is Arturo DeVille's sister."

Slowly, I turn around and stare at the sparkling girl. She's still talking, waving her hands in excitement, multiple gold bracelets dangling on her wrists. I focus on her lips.

"He's dying because of a wound in his chest. The one he got when he fought her mate in his wolf form."

I look at my second-in-command. "Are you sure?"

"Yup. Do you want me to call Ajello and say you won't do it?"

"Not yet."

I turn back toward Sienna DeVille, take another sip of my whiskey, and wait to see what happens with the wolf man.

"And she rushes into the room and sees him covered in blood. Bam! Cliffhanger. What do you think?"

The blonde girl tilts her head, so I'm unable to catch her reply. She laughs, then nods her head toward the crowd, saying something else.

"I don't think so," Arturo's sister replies. *"I only saw a few pictures of him, but the shots were taken from behind. I hope he's hot. But even if he's not, that's okay. Based on what I see here, he's loaded. I can't wait to start spending his money. So exciting!"*

She giggles, reaching for her drink. I shake my head and turn around, intending to find Filip and have him call Ajello. If there is one thing I can't stand, it's a gold digger. And I'm not saddling myself with one, business be damned. I throw a final look at the booth. The blonde girl is leaning to the side, searching for something in her purse. Nino is still fumbling with his phone. But the thing that catches and holds my attention is the expression on Sienna DeVille's face. Instead of the mischievous smile of only a few seconds earlier, her face is completely blank. The drink she's holding seems to be forgotten as she vacantly stares somewhere in front of her.

When one of your senses gets compromised, the body adapts, heightening the ones you have left. I've had two decades to adapt and hone various ways of perceiving things. Body language. Facial expressions. The look in a person's eyes. All those things say so much more than the words people actually speak. I lift my glass to my lips, watching the girl. The outfit she is wearing might be glittering like a damn Christmas tree, but there isn't even a hint of a spark in her eyes. Nope, Sienna DeVille is not thrilled with the idea of marriage any more than I am. No matter what she says.

The blonde girl pulls out the phone from her purse and turns back to Arturo's sister. A beaming smile overtakes Sienna's face as she wraps her arm around her friend, posing for a photo, laughing. I don't think I've ever witnessed a person changing both their facial expression and their body language so fast. She seems to be genuinely enjoying herself now, and no matter how hard I try, I can't decide which of those expressions was the true one.

Sienna

"So? Is he here?"

Nino ignores me, too focused on his phone.

"Nino!" I pinch his arm.

"What now?"

"Is Popov here?"

He rolls his eyes and takes a look around. "No, he's not. As I've already told you at least seven times in the past hour."

"It's been two hours. Why isn't he here? It's his club."

Nino mumbles something and looks down at his phone again.

Sighing, I grab Luna's forearm. "Let's go dance."

I pull my friend toward the dance floor, swaying my hips to the beat. It's difficult with four-inch heels, but I try my best. There aren't too many people dancing, maybe twenty, and a good number of them are throwing curious looks in my direction.

I'm used to people staring. It's unavoidable, considering my fashion choices. So, let them stare. Let them believe the persona I project—a carefree girl so sure of herself that she'd come into an upscale club dressed in a glittering outfit and feel good about it.

My brother thinks I accepted the arranged marriage because I'm bored and want to get back at him for being too protective. He said so himself while berating me and trying to change my mind. The don believes it's because he threatened my brother's life. I'm not sure what Luna thinks, but considering the number of times tonight I've mentioned how loaded Drago Popov must be, she probably believes I want to marry for money. It always amazes me how easily people come to conclusions when I let them see what they expect to see. I guess no one would believe I'd marry a stranger because I'm afraid to be alone.

I pass my eyes over the crowd, looking for a man in jeans. This doesn't seem like a jeans-friendly place, but in all the photos I've seen, Drago Popov is wearing them. Nope, no jeans anywhere in sight. Only bespoke suits.

A tall figure leaning on the bar attracts my attention. He's partially in shadows, but based on his posture, I'd say he's in his thirties. The black dress pants he's wearing are immaculately tailored and his black shirt, with the first button undone, stretches over his wide shoulders. He's not wearing a jacket, and the sleeves of his shirt are rolled up to his elbows. There's something familiar about him, but I can't pinpoint it. He's been looking my way ever since I noticed him standing there, but I've ignored him, just like I've ignored the rest of the men at this club who've been ogling me.

He leans forward to place his glass on the bar, and suddenly I can *see* him. Short dark hair, a little longer at the top. Olive skin that speaks of time in the sun. And finally, the sharp lines of his face, illuminated by the light from the sconce on the nearby pillar. He's handsome, like many others in the club. But there's a striking difference that sets him apart from other men here. While they have been gaping at my ass and cleavage, this guy is focused solely on my face.

I meet his eyes and smile. By all accounts, I'm still an unattached woman, so I don't see anything wrong with a bit of benign flirting. He doesn't smile back. How rude! I turn my attention back to the rest of the crowd but, somehow, my gaze wanders back to the brooding man. He's still looking at me. Another guy in a gray suit approaches from behind and places a hand on Mr. Tall, Dark, and Handsome's shoulder. Without breaking our eye contact, the rude hottie shakes his head and sends the suit guy away.

The song changes to a slow melody—"The Sound of Silence" performed by Disturbed. I've always preferred this version.

"I don't like slow songs. Do you think Nino will let us get another drink?" Luna asks and heads back to our booth.

I don't reply. I don't even move because I'm rooted to the spot, staring at the man from the bar as he walks directly toward me.

Something in the way he carries himself commands attention. An air of danger surrounds him, the scent of it heightened by the way he walks. Each step is slow and deliberate as if he's a wolf on the prowl. The intensity of his gaze is petrifying and enticing, like he's somehow sunk invisible claws into me. I can't look away.

The song blasting from the speakers rises in pitch, each word louder than the previous one. My heart matches the rhythm, beating faster and faster, and by the time he stops right in front of me, it seems like the damn thing is going to break out of my chest.

"Dance with me." The deep timbre of his voice rolls over me, and it's as if it brushes over every inch of my exposed skin. I'm convinced that I wouldn't have been able to reject him even if he bothered to actually ask. His hand slides around my waist. Certainty sets in as I stare into his green eyes. My chance to escape whatever darkness he offers has long passed.

He tilts his head up, breaking our eye contact, to look at something behind me. Shit. I completely forgot about Nino. I glance over my shoulder, expecting to see Luna's brother rushing toward us. But instead of coming over to stop the stranger's advance whether I want him to or not, Nino is standing at the edge of the dance floor, glaring at the hottie. As I watch, Nino nods and remains in place. Immediately, the arm around my waist tightens, pulling me closer against the hard chest, demanding my rapt notice.

"Your babysitter decided not to bother us."

He has a strange accent, rolling the *R*, which makes his voice sound kind of growly. My sister's husband is Russian, and while Pasha has no accent at all when he speaks English, some of his friends do. This man's accent is similar, but not exactly the same.

"I guess it's your lucky day." I smile, trying to hide my nervousness. Talking or flirting with men has never posed a problem for me before, but I find it hard now.

His hands move to the small of my back, just above where the low waistband of my jumpsuit rests. I know I should hook my hands behind his neck, but he's much taller than me, so I just place my palms on his shoulders.

"It seems like it." One of his palms drifts up slightly, touching my bare skin. "I don't remember seeing you here before."

"I came to have a look at someone."

"Is it a male someone?"

His thumb strokes the skin along the beltline of my jumpsuit. With every brush, a spark ignites, sending a wave of heat through me while his eyes bore into mine. I blink a few times, trying to pull myself together.

"Maybe," I finally say.

"Hmm. I wonder, what will your *male someone* think about your . . . attire."

I grin, intending to give him a witty retort as I usually do in similar situations, but the fierceness of his stare is messing with my concentration, and I end up blurting out the truth instead. "I don't really give a fuck."

Something flashes in his eyes, and a corner of his mouth curves upward.

"Interesting." He lifts his hand and traces my lower lip with the pad of his thumb. "Tell me, what happened with the wolf girl?"

"The wolf girl?" I chuckle. "What are you talking about?"

"The girl who found her man covered in blood. Will she save him?"

My jaw hits the floor. What? How?

The hot guy moves his forefinger under my chin and taps it lightly. I quickly close my mouth, then open it again to ask how the fuck he knows about my story when the song ends. A fast tune starts playing, and I realize we haven't been dancing at all. We've just stood there, unmoving, this whole time.

"It was a pleasure meeting you, Sienna DeVille," he says, and my eyes flare in surprise. "Call your don. Tell him Drago said yes."

I gape at him, at a loss for words.

Drago's hand falls from my face, and he turns away, heading across the dance floor and signaling to the man in a gray suit to follow him. They walk toward the back and, a moment later, disappear through a black door.

That is my future husband?

CHAPTER

Drago

I PARK MY BIKE A FEW SPOTS AWAY FROM THE WHITE CAR I've been following for the past hour and watch as the driver opens the back door. Sienna DeVille exits, wearing a wide smile and the most bizarre outfit I've ever seen. At first, I wonder if she went out in her pajamas because that's what this matching set of pants and a blouse looks like. It's white, with black blotches all over, making it look as if she put on a cow's hide. Her heels are orange like her coat, and she has a big orange bow on the top of her head, fastened to her high ponytail. She says something to her driver and walks inside a bookstore that faces the street. I wait for a few moments, then take off my helmet and follow.

The bookstore is huge, with several large tables laden with stacked books at the front and wall-wide bookshelves in the back. I don't have to search for long to find my future wife, because it's impossible to miss her in that outfit. She's standing by one of the shelves, holding a thick paperback in her hands. I look at the big sign suspended from the ceiling, expecting it to say *beauty* or *fashion*. It doesn't. It looks like she's browsing the business section.

A store attendant approaches her, an older woman with a sour face. Sienna smiles and leans forward to whisper something in her ear. The grim attendant widens her eyes, then bursts out laughing. They spend a few minutes discussing something, and when the saleswoman returns to the counter, she's wearing a bright smile on her face. My future wife checks out a few more books in the section before strolling around the store. I lurk amid the displays of books on politics and continue watching her.

A teenage girl is crouching by the shelf of romance titles when Sienna walks up to her and bends, saying something. The girl shrugs and shakes her head. Sienna sits down on the floor, cross-legged, and starts taking the books off the shelf one by one and passing them to the teenager. Every time she pulls out a new paperback, she leans toward the girl and comments as she holds out the book. With her hand covering her mouth, the girl snickers.

I slip behind the bookshelf just on the other side of them, and now I have a direct view of Sienna's face through the void over the shorter books lined up in a row, allowing me to focus on her lips without being seen myself.

"... *my favorite. He's a grumpy CEO, and she's his secretary who's been in love with him since they were kids.*" Sienna grins and takes the next book. "*Oh, and this one is so good. She's a model, and there's some psycho pestering her. So, her father hires a bodyguard who's a retired SEAL, but the guy can't stand her. It's an age gap, grumpy-sunshine trope. You're going to love it.*"

I spend almost an hour stalking my future wife around the store, watching as she chats with random people as if she'd known them for years. Some don't seem interested in the beginning but, sooner or later, they all end up pulled into a conversation with her. When they leave, smiles light up their faces. It's as if she's bewitched them. And it seems, I'm falling under her spell as well, because I have forgotten about the meeting I have with her brother today.

I turn around and exit the bookstore, leaving my future wife to spread the obviously contagious happiness all around her.

"There won't be a wedding reception, Arturo," I say. "We'll sign the papers at city hall and that's it."

Sienna's brother stares at me from across my desk, his jaw clenched tight. Arturo and I had a rather nice business relationship before the whole Pisano fuckup.

"Why?" he asks through his teeth.

"The civil marriage ceremony will take place on Saturday. There isn't enough time to organize anything else."

"Why so soon?"

"Because I said so."

He gets in my face. "Who the fuck do you think you are?"

"Someone who agreed to work with you again even though Rocco Pisano killed one of my men."

"You sent your bikers to storm the Natello shindig. There were civilians there! God only knows how none of them ended up dead."

"There are no civilians in our business, Arturo. We have dead people on both sides, but Cosa Nostra started this shit. If you want a truce, it'll be on my terms."

Arturo glares at me, his nostrils flaring. I can see his control slipping as fire burns in his eyes. A heartbeat. An invisible snap, and he hits the top of the desk with his palm. "Fine." He turns and marches out of my office.

I take my phone off the desktop and shoot a message to Filip, saying that the wedding date has been confirmed and we're a go.

My insistence on having the wedding on Saturday has nothing to do with mending the feud between us and Cosa Nostra. But the timing is perfect, and if we're going through with the truce, I want it to come into effect before our first weapons delivery crosses the border on Sunday.

With any luck, it will take the Romanians at least a week, maybe more, to realize what's happening. In the meantime, I'm not willing to risk that someone may talk. As soon as Bogdan finds out I'm planning on taking over his market, the Romanians will attack. We'll fight back. In less than a month, we'll have a full-blown war. And I need Cosa Nostra to stay out of it.

But more importantly, I want the bundle of joy that is Arturo's sister in my possession as soon as possible.

Sienna

"What do you mean there won't be an actual wedding?" Asya's voice comes through the line. "I only have one sister. I want to see you in a wedding dress going down the aisle!"

"Yeah, well." I shrug and continue painting my toenails. "Maybe next time."

"Next time? And how many times are you planning on getting married?"

"Three. That's my lucky number."

"Jesus, Sienna. Why are you doing this? If you don't want to get married, just tell Arturo. He'll call off the engagement."

"I don't want him to call off the engagement. This Popov guy is really handsome. I think I'm in love with him already." I snort.

"After spending a whole minute with him. Yeah, sure. What's going on?"

"The guy is hot! And he's rich. What's not to love? He ticks all my boxes. You know I'm shallow like that."

"You are not shallow. You just pretend that you are."

I tighten the lid on the nail polish and drop the bottle onto the bed while Ajello's words from two months ago run through my head.

"You have Pasha now," I say, staring at the ceiling. "Arturo will find someone and marry, eventually. Have kids."

"So?"

I close my eyes. "I can't bear the idea of being alone, Asya."

"Arturo will never let you be alone, even when he marries. The house is large enough for ten people to live in without ever stumbling over each other."

"I will never force myself on my brother's family."

"He doesn't even have a girlfriend, Sienna. And you're only twenty. You'll find someone."

"Yeah."

"I can ask Pasha to hook you up with Kostya if you want?"

"Thanks, but no thanks. That man has slept with every woman in the Chicago area. He's good-looking, but not my type."

"And what is your type, sis?"

"A big, mean wolf-shifter alpha who hates everyone but me, and who'd make me the queen of his pack," I declare and burst out laughing.

"Please, be serious."

"I am!"

"You accepted an arrangement to marry a guy before you even met him! That's not normal, Sienna! Please, be reasonable and call off the engagement. Please."

"I'll send you pictures. Love you," I chirp into the phone and end the call.

It starts ringing again moments later, so I turn on "do not disturb," snuggle under the blanket, and then peer out the window without actually seeing anything at all.

Can I pull this off? Live the rest of my life with a man I know nothing about? Pretend innocence while secretly collecting info and relaying it to my don?

Probably.

I've been pretending most of my life.

Chapter
five

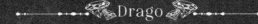 Drago

"**D** EAR GOD," FILIP CHOKES OUT, STARING AT something behind me. "What the hell is that thing she's wearing?"

I turn around just in time to see my bride exiting the car. She's got on what some may call a puffy faux fur jacket. It might look rather nice if it was in another color, but hers is yolk yellow. And she's wearing silk pants that are the same shade.

Sienna catches my eye, says something to Arturo, then rushes toward us, expertly jumping over the rain puddles in her sky-high heels. And those are the same color as the rest of her outfit. She reminds me of a baby chick on LSD.

My bride stops in front of me, speaking while she searches in her purse, but with her head bent, I can't read her lips. She finally finds whatever she was looking for and looks up at me with a big grin. "If that's okay with you?"

"Yes," I reply with no idea what she said.

Her smile widens. "Perfect." She leans her back on my chest, raising her phone in front of us. "Say cheese."

She looks toward the phone and snaps a selfie.

"What are you doing?" I ask, staring at her yellow-painted nails as her fingers fly over the keyboard.

"Sending the photo to my sister. She asked why I accepted an arranged marriage to a stranger."

I reach out and take her chin between my fingers, tilting her head up. "And why did you accept, Sienna?"

She blinks at me and, for a quick moment, a smidge of panic flashes across her face, but the next second it's gone, replaced with a grin. "Because you're hot. And rich."

Her smile seems genuine and her tone sounds sincere, but as I focus on her eyes, I notice something else. Something she's trying her best to hide with her sunny performance. It looks very much like hurt.

I move my thumb to trace the curve of her lower lip. It trembles slightly under my touch.

"Come. Let's get this over with." I turn to Filip. "You can go. Call Keva and let her know I'm bringing Sienna home with me."

Sienna doesn't say anything when I take her phone from her and drop it back into her purse. She stays silent as I take her hand and lead her up the wide stone steps to the city hall entrance, Arturo following a few paces behind. We are at the top when Sienna suddenly turns around toward the parking lot. I follow her gaze, spotting a heavily muscled man exiting a car, and immediately push Sienna behind me. I'm reaching for my gun when Sienna pulls her hand from mine and dashes around me down the steps toward the ripped bastard.

Rage sparks inside me until I notice the guy is helping a woman out of the vehicle. I release the hold on my gun as I watch the spitting image of my bride, minus the crazy outfit, make her way toward Sienna.

"It's my sister and her husband," Arturo's deep voice penetrates my momentary daze.

He comes up to stand beside me. For just a moment, the

ever-present lines of worry on his face ease as he looks at his sisters and gives a brief nod to his brother-in-law.

Well, shit . . .

I knew Arturo had two sisters, but I wasn't aware they are twins. My heart squeezes and bleeds as I behold the two women falling into each other's arms. Sienna says something and hugs her sister again. Then, she leans and drops a kiss on her twin's cheek before tucking a strand of hair behind her ear. Her sister does the exact same thing to Sienna. Even their mannerisms are identical. I forgot how twins can be sometimes.

It hurts to watch them, so I turn away from the sight and open the door to the building.

Sienna

I regard my new husband from the corner of my eye while he drives. He was very closed-off during the quick wedding ceremony, and also after, when everyone was leaving city hall. We've been on the road for almost two hours, and he hasn't said a word to me. I spent the time sorting through my photos and posting them on social media, but I finished that five minutes ago.

"Is everything okay?" I ask.

Drago throws a sideways look at me, then returns his attention to the road. "I don't talk while I drive."

Raising my eyebrows, I mouth, "Oookay." I type a message to Asya, asking if she and Pasha got to the airport. I still can't believe she actually came. It's not as if it was a real wedding. It felt more like going to a bank to open an account. The rings were a nice touch, though. Drago's is a thick gold band and mine has a huge pale-yellow diamond. It goes quite nicely with my jacket and reflects the light beautifully. I lift my hand and snap a picture to upload to my Insta later.

We make a right turn, and I look up from the phone to see a narrow road leading to an entrance set into a high fence. The gate slides to the side, and we continue along the tree-lined driveway toward the beautifully landscaped island with a marble fountain in the middle. At the end of the lane, stands a massive four-story mansion. The light-beige brick and brown woodwork of its façade glows in the late afternoon sun. The house is so big, it looks more like a hotel than a residential home. I count the windows on the upper floor. Ten are facing the front. Just how many rooms are there? Greenery and trees surround the palatial citadel, making it look like a setting of a fairytale.

"We're here." Drago exits the vehicle and walks around the back to open my car door.

I step out, still gaping at the beautiful house, just as the front door flies open and an apron-clad woman in her late sixties rushes outside. She marches toward us, yelling something in Serbian so fast that I can't grasp the meaning, only catching random words.

". . . dinner . . . Filip just told me . . . married . . . no cake . . . kill you . . ."

Stopping in front of Drago, she pokes her finger into his chest. "*Sram te bilo.*"

I'm still processing the fact that my husband allows a woman, who seems to be part of the staff, to yell at him and tell him he should be ashamed when she turns to me and grabs me in a tight hug. Three loud smacks explode in my ears as she kisses my cheeks in quick succession—right, left, then right once again.

"Drago didn't tell me he was bringing you today. I thought he went to a business meeting! Let me look at you." She leans away and takes my face between her palms. "Oh, you are so pretty and . . ." Her eyes move down over my outfit. "Why are you wearing a chicken costume, sweetie?"

The look of confusion on her face while she's staring at my jacket is so hilarious, I burst out laughing. When I catch my breath, I say, "I'm Sienna."

"I know, sweetie. Drago was so nice to inform me he was getting married." She looks up at my husband, who's been watching the whole exchange in silence, annoyance written all over her face. "But he must have forgotten to tell me that it would be *today*."

"Sienna." Drago places his hand on my lower back, and an excited shiver passes through my body from the light touch. "This is Zivka, my late father's ex-wife, who should have introduced herself first."

"Just call me Keva," she says. "Let's eat. Everyone has been waiting for you in the dining room for almost half an hour."

I furrow my brows. Keva? Drago just called her Zivka, so is Keva a nickname?

As we follow Zivka into the house, I try to think of a reason why Drago would have his father's ex at his home, but I lose my concentration as his hand slips under my jacket. My pants have a low waistline and my blouse has ridden up, so his fingers are touching the bare skin at the small of my back, igniting a small shiver of pleasure that shoots up along my spine. I steal a look at him to find him typing something on his phone with his free hand, seemingly oblivious to what his touch is doing to me.

We step inside the house where a man in jeans and a plain black T-shirt, and wearing a shoulder holster carrying two guns, greets us. Drago's hand slips away from my back, the tips of his fingers brushing my exposed flesh in the process. It's just a light stroke, there one moment and gone the next, but it still feels like I'm on fire where his caress slid across my skin.

The man with the holster nods at Drago and takes his jacket, then moves to help me take off mine. My husband's hand wraps around the guy's wrist before he has a chance to reach for my faux fur.

"No touching my wife," Drago says in Serbian. His tone is calm, but the hold he has on the man's wrist tightens. "Make sure everyone in the house knows that."

The guy freezes and blinks nervously.

When Drago turns toward me and helps me take off my yellow jacket, I pretend to be confused, expecting him to explain what just happened. He doesn't, just passes my coat to the man, who's now pointedly looking at the floor. Drago places his hand on the small of my back again and ushers me across the foyer.

We walk toward the double wooden doors, which seem to contain cheerful and boisterous chatter behind their solid frame. As we approach, the voices become a cacophony, dozens of people in a battle for who can hold the loudest conversation. The moment we step through the doorway, all noise ceases, and silence descends over the huge dining room like a blanket. I stop midstep and gape at the long table which has at least forty people sitting around it. Most are men, casually dressed—more or less—but all of them wearing a shoulder holster with one or two guns. And every single person is staring at me.

"This is Sienna," Drago says and guides me toward three empty chairs at the head of the table. He stops and pulls out one to the right of the host's—the place of honor. Before I can take a seat, the sound of several dozen chairs scraping the floor fills the room as everyone around the table stands up.

"Um . . . what's going on?" I mumble and look at Drago sideways.

"Sit."

I lower myself onto the chair. Drago takes a seat at the head of the table, and everyone else sits back down.

I turn to face my husband and whisper, "Is there a hidden camera?"

Drago's gaze moves from my mouth to my eyes, and the corner of his lips lifts. "No."

The door on the other end of the room bursts open, and Zivka, followed by four women and two men, walks in. They bring in enormous platters of food and set them on the dining table, then return to, what I assume, is the kitchen. Moments later, they come back with salads and bread. When they're finished, Zivka sits at Drago's left and the other serving staff take the remaining empty chairs around the table. Everybody looks at Drago, waiting. He nods. The chatter resumes as people start spooning food from the big serving dishes onto their plates. I blink at the strange scene several times, then shrug and grab the salad bowl nearest to me.

Drago

Laughter and loud conversations ring all around as I covertly observe my young wife. Other than Keva, I didn't introduce her to any of my people, and I did that on purpose so I could see her reaction. I expected her to be uncomfortable. Intimidated, even. It seems I may need to alter my assumptions because, since the meal started, she's been happily babbling nonstop with Jelena, Jovan's wife. From what I managed to catch, they are discussing a book.

High-pitched sounds are the hardest for me to hear. Sienna has a moderately high voice, so it's difficult for me to grasp her meaning when she talks, even if there are no competing auditory distractions. I can hear her speaking, but I miss too many words. With so many people in one room talking at the same time, the background noise makes hearing her impossible. And since she's turned toward Jelena, I can't even read her lips.

I take her chin between my thumb and finger, turning her to face me. Everyone living in this house knows about my situation, so they make sure they look at me when they speak. I'm not sure why I haven't told Sienna about my hearing loss yet, but she'll find out soon enough.

"Making friends already?" I ask.

"It looks that way." Her lips widen into a smile. "Do you have something against it?"

She has an amazingly sinful mouth, and the way it curves as she speaks makes me want to take her lower lip between my teeth and bite it. "No. I don't have anything against it."

People start leaving the table, each taking their plate and carrying it to the kitchen. Sienna watches them with amazement in her eyes, then looks down at her own empty plate and reaches for it. I take her hand, moving it away from the plate and back to the table, but I don't release my hold.

"I think you need to explain to me the rules you have around here." She smirks, pretending she doesn't notice I'm still holding her hand.

"What rules?"

"People clearing their own plates. Don't staff do that? And why was everyone armed at dinner?" She drops a quick look at our joined hands, then snaps her eyes back to meet mine.

"There are seven women and two men in charge of tending to various things around the house like cleaning, preparing food, and keeping up with grounds. But they aren't staff. It's just what they do around here." I reach out and move a strand of her hair over her shoulder. "And when we finish with our meal, we all take our plates to the kitchen to lighten their workload."

"They are not paid to do that?"

"They get paid. But we still take our plates to show our

respect and appreciation. As for your second question—we like to be prepared."

"For what?"

"Anything and everything."

"Don't you have security?"

"Every man in this household is an excellent shot. All of us are part of security." I lean forward and place my hand on the back of her neck. "You have nothing to fear while you're in my home, *mila*."

She narrows her eyes at me. "My name is Sienna. Not Mila."

"I know." I pull her closer until our lips almost touch. "I also know you didn't agree to marry me because I'm 'hot and rich.'"

Sienna's eyes flare at my words, and I expect her to try to pull away, but she just grins. "You don't think it's a good enough reason to marry someone?"

"No. You see, I had a very specific reason for saying yes to this marriage. But I have a very hard time deciphering *your* motive for agreeing."

The phone in my pocket vibrates with an incoming message. I fish it out with my free hand and look at the screen.

> **16:22 Filip:** Our truck crossed the border early and arrived at the warehouse ten minutes ago. Someone talked. Romanians just got here. Bogdan is demanding your presence and explanation.

"I have to go." I release Sienna's hand reluctantly and stand up. "We'll continue this conversation tomorrow."

I head across the dining room, and I'm almost at the door when a hand grabs my forearm. When I look down, my wife is standing next to me, a questioning look in her eyes.

"What is it?"

"I asked if I could come with you?"

"I'm going to a business meeting, Sienna. One that may very well end up with blood being spilled. Of course you can't come with me."

"Oh, this is an old blouse. I'll just throw it away if I get blood on it." She waves her hand through the air.

I lower my gaze, taking in her shirt. It's white with an image of a yellow, cross-eyed rabbit holding a carrot. Both the carrot and rabbit's ears are covered in tiny orange sequins. Why am I not surprised she got married in that? When I look back up, I find her still smiling at me. Is she fucking with me or is she just plain nuts?

"Go find Keva. Your things were probably taken to the bedroom already. She'll show you where it is." I nod toward the kitchen door and head out.

It takes me an hour to reach the abandoned house we use as our storage facility for drugs before shipping them out. We still haven't received the next load from Ajello, so I decided to use the place to hold the first firearms shipment for the time being. Six of my men, weapons in hand, are guarding a big truck parked in the back. Only half of the cargo has been unloaded. Several yards to the right, there are two black cars. Bogdan, the head of the Romanian crime organization, is leaning on the hood of the car closest to the truck, his arms crossed over his chest.

I park my bike between the truck and Bogdan's car, remove my helmet, and face the Romanian leader. "You wanted to meet."

"I want an explanation," he bites out.

"About what?"

"That!" He points toward the crates piled next to the truck. "We've had a nice collaboration for the past ten years. I gave you the best product and great rates. So, I want to know why you suddenly started buying weapons from someone else, and what the fuck are you planning to do with ten times the amount you usually order."

I take a quick look inside the cars. There's a guy in the passenger seat of the vehicle Bogdan is leaning on, and one more in the other car. Someone obviously told Bogdan I had a truck full of guns and ammunition arriving, but he doesn't know I plan on reselling the goods. If he did, he would have brought more men with him. I could tell him my needs have changed, that I need more weapons, but he'll soon realize what's happening.

"I made a call to the home country," I say, "and struck a deal with Lutovac. As it happens, we went to school together. He knows what I like, and we came to an understanding that a partnership would be to both our benefits."

A mix of surprise and anger flashes across Bogdan's face the moment he hears the name. There are two major dealers of small firearms and ammunition in this part of the US— Bogdan and Endri Dushku. They both get their product from Lutovac, a Serbian supplier based in Belgrade. The fact I'm now working directly with Lutovac makes it clear I have the product available for resale.

Bogdan pushes off the car. He's nearly shaking with rage, fists balled at his sides as he comes right up to me. "You won't be selling arms on my turf, Drago."

"There is nothing you can do about that, so I advise you to accept the new situation and walk away. For old times' sake, don't make me kill you."

"We'll see about that." Bogdan's nostrils flare as he grinds his teeth, but he turns and gets inside his car.

I watch both vehicles leave, then dismount my bike and head toward my men standing by the truck.

"Load everything back inside. We need to move the goods to another location. This site can't be used anymore." I turn to Filip. "How the fuck did the Romanians find this place?"

"The driver says they followed him from the border. He thought he lost them at one point, but they turned up here while the guys were unloading the crates."

"Who talked?"

"It can only be the man we bribed to arrange for the truck to bypass cargo inspection. Wesley P-something."

"Find out his full name and address. I'll pay him a visit tomorrow," I say.

"What are we going to do with the Romanians? Bogdan isn't likely to let this go."

"He won't. I need you to add more men at each storage location."

"You think Bogdan will try something? Why not kill him now?"

"If you go around offing past business associates, no one will do business with you. Unfortunately. But if he attacks first, I'll have cause to dispose of him." I bend and grab the closest box of ammunition.

It's almost six in the morning when I get home. I climb the stairs to the top floor, heading for the last door at the end of the hallway. The lights are off in my bedroom, but the curtains are pulled back, allowing the faintest morning glow to fall onto the body curled up on the left side of my bed. The plush carpet muffles my steps as I walk across the room and come to a stop next to the footboard.

Sienna is sleeping on her side, clutching a pillow between her arms and legs. Her hair is loose, and some of it has fallen over her face. I cast my eyes down her curled form and feel my lips tilt upward. It seems that my wife's eccentric fashion extends to her nightclothes, as well. She's wearing silk pajamas—pants and a top with spaghetti straps. It's a zebra print set, but the colors are purple and pink.

I watch her for a few moments, wondering why I'm so fascinated by her. From the moment I left her in the dining room earlier this evening, I couldn't stop thinking about her. I don't like it. The only thing that should interest me as far as my young wife is concerned is her ulterior motive for marrying me, but I find myself completely captivated by her strange essence. It's as if I've discovered a previously unknown creature, one whose behavior is completely contrary to what would be expected.

For a girl as sheltered and spoiled as she probably has been, coming to a new place where she doesn't know anyone should be stressful. Uncomfortable. I expected her to start whining, asking me to take her back to her brother. Instead, she took it all in stride. All along, she wore a mischievous smile on her face and emanated that irritatingly cheerful energy. It's as if she's not bothered by this whole situation in the slightest.

Sienna DeVille is a surprise.

And I hate surprises.

With one last look at my stunning bride, I head into the en suite on the other side of the room to take a shower. Ten minutes later, I climb into bed and sprawl next to my wife. She's turned away from me, and hell if I know why, but I don't like it. I wrap my arm around her waist and pull her closer until her back is plastered to my front. Then, I throw one leg over hers, entangling her body with mine, and close my eyes.

Chapter
six

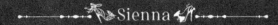

I AWAKE COCOONED IN SOMETHING WARM AND BIG. It feels nice. I sigh and bury my face into the pillow. The hold around my body tightens slightly, and my eyes pop open, zeroing in on a thick tattooed arm wrapped around my waist.

There is a man in my bed.

I blink. Why the hell is there a man in my bed?! Screaming, I try to untangle myself, but the grip on my middle only grows stronger.

"Stop." Drago's husky voice rumbles behind me. "I'm trying to sleep."

I push against his forearm, only managing the tiniest movement, then twist around, ending up with my face pressed into his neck. My God, he smells amazing. I tilt my head slightly and inhale. It's something woodsy with a mix of—I breathe in again—oh, a touch of mint.

"Stop sniffing me, Sienna, and go back to sleep."

"I'm not sniffing you," I mumble and resume trying to free myself from his embrace. "Let me go."

Drago doesn't move a muscle. I press my palms to his hard chest and push. A heavy sigh sounds above my head, and his hold on me loosens. I roll to the other side of the bed and spring up.

"What are you doing in my bed?" Hands on my hips, I glare down at my husband, who's watching me with hooded eyes.

Drago is stretched out on the bed, his right arm tucked under his head. He's not wearing a shirt, but a sliver of navy-blue pajama bottoms peek from under the sheet.

"This is *my* bed. You were in it when I came home."

"What? When Zivka brought me upstairs after dinner, she told me this would be my room. All my suitcases were already here."

"And you are my wife, so it's expected that both you and your suitcases would be here."

I scan the room and realize that it does look like it belongs to a man. I was so mentally exhausted last night that I just changed into my pj's, brushed my teeth, and went to sleep without actually paying attention to my surroundings.

"I think both my luggage and I would prefer to have a separate room." I glance back at Drago. His eyes are closed, and his chest rises and falls in a slow rhythm.

"Drago?"

He's asleep. Fucking great.

I should go take a shower and get dressed. Then, I need to find Zivka and ask her if there's another room I could have. That would be a smart thing to do, but I can't take my eyes off my husband. He looks different when he sleeps. Less . . . brooding somehow.

There's an area of patchy skin on his neck. I noticed it during dinner yesterday, but his shirt hid most of it from view. What I could see looked like a small scar. Now, however, it's clear that the bit I spotted yesterday was only a part of something much larger. The skin on his shoulder and down his left arm, all the way to his elbow where his tattoos start, is discolored and has a slightly bumpy texture. I put my knee on the bed and slowly lean forward to have a better look. Drago's hand suddenly shoots up, his fingers wrap around my arm.

"Changed your mind about coming back to bed?" he asks and focuses his gaze on my lips.

"No." I smile. "I don't sleep with men I haven't personally invited into my bed."

Something dangerous flashes in his eyes the moment the words leave my mouth.

"If I catch any man touching you, even with just the tip of his finger, he'll lose much more than his hand." The hold he has on my arm tightens. "This marriage might have been arranged, but from this point forward, the only man allowed to look at you, touch you, or fuck you . . . is me."

A pleasant shiver runs through me, and I bite the inside of my cheek. "Why don't you, then?"

Drago tilts his head to the side, scrutinizing my reaction. He releases my arm, and his fingers glide over the swell of my breast, down the valley of my chest, and then lower, past the waistband of my pajama bottoms. My breaths quicken. His touch may be light, but my body's response is anything but. I'm not accustomed to being touched by men I don't know, and I've never spent a night in bed with one. I should be concerned, not turned on by his gentle strokes. Not wishing for his hand to slide lower. But I do.

How would it feel to be pinned under that big body while his heated touch sears my naked flesh? A pleasant shiver runs down my spine from the mere thought. Drago's palm slips between my legs, pressing on my pussy over the silky fabric while his gaze captures mine, and I have to bite my bottom lip to stop the moan from escaping. I've never been attracted to hard, grumpy men, but for some remarkable reason, I'm absolutely enthralled by my stranger of a husband.

"I would enjoy that very much." He puts more pressure on

my quivering center, and I feel myself getting wet. "But I don't fuck liars, *mila moya*."

With one last caress, Drago pulls his hand from between my legs and turns his back to me. I grind my teeth, then get off the bed and march across the room into the bathroom, making sure I slam the door closed with all my strength.

Ten minutes later, I crouch in front of a suitcase and rummage through its contents, searching for something nice to wear. Bright clothes make me feel happy even when I'm not. I find underwear and a blue blouse, but my favorite orange jeans are not in there. I slam the lid of the suitcase closed and move to the second one. Drago keeps sleeping, absolutely oblivious to the racket I'm making. In the third suitcase, I finally find the jeans I'm after and the fluffy slipper booties. Sitting on the edge of the bed, I unwrap the towel from around me and start getting dressed.

He called me a liar. I guess he's right, in a way. I did, after all, come here to spy on him for the don. But it still hurts. And the fact that it does, bothers me. There're only two people whom I allow close enough to be bothered by—my brother and sister. As far as other people are concerned, I let their actions or remarks slide. If I don't care about them, their opinions or behavior can't hurt me. And I don't give a fuck what Drago Popov thinks of me.

Once I'm finished getting ready, I grab the towel off the bed to take it back to the bathroom, but I stop halfway there and look over my shoulder at my sleeping husband. Chuckling quietly, I throw the towel at his face and run out of the room as fast as I can.

One of the women who looks after the house passes by me on the stairs, carrying a stack of sheets on her way to the upper floor.

"Good morning!" I chirp.

She gives me a somewhat hostile look, but her expression

transforms into confusion upon seeing the fuzzy slipper booties I'm wearing. They're orange and have big white polka dots
all over. The middle of each dot is nested with a small orange
sequin.

"Nice shoes," she mumbles.

"Thank you." I beam as I respond.

When I reach the ground floor, I notice several men standing by the front door, taking off their coats. I recall seeing them
at the dinner last night and remember they mentioned heading out for night guard duty after the meal. Why would they
come back here instead of going home?

I enter the great dining room, only to stop barely a step
over the threshold. Almost every chair at the long table is occupied. Do Serbs celebrate special events for several days? The
spot at the end of the table where I sat yesterday is vacant, and
I make my way toward it, voicing a cheerful "good morning"
as I pass. A few people nod, but most just glare at me. Looks
like I'm not winning any popularity contests around here. I
take my seat and lean toward Jelena, the red-haired girl with
freckles I chatted with last night during dinner.

"So, what's the occasion today?" I ask.

She furrows her brows. "Occasion?"

"Yeah. I see we have guests again." I gesture toward the
people sitting around the table.

"Oh . . . they are not guests." She laughs. "They live here."

"Here? In this house?" I gape at her. "But, that's like . . .
like forty people."

"Forty-eight, actually. The first guard shift already had their
breakfast, and others aren't here at the moment."

I look down the length of the table. Jesus Christ.

The door leading to the kitchen opens, and women carrying multiple plates over their arms and in their hands rush inside. Two take the right side of the table, while the other three

take the left. They begin placing plates loaded with scrambled eggs and bacon in front of each person.

A guy in his early twenties sitting a couple of seats down from Jelena reaches for a plate being lowered before him, but the girl putting it down quickly moves it out of his reach.

"Keva said you're on a diet. She's making you a salad." The girl slaps the back of his head and then sets the last two plates down on the table.

"Nato, sweetheart, don't do this to me," the guy calls after her as she heads back into the kitchen. "I'm starving. You know I can't work when I'm hungry."

Everybody ignores his whining and digs into their food. I grab a piece of bread from the nearby bowl and start eating, pretending to be solely interested in my meal while listening to the conversations going on around me.

I'm having a hard time understanding complete sentences because I don't have experience with conversational Serbian, especially with so many people talking at once. My attention shifts from one exchange to the next, but all I can grasp is bits and pieces, and just some of the meaning. It seems most conversations revolve around a big deal that has been made and the new security measures.

"*Pop treba da se vidi sa ludim Rusom u vezi isporuke,*" the big tattooed man sitting across from Jelena says.

The fork stills halfway to my mouth. Pop? That means priest. *A priest is meeting the crazy Russian for something related to a shipment?* Do they have a priest among them? What does the priest do, bless the drug containers? I try listening in to what he'll say next, but the guy is back to stuffing eggs into his mouth.

At the other end of the room, the kitchen door is pushed open again, and an older man enters. His hair is completely white and gathered into a short ponytail. Combined with his long white beard, it makes him look like Santa Claus. A really weird Santa Claus, since he's wearing army-green tactical pants, a matching T-shirt, and a shoulder holster with two guns overtop. He also has a knife sheath strapped to his thigh. The badass Santa takes a seat, pulls out a wicked-looking knife from its sheath and starts cutting the bacon with it.

"Who's that?" I nudge Jelena.

"Oh, that's Beli. Our gardener."

"A gardener? What does he garden, exactly?"

"Tulips are his favorite, can you believe?"

"Nope." I snort.

"He and Keva hate each other. A couple of years ago he planted white lilies all around the house, and Keva had one of the guys mow them down because she says those are funeral flowers. Beli makes sure he plants them every year now, picking a different place every time."

"Well, doesn't seem like things are dull around here. And what's your role?"

"Most of the time I work with Mirko. He's in charge of logistics." She nods toward the salad guy sitting close by. "He arranges the trucks and the routes, and I help him with that. But he's also in charge of surveillance here and at Naos. Oh, and I also help Keva to launder the money."

"Keva?" I look toward the end of the table where the woman in question is pouring a cup of coffee for some guy. "I thought she's the cook."

Jelena laughs. "Yes, she prepares meals for everyone, provides first aid when necessary, and makes sure all the money that's brought in passes through Naos and comes out clean."

"Wow." I shake my head. "And why do you call her Keva? Is that a nickname?"

"It's slang. *Keva* means mom. Fitting, since she orders everyone around."

"It must be weird to have fifty people calling you 'mom.'"

I glance down the table one more time. "I can't believe that all of them live here. It's like a hotel."

"Oh, it's nothing like a hotel, believe me." She snickers. "More like a military base."

"So, Drago insists on everyone living here?"

"God, no. He often grumbles about it, but he lets us stay," Jelena says between bites. "When Jovan and I joined the organization a few years back, we got a room on the second floor. It was meant to be temporary, a way for us to get to know everyone and see how everything works since this is the main base of operations. But we ended up staying." She motions with her hand down the table. "It was kind of the same for the rest. They feel safe here."

"Because the house is well guarded?"

"No. It's because of Drago. People tend to gravitate toward him. *He* makes them feel safe."

I try to imagine living in one house with so many people. Unbelievable. Absolutely crazy. A small smile pulls at my lips. It's almost . . . like the wolf pack in my story.

"I think it's because they know Drago will take a bullet for any of them," she continues. "They've witnessed it happen more than once."

My head snaps back to Jelena, a smile vanishing off my face. "What?"

"He got shot during an attack on the compound a few years back. Even though there were plenty of guys on guard shift to fight the attackers off, Drago was the first to rush outside. He got hit while covering a position left exposed because one of the soldiers got wounded."

I imagine a bullet piercing my grumpy husband's chest, and a shudder racks my body. Jelena doesn't seem to notice my distress because she keeps blabbing.

"And it's more convenient when most of the people are in the same place. It makes organizing things much easier." She gestures across the table, toward the guy who was talking about the priest. "That's Adam. He's been friends with Drago for a long time, even back in Serbia, and moved here fifteen years ago or so. He is in charge of the foot soldiers. As for the rest of the guys, there aren't any strict job definitions. Everyone does what needs to be done. Transport. Delivery. Guard shifts. Some of them work as additional security at the club when needed."

"Okay . . ." I nod as if it all makes sense. Only, it doesn't. In Cosa Nostra, every member has a very strict job description and obligations. Cooks prepare food. They don't launder money. I look again at everyone seated around the table. How can a crime organization function with such an undefined structure? "So, one big happy family."

"Oh! I forgot Tara. Drago's sister," she adds.

"Drago has a sister?"

"Yes. She lived here, in this house, but she moved out last week."

"Why?"

"Well . . ." Jelena cringes and avoids meeting my eyes. "There was kind of a confrontation between us and Cosa Nostra two years ago."

"Yes, I heard about that." I nod. It happened while Asya was missing, so I didn't pay much attention to what was happening within the Family.

"Tara's boyfriend got shot and died."

"Shit." I look down at my plate. "So, she left because of me?"

"Yeah. She didn't take it well when Drago told her that his bride was from Cosa Nostra."

I continue to nod like I've turned into a fricking bobblehead all of a sudden and focus on my food. No wonder most of the people here have been glaring at me.

"If you want, I'll show you around the house later," Jelena

says between bites. "Also, did Drago tell you? Don't go outside by yourself at night."

"No. Why?"

"Because of the dogs. They're not really sociable, I'm afraid. It's best not to wander out there until Drago takes you to meet them."

An image of my dog Bonbon rises before my eyes. He passed away last year, and I'm the one to blame for that.

"Sure," I mumble, even though I have no intention of meeting my husband's dogs and reopening that wound.

When I finish breakfast, I carry my plate into the kitchen, almost colliding with one of the girls holding a stack of dirty dishes. Four other girls are running around the room, cutlery clinking against the china as everything is being loaded into the dishwashers. This must be the biggest kitchen I've ever seen.

A long, wide island—piled high with used bowls, baking trays, and dishes—takes up most of the central part. An industrial fridge takes up space at the end of the counter and, based on its size, it can store food for a small army. Dozens of glasses, cups, and plates sit behind the glass doors of the white wood cupboards. The smell of freshly brewed coffee mixes with the sweet scent of baked apples coming from an enormous pot placed atop the stove. One of the guys I saw returning from the guard shift is reaching a spoon into the pot.

"Relja!" Keva yells, rushing toward him, and smacks his arm with a kitchen towel. "Don't touch that!"

"I just wanted a taste. It smells amazing."

Keva snatches the spoon out of his hand and scoops up something that looks like grated apples from the pot.

"Get lost." She thrusts the spoon back into his hand, then turns toward the girl putting groceries into the fridge, shouting to her to make haste.

My eyes wander across the room to where Drago is leaning on the wall by the back door that leads to the yard. I thought he was still asleep. The guy who was at city hall with him is standing close by, and they seem to be talking about a shipment scheduled to arrive next weekend. I can't hear everything they are saying from this distance, but something feels slightly off about their exchange. I just can't pinpoint what it is. Instead of maintaining eye contact, Drago's eyes are cast lower, as if he's looking at the ground and not overly interested in what the other man is telling him. He grumbles a response I don't catch and nods, then his gaze shifts to me.

Even though he is all the way on the other side of the room, it's like I've been hit by a bolt of lightning when his eyes pin me with their power. I can still smell him on me even though I took a shower earlier. It's as if, while spooning me, he somehow imprinted himself on my skin.

"We'll speak later, Filip," Drago says and heads toward me.

With each step he takes, my pulse skyrockets. When he finally stands before me, I can barely swallow over the cotton ball that has suddenly lodged in my throat, and my breaths become rapid and shallow.

He braces his hands on the kitchen island, caging me between his arms, and lowers his head. "Did you sleep well last night, *mila*?"

"Nope, not really. The mattress was too hard, and then an intruder snuck into my bed." I smirk. Earlier, I googled the translation for "mila," expecting to find a derogatory term of some kind, but instead, I was rather surprised to see that it's a bit antiquated but still highly regarded Serbian endearment that means "darling".

"I didn't notice you complaining while you slept nuzzling my neck. Snoring."

"What?! I do not snore."

Drago leans in even further, his mouth just next to my ear. His breath teases my skin as he speaks.

"Yes, you do. It's very subtle, like the purr of a kitten." His lips press to the side of my neck, and a low rumbling sound sends a shiver down my spine. "Just like that, Sienna."

I bite the inside of my cheek and close my eyes, trying to extinguish the urge to wrap my arms around him and pull him even closer. My body is somehow gravitating toward him, and I'm barely maintaining control.

"I wonder," he continues, and the tiny hairs at the back of my neck rise. "Do you have claws, too?"

I shake my head and bite my cheek harder.

"Liar." The word, delivered in his gravelly timbre, rolls over me.

A pleasant shiver runs down my spine, and I lean into him, wanting more of that sensation. Quickly though, I realize what I've done and pull away. He still has me caged between his body and the counter, so there's only so far I can move.

"I promised some friends I'd meet them for lunch later today, and we'll probably go to the mall after. Can someone drop me off?"

"Jovan will drive you." He takes his wallet out of the back pocket of his jeans and lifts a credit card in front of my face. "For your shopping."

"I have my own card," I mumble.

"But I thought you married me for my money."

Shit. I forgot about that. "Yup, that's correct." I grab the card out of his hand and grin. "Just a heads-up . . . you'll probably regret marrying me."

He lowers his head until his lips brush my ear. "I don't think so."

Drago's breath and warmth are suddenly gone as he walks away and leaves the kitchen. I have a silly urge to go after him and insist that he should drive me to the mall himself.

"So, ahem." I clear my throat and turn to Keva who's drying a glass. "Jelena told me there's a fountain out front. Can someone point me in the right direction? I want to take some selfies."

"I'm fine Arturo, as I already told you ten times today! Please stop calling."

I shove the phone into my pocket and roll the last suitcase inside my new bedroom. It's all the way on the other end of the fourth floor, the farthest from Drago's. The space is small and has only one window that doesn't even have curtains. A faint smell of fresh paint lingers in the air, hinting that the room was probably renovated recently. My eyes fall on the narrow bed next to a wall and stay glued to it.

I don't like sleeping alone.

The night after my parents' deaths was the first time I snuck into my sister's bed to sleep. Arturo found me there when he came to check on us in the morning, but he said nothing. I kept sneaking into Asya's bed every night after that, for years. I had a bone-chilling fear rooted deep inside my mind that Arturo would wake me one night to tell me that Asya was gone, just like our mom and dad. I was convinced that if she was next to me when I fell asleep, she would be there in the morning, as well.

Asya never asked me to go back to my bed. Not once. Even when her bed became too small for the two of us. My twin sister. My other half. People have often made the mistake of assuming she was the more fragile one. Asya has always been an introvert, the quiet one, and nothing other than her music held her interest for too long. But she is so much stronger than me. I'm just better at pretending.

As we got older, I stopped sneaking into her bed. I was a big girl, and it was expected that I would sleep in my own. It was always cold and lonely, never peaceful. Most nights, I managed, but there were times when I couldn't rest. I would toss and turn until the bed beneath me would squeak as Asya climbed in next to me. She always knew. God, I miss her so much.

I'm so glad she found Pasha, though. The day of her wedding was the most joyful day of my life. Seeing her happy and smiling, after everything she'd been through, was a wish come true for me. Even if, in a way, it meant losing her.

I take my phone out again and stare at the screen. It's too late to call Asya now, and we already chatted this afternoon. Throwing the device on the bed, I crouch next to my yellow suitcase that holds the essentials and start digging around, searching for my notebook. Writing always helps lift my spirits when I'm feeling down.

Five minutes later, I'm sprawled on top of the duvet, leafing through my thick glittery notebook when a thought strikes me. I never did ask Drago how he knew about my story.

Drago

The blond man sitting across from me in the booth leans forward and points his finger at me. "I don't like you, Drago."

"Well, I don't like you either, Belov, but, as it happens, your pakhan likes the ammunition I'm offering. So, are we doing business or not?"

The Russian narrows his eyes at me and bursts out laughing, then takes his phone and calls someone, probably Petrov. Sergei Belov has a deep voice so I can hear everything he says, but it doesn't give me much insight into the conversation he's having in Russian with the Bratva pakhan.

"Delivery every two months," he says when he ends the call. "And Roman wants to meet you in person. Next month."

"All right. I'll let you know the time and place."

Belov nods and stands up to leave, then looks down at the armchair he just vacated. "Mind if I take a picture of the booth? I keep trying to convince Pasha to change the interior of our clubs to white. He said he'll consider it when I retire."

I raise an eyebrow. "Any particular reason for that?"

"Yeah." He lifts his phone and snaps a shot. "It's a bitch to get blood out of the light-colored upholstery, apparently."

I follow him with my eyes as he strolls toward the exit, whistling along the way. It seems the guy is as crazy as I've heard people say.

Picking up my phone off the table, I check the message Filip sent me earlier—an address for the man who squealed to the Romanians about our shipment. It's a couple of hours away, but there's still time to drop in and see what my sparkling wife is up to before I head out. Jovan has been sending me hourly updates, and the last one said Sienna and her friend just entered a restaurant that's fifteen minutes from the club.

The underground garage below Naos is filled with several vehicles, including the SUV I drove here and two beat-up cars I use when I don't want to be noticed. I move past all of those and approach the black bike I parked in the far corner. Riding on two wheels is a much wiser choice when handling delicate issues. Our snitch, Wesley, has become one of those issues and needs to be made into an example so our other associates know what will happen if they follow his lead.

When I reach the restaurant, I park my bike on the driver's side of Jovan's white sedan and raise the visor on my helmet. My wife is sitting at a table next to a floor-to-ceiling window, and the blonde girl from Naos is with her. They are laughing about something. Sienna is wearing a sweater in an awful shade of blue. As if that's not enough, it has glittery gold detailing that sparkles whenever the sunlight falls upon her. My eyes slide down to her legs, clad in shiny gold skinny pants, and stop on the shoes. Same blue hue as her sweater, with small bows on the heels.

"I'm listening," I say and turn to Jovan.

He leans his elbow out of the open window and nods toward the women. "She met up with this girl, Luna, and another friend at the mall. They went to a few boutiques to buy some trinkets, then she dragged them to a store that sells stationery."

"What did she buy there?"

"A few notebooks and some pens. And a pen holder that looks like a rabbit." He rolls his eyes.

"And after?"

"They strolled around the shopping complex for a bit, taking selfies, and then we dropped off the other girl at her home and came here."

"Anything else?"

"Her brother called her on our way to this place."

"What did they talk about?" I ask.

"I couldn't hear his side of the conversation, but based on her replies, I think he wanted to know if she was okay. She said she's having a great time spending your money."

I look back at my wife. The bank sends me a text message every time my card is used. I didn't receive any today. She was paying for her purchases with her own money.

Jovan says something else, but with the helmet on, I don't catch it.

"Repeat," I say and turn to face him.

"She got another call just before we reached the restaurant, but didn't answer it. When she looked at the phone, she must have declined and put it back into her purse."

"Interesting. If she gets any more strange calls, let me know."

"Sure."

I switch my gaze back to my wife who's currently giggling with the waitress, motioning with her hands through the air. Her nails are gold today. I move my eyes from her hands to her lips wondering what got her so excited. Her lips are moving, and I can see them clearly, but I can't decipher anything she's saying. The waitress responds, but I don't catch what the young Asian woman says, either. I look up at the sign above the entrance. It's a Japanese restaurant. No wonder I can't get a read on their conversation. I don't speak Japanese, but it looks like Sienna does. Well, isn't my glittery wife full of surprises?

"Call Keva," I tell Jovan. "After dinner, I want her to ask my wife to help around the kitchen."

Jovan stares at me, his eyebrows hitting his hairline. "All right," he mumbles, confusion written all over his face.

"Small tasks, nothing hard. If Sienna says no, tell Keva not to insist."

"Is that all?"

"I'll be dealing with Wesley tonight and won't be home before midnight. Tell Keva to message me with what happened in the kitchen."

Jovan responds, but I don't pay any attention to him, my eyes back on my wife. This morning, I woke up with Sienna in my arms, curled up like a kitten. I wished I didn't have to leave her. Staying in bed, with her snuggled into my body, sounded like a much better option than heading to work, even without sex in the picture. I tried to recall if I ever had an urge to spend a night with a woman if there wasn't sex involved and came up blank. And I most certainly have never delayed business obligations so I could check up on one, either. But here I am now, spying on *my wife*, instead of heading to off the fucker who couldn't keep his mouth shut. And wondering who the fuck was on the other line of the phone call she disconnected.

"If any man approaches my wife, take care of him," I growl and lower my visor. Time to pay a visit to the snitch.

"Take care of him?" Jovan asks. "In what way?"

I meet his gaze through the tinted shield. "In any way that ends with requiring a spot at a cemetery, Jovan."

It's well after midnight when I finally arrive home. I had to take a longer route back because the police presence around Wesley's block was heavy. Someone probably reported screaming.

I nod at the man on guard by the front door. "Anything?"

"No. The guards outside the perimeter fence confirmed there is nothing suspicious."

"Good," I say and head upstairs.

It's just a matter of time until Bogdan makes his move. He'll probably hit one of our warehouses or maybe the club, but I prefer to cover all my bases, so I made sure we have men positioned along the road leading up to the house.

I step inside my bedroom and instantly know something isn't right. The pile of colorful suitcases is gone. My bed is empty. Looks like my wife thinks she has a say about our sleeping arrangements. I throw my jacket onto the recliner next to the balcony doors and head into the bathroom.

After a much-needed shower, I walk down the hall, checking the rooms along the way. There are several unoccupied suites on this floor because I'd rather not have anyone around me for the few hours I allow myself to rest, so she could be in any of them.

The first few rooms I pass are empty. I slip by Keva's and Filip's without checking, as well as some others used by my men, and proceed further down the hallway. My wife is in the last bedroom on this floor, sleeping under a thin blanket on a tiny-ass bed that could never fit my large frame. Her suitcases are stacked in the corner, all eight of them.

Leaning my shoulder on the doorframe, I watch her sleeping form. I was convinced she would decline to help around the kitchen. But the message I received from Keva wasn't a text, it was a photo of my wife standing on a small stool in front of a sink, scrubbing an enormous, burned pan. She was wearing the same gold pants and blue sweater she had on at the restaurant, only instead of high heels, she had on some fuzzy monstrosity on her feet. Several more photos followed. Sienna placing glasses into a cupboard. Leaning over the stove, looking inside a steaming pot. Carrying dirty dishes while clearly laughing over something. I was seriously tempted to leave my task of killing Wesley for another day and head home just so I could watch Sienna while she appeared to be enjoying her tasks.

The Italians in Cosa Nostra are a very special lot. Those at the upper levels of the hierarchy are treated almost like royalty, and a lot of them act as if they actually are. Especially women. I went out with the sister of one of the capos a few years back and was tempted to off myself twenty minutes into our date. I don't even remember the name of the woman, only the feeling that I was sitting across an empty shell of a person. A mannequin in a shop window whose only purpose in life was to showcase the expensive clothes she had on. Peel those away, and nothing but a plastic dummy remained.

My wife may wear equally expensive attire, but I have a feeling that there are many, many more layers under her surface. And I intend to peel every single one of them and find out what hides beneath.

Walking toward the suitcases, I pick up the first two and carry them back to my room. After repeating the act three more times, I approach the bed where Sienna is sleeping and slide my arms under her slight frame. I may not have any intention of having sex with her yet, but there is only one place she's allowed to sleep. In my bed.

Sienna stirs, mumbles something, and buries her face in my chest. I carry her back to my bedroom, carefully lower her onto the bed, and climb in to lie behind her. She keeps sleeping even when I wrap my arm around her waist and pull her against my body.

Chapter
seven

THE MOMENT I OPEN MY EYES, I KNOW I'M IN THE wrong room. Instead of a small curtainless window, I'm looking at long navy drapes covering French doors that lead to a balcony. My husband's room. He probably carried me here while I was asleep. And my suitcases are back as well, lined along the wall. A small smile pulls at my lips.

I roll over, finding the other side of the bed empty, and an unwelcome pang of disappointment stabs me in the gut. Did I secretly hope Drago would be next to me? I guess I did, a little. The bedroom door is shut, and he's nowhere in sight. I reach for his pillow and pull it to my face. It smells like him. I might like waking up in Drago's bed, but I'm still going to move my stuff back into the small room again, later. I'm not sleeping with a man I don't know, no matter how hot he is.

The thump of approaching footsteps resonates in the hallway. I throw the pillow away as if it burned me, jump out of bed, and head toward the suitcases.

"You missed breakfast," Drago's voice rumbles through the room from the doorway. "Keva put something aside for you in the kitchen."

"Thank you, dear," I say as I rummage through the contents of a suitcase. "Hey, I was wondering—"

"We're taking a quick tour of the property before I'm headed to work," he interrupts me midsentence. "I'll be waiting for you in front of the garage. Hurry. I don't have all day."

"Oh, that's so nice of you to offer, but I'm not into taking a stroll this early in the morning. How about we leave it for the afternoon, huh?" I look over my shoulder. He's already gone.

"That was rude!" I yell after him.

I dress in under ten minutes and dash down the wide stairwell to the ground floor. Two of Drago's men are standing by the front door, completely engrossed in their discussion while getting their coats on.

I approach and offer them a beaming smile. "Such a lovely morning. Going to a meeting?"

They both glare down at me. The man on my right is wearing a black suit and a crooked, half-knotted tie around his neck. I think his name is Iliya. I had a chance to explore the house with Jelena yesterday, and she pointed out a few people we passed. There are so many who live here, though, it's going to take me a while to get to know everyone.

"Oh, you can't go out like that, sweet cheeks." I shake my head and adjust his tie. "There. Much better. Did you two have breakfast?"

When I look up again, I find them both looking at me with wide eyes and brows creeping toward their hairlines.

"Yes," they mumble in unison.

"Oh good. Have a nice day, then." I wave and head across the foyer.

As I make my way to the kitchen, I think back to last night's after-dinner episode. The kitchen looked like a bomb went off there—stacks of dirty dishes everywhere, and the girls running around, putting away the leftovers and stuffing plates into dishwashers. There are three, and I'm certain they are constantly running with the number of dishes that every meal produces. I'm surprised they don't have one of those commercial units, like a restaurant. The scene was chaotic, but I actually found it calming somehow.

Drago wasn't at dinner, as I hoped he would be, and I was feeling a bit down because of it. So, when Keva noticed me standing in the doorway, she asked if I'd like to help. I shrugged and readily agreed. The next second, she shoved a burned pot into my hands. It took me more than thirty minutes to scrub that thing, but it probably would have been two hours if Nata hadn't noticed that I was using a sponge and gave me a metallic-looking thingy to use instead.

I'm not accustomed to housework—we had a maid for that—but I quite enjoyed helping Keva and the girls. The women laughed and gossiped about their boyfriends, throwing curious looks in my direction every once in a while. Then, at one point, they suddenly switched to English and pulled me into a conversation. We busied ourselves until Keva shooed us out. I ended up with a chipped nail, but it was fun.

The kitchen is less frantic now, but there are still plenty of activities happening. The morning meal is long over, so three girls are loading up the dishwashers and tidying up. I spot Filip and a couple of other guys having their breakfast at a small table off to the side. They must have missed the main event just like I did. Keva is across the room, absently stirring the contents of a big bowl she's holding, her eyes on the TV suspended over the counter. She stills, her attention completely engrossed on the screen blasting the local news. There's never a shortage of drama in New York.

I spy an almost empty juice jug in the middle of the table the guys are sitting at, so I head over to the huge fridge and take out a full one. I noticed Keva putting a few of these in to chill yesterday.

"Here," I say as I set the juice on the table and smile before I take the empty jug to the dishwasher.

Adam, the big dark-haired guy who's in charge of the foot soldiers, according to Jelena, enters the kitchen.

"*Pop se zabavio sinoc, vidim.*" He nods toward the TV as he takes a can of soda from the fridge.

The priest had fun last night? What is considered "fun" for Serbian priests? Maybe he runs a church choir? I look up at the TV screen. A reporter is standing in front of a five-story building, speaking to the camera. Several police cars are parked behind him, and a yellow crime scene tape restricts entry to the premises.

"*. . . what is possibly another gang-related execution. The victim, Wesley Powells, was found by a neighbor. According to the eyewitness, Mr. Powells was nailed to a wall with spikes thrust through his hands. A sign of a cross was carved into his chest. Police, however, have not provided a further statement at this time.*"

"Dear God," I mumble as a shudder passes through me. Their priest must do much more than give spiritual guidance. "You need to be seriously disturbed to do that to a person."

Keva grabs the remote off the counter and quickly turns off the TV.

"I didn't notice you there," she says and resumes mixing whatever she had in the bowl. "I left those sandwiches for you."

"I kind of lost my appetite."

"You won't be leaving my kitchen until you've had your breakfast, Sienna."

I sigh and pick up the smallest sandwich off the plate. Her nickname definitely suits her.

"Why are you still in your pajamas?" she asks.

My mouth is full, but I mumble, "They're not pajamas."

Keva's eyes slide down my body, over my matching set of turquoise silk pants and a blouse with big fuchsia flowers on it. "Are you sure?"

"Yup."

She laughs, sounding like a mischievous squirrel. "Drago is going to love it."

"I was thinking the same thing." I grin.

I leave the kitchen and hurry across the dining room and entry hall. My yellow jacket is hanging on the wall next to several dozen other coats. I slip it on, smile at the scowling dude standing by the door, and head out of the house.

Drago is standing by a car parked on the driveway, speaking with the two guys I met by the front door earlier. They see me coming, give a head nod, then get inside the car and drive off. Well, a nod is better than nothing.

"I'm not sure that outfit is a good choice," Drago says, looking me over.

"Oh? Why?"

"You'll scare my dogs."

I stiffen. "I'm not interested in seeing your dogs."

"You don't like dogs?"

I meet his piercing gaze and smile while bile rises up my throat. "I hate dogs."

"Too bad. You're meeting them, anyway." He takes my hand and leads me across the lawn.

"I don't want to see your damn dogs!" I try to pull away as we walk around the house. "Drago!"

He stops and takes my chin between his fingers. "They're guard dogs, Sienna, but they don't know you or your scent. You need to meet them so they can take a sniff and see that you're with me. You don't have to be scared."

"I'm not," I choke out.

"No? You seem pretty terrified to me." His thumb

brushes the side of my chin and stops at the corner of my lips. "Nothing will happen while you're with me, *mila*."

I close my eyes, enjoying his touch. His other hand is still holding mine, and I'm overwhelmed and so damn tempted. I'm trying hard not to lift onto my toes and kiss his hard mouth. We didn't kiss at city hall before we signed the marriage certificate. How would it feel to have his lips on mine?

Loud barking erupts on the other side of the back lawn. I open my eyes and look behind Drago. An iron fence divides the area, and beyond it, three rottweilers are jumping around, barking in our direction. They look excited, chasing each other and rearing back on their hind legs to brace their front paws on the barrier.

"Let's go say hi." Drago's hand falls away from my face.

While we slowly approach the fence, he keeps squeezing my hand lightly, as if to assure me that everything is going to be okay.

"Sit," he commands when we reach the enclosure. All three dogs immediately sit down, their eyes focused on him. Drago moves to stand behind me and wraps his arms around my middle.

"What are you doing?" I ask but completely forget about the question when a kiss lands on the side of my neck. The hold on my waist tightens as his lips move up to my chin.

"Keep your eyes on the dogs," he says next to my ear and wraps his fingers around my wrist, raising my hand to his lips.

The dogs are watching us with interest, their heads slightly tilted to the side. I keep my gaze on them as Drago's lips press to the back of my hand. My fingers begin to shake slightly as he turns my hand and kisses the center of my palm.

"Now, the other one," he says.

The simple act of breathing becomes hard as I lower my right hand and lift the left one, because I can still feel the caress of his lips on my skin. He takes my hand and pulls it closer to his mouth, but not close enough for another kiss. His hot breath fans across my palm. He's obviously doing this for the sake of the dogs. I don't understand the reasoning behind his actions, but I'm certain it has something to do with them. And I wish it didn't.

Drago runs his lips across my wrist, just over my pulse point, and I swear my heart skips a beat. It's as if a low-intensity electric current is running through me. Everywhere his lips touch, thrilling energy enters and spreads through my body, zapping every nerve ending in its path. Another kiss falls to my wrist, and then he moves my hand and presses my palm against his cheek. I take a deep breath and lean more onto him, my entire back plastered to his front.

"I think I've made my point." Drago lowers my hand and ushers me closer to the fence, beyond which the dogs are still sitting at attention.

"What point?" I ask and look up to find him watching me.

"That you're mine."

Not breaking our eye contact, he lifts my hand to the gap between the iron posts. All three rottweilers rise and, one by one, come over to sniff my hand. A wet, warm tongue licks my knuckles. Bonbon loved licking my hands and face.

I close my eyes for a second, then pull my hand out of Drago's. "Well, I've met your dogs, so I'll be on my merry way now. Have fun at work."

I turn toward the house, but his arm wraps around my waist, pulling me back and crushing me to his body.

"I'm sorry if they scared you," he says next to my ear. "I'll tell my men to only let them out to run around at night."

"Thank you," I say.

Apparently, he still thinks I'm afraid of dogs. Whatever. I don't plan on explaining myself.

Drago

She's not afraid of dogs.

I pause with my hand on the doorknob. I'm not exactly sure why that realization suddenly hits me now, hours later, but I know I'm right. Whatever the reason for Sienna's reluctance, it wasn't fear.

"Where is my wife?" I ask Jovan who's on guard duty at the front door.

"In the rec room."

I step inside and turn right toward the great rec room that takes up a good part of the ground floor on this side of the house. There are several big-screen TVs and gaming consoles, as well as a pool table and pinball machines Mirko bought last month. A small wet bar with a variety of beverages is in one of the corners. With nearly fifty people under the same roof, you need to provide some sort of entertainment unless you want your life to become a living hell. Especially during evenings.

As I enter the room, I expect to find my wife watching a movie or gossiping with a few of the women. Instead, I find her sitting with three of my men at the poker table that's set up close to the bar, with half a dozen people watching the unfolding game. The main overhead lighting is off, and only a pendant light above the table is illuminated, creating a very film noir ambience in the room. I stop by the bar to pour myself a drink, then lean on a nearby wall and observe what's happening.

My wife is perched cross-legged on a chair, holding the cards in her left hand while chewing on the pad of her right thumb. Mirko is to her right, wearing a smug expression. On her other side is Adam, and while his poker face doesn't show it, he believes he's going to win. We've been friends since high school, and I know all his tells. Across from Sienna is Relja. I found him freezing on the streets when he was still a kid and brought him here. As usual, he's completely enigmatic. I'm not sure I've ever met a man who's been as hard to read as Relja.

There's a minuscule heap of money at the center of the table, probably no more than a couple of hundred bucks in small bills. Hardly a high-stakes game; they're obviously playing for fun. My attention shifts back to my wife as she takes off her big gold hoop earrings and drops them on top of the cash pile. Sienna resumes chewing on her thumb, her eyes flitting from one man to another in rapid succession. Anyone else may think that her cards are crap. My lips tug into a smile.

All three men at the table think that my wife is losing.

And all three of them are wrong.

I leave my empty glass on the counter and stride toward the group, then come to a stop behind Sienna. Grabbing the side of her chair, I turn it one-eighty and shove the back of it against the table's edge. She must have given a little yelp when I spun her around because she's looking at me with a slightly wild look in her eyes.

"Drago?" she gasps. "What . . ."

My hands land on Sienna's waist. I lift her off the chair and take her place, then deposit her astride on my lap. Blinking at me in confusion, my wife presses the cards to her chest to hide them from view of her opponents. I can hear the guys behind me subtly clearing their throats as they take in our new position, and spot more than a few curious looks in my peripheral vision from the onlookers around the room.

"Feel free to continue," I say, my eyes sliding back to Sienna's face, just inches away from mine.

"Like this?"

"Yes."

Her lips curve into a mischievous smile. She looks down at the cards in her hands, then leans toward me, reaching over my shoulder for a card on the table. I move my hand to the small of her back and pull her closer until her breasts are crushed against me and her pussy settles over my rapidly hardening cock. The chatter around the room dies down. By all outward appearances, Sienna remains unperturbed, but she can't hide the rapid rise of her chest from me.

"Getting distracted?" I ask and lean back slightly so I can see her reply.

"Not at all."

"Hmm . . ." Taking the cards from her hand, I throw a quick look at what she's got.

A winning hand, just as I thought.

"She won. You can all leave," I say and toss the cards over my shoulder onto the table.

There is a sound of chairs scraping the floor and footsteps hurrying away behind my back. The crowd around us slowly disperses, as well.

"You ruined my game," Sienna whispers, staring into my eyes.

"I did." I lift my hand and stroke the line of her jaw. "What's the deal with the dogs, Sienna?"

Her body goes utterly still, but the very next moment, she relaxes and smiles. "What do you mean?"

I tilt my head to the side and just watch her face. Her smile seems genuine. But it doesn't reach her eyes. And she knows exactly what I mean.

"Well, I should get going now. I need to wash my hair," she blurts out and climbs down off my lap. "See you later."

I follow her with my eyes as she rushes to collect her earrings and the money from the table, then quickly leaves the room. Crossing my arms over my chest, I regard the door she disappeared through.

I will find out her secrets. It may take time since I suspect pushing her won't yield any results. Doesn't matter. I am a very patient man.

Chapter eight

I WAKE TO THE SOOTHING SOUND OF THE SHOWER drifting from the bathroom, but I didn't need to hear it to know that Drago is no longer in bed with me. His warmth is absent, and I miss the sense of peace I've gotten used to over the past ten nights.

After my first endeavor to sleep in a separate room only to find myself back in Drago's bed in the morning, I attempted that stunt twice more. Each time, my husband carried me to his room. I stopped trying to "escape" after that because I like sleeping with his body spooning mine more than I care to admit. And that's all we've done so far. Sleep.

Other than holding me, he hasn't *touched* me. I wish he would. A few times when I woke while he was still in bed, I pretended to still be asleep, enjoying being pressed to his hard chest. His chest wasn't the only thing that was hard, and it freaked me out a little. I've never had sex before.

I've had a couple of boyfriends, but we never went further than first base. It's not as if I was saving myself for marriage, and I'm not scared of the intimate act itself. It's just . . . being attracted to someone physically has never been enough for me.

An alluring body that had no impact on me mentally held as much of my interest as a bedazzled paperweight. Pretty to look at, but not essential in my life.

Whenever a guy pressed to have sex, I would break up with him. I just couldn't handle the idea of getting that close to anyone. I had my reasons. Usually, when relationships reach a certain level, people tend to believe they're entitled to "more." More talking. More explanations. More of *you*. But the pieces of *me* were always locked away. Always hidden, especially from whatever man I happened to have been seeing. What if I did open up, letting him glimpse what hides behind my carefully composed facade, and he decided to leave? Or even worse, he stayed, and I developed feelings for him. No.

No feelings meant no hurt if anything bad happened. The pain and heartbreak weren't worth the carnal experience.

My sister knows this about me. She's always known *me*. Asya once said that I need a man who can seduce my brain before I would allow him to fuck my pussy. Whatever the hell that means.

I roll over onto my back and stare at the ceiling, contemplating how lonely this enormous bed feels when Drago isn't here with me. What would he say if I asked him to come back to bed after the shower so we could cuddle a bit longer? He would either laugh or think I'm trying to tempt him to have sex with me. If he acted like he wanted to, I would have jumped all over him, consequences be damned. But it's not sex I'm after. I have this strange urge to just be close to him, to bury my face into his neck and absorb his scent. It's stupid, I know, but I can't help it.

The water shuts off, and two minutes later, my husband comes out of the bathroom wearing only a towel around his waist.

I pretend I'm still asleep and watch him from beneath half-lowered lids. He has one of the most beautiful male bodies

I've ever set eyes on. It's not like I've seen many, but still. Wide shoulders and heavily muscled arms. Hard, chiseled abs that I could probably bounce a quarter off if I threw one. He walks toward the closet on the other side of the room, and I move my eyes to his back, observing the burn scars that cover the left side of his body. They are mostly concentrated across his shoulder blades and just below, but there are some on his forearm and the back of his hand. I noticed those only recently because they're covered with tattoos.

I googled burns the other day and, based on everything I read and the images that showed the different stages of healing, I concluded that Drago has had skin grafts. Was he caught in a fire when he was younger?

Drago removes the towel, and I snap my eyes closed. An instinctive act for someone who's not used to seeing a naked man. But my curiosity gets the better of me, and I lift my lids to ogle his ass. When he reaches to take something off the shelf, I glimpse his cock and squeeze my eyes shut again. Should it be that huge? I imagine his big cock sliding into me, wondering how it would feel, and bite the inside of my cheek to stifle a sigh.

The echo of approaching steps reaches me a split second before the duvet flies off my body.

"Get up."

I keep my eyes closed, pretending to still be asleep.

"I know you're awake."

Crap. Does he know I was gaping at his cock? I crack my lids open and find Drago standing at the foot of the bed. He's wearing black sweatpants and a red hoodie.

"What time is it?" I ask. I missed breakfast yesterday and had to go to the kitchen to ask Keva for some leftovers. The meal schedule they have here doesn't work that well with my biorhythm. Breakfast at eight? That's tyranny.

"Six thirty. You're going for a run with me."

"I don't think so." I snort and bury my face into the pillow.

A hand wraps around my ankle, pulling me toward the edge. I yelp and try to push him off with my free leg. Drago bends, picks me up, and carries me to the en suite. I'm kicking my feet in front of me while squeezing his forearms, trying in vain to free myself. The moment he sets me down inside the bathroom, I shove at his chest.

"I'm not one of your subordinates, Drago!" I jab him again. "You can't order me around."

"You're not my subordinate." He takes a step forward, making me take two steps back. "But you belong to me. And I won't let you go around as pale as a sheet of paper. We're going for a run, and we're not coming back until you get some color in your face."

"I'm not your property," I meant to say it with a grin, but it ends up being a semi-sneer through my teeth. For some reason, my "nice persona" filter doesn't seem to work that well when he's around.

Drago looks down at my hand, which is still pressed against his chest. "That says you are."

I follow his gaze and see it focused on my wedding ring.

"Oh, really? I thought it meant we signed a marriage certificate, not a bill of sale. But I guess that misunderstanding is easy to correct." I lift my hand in front of his face, planning to take off the wedding band. The moment he registers my intention, he grabs my chin and tilts my head up.

"Feel free to take it off if you want," he says casually, then leans until our faces are at the same level. "But know one thing, *mila moya*. Any man who sets his eyes on you while you're not wearing the wedding ring is going to die."

I roll my eyes. Yeah, sure. He probably forgot that I was present when he got yelled at by Keva and did nothing about it. He's not going to kill anyone, especially for just looking at me. I guess I was lucky to have ended up with Drago rather than someone who does go around killing people. It's a risk with arranged marriages. I could have wedded someone like the priest guy. It's obvious that man handles the offing of the people for Drago, or Adam wouldn't have made that comment in the kitchen when we saw the news report.

"I'll be waiting for you outside." He releases my chin and leaves.

I shake my head and grab a toothbrush. There's no way I'm going for a run with him. Even if I didn't hate running—which I do—I don't have anything suitable to wear. But maybe I could take a stroll around the property and check the number of guards. Ajello has called me twice since I got here, but I couldn't answer either time because there were people around. I did send him a text saying I haven't learned anything important as of yet, but I will have to call him soon to tell him *something*.

The mirror above the sink is still foggy from Drago's shower. I swipe my palm over it and stare at my reflection. It doesn't feel right to gather info about my husband and pass it to the don, but I don't have a choice. Family always comes first, that's the Cosa Nostra motto.

I'm descending the stairs when an idea pops into my mind. Smirking, I take off the wedding ring and stuff it into the pocket of my pink jeans. The front door is open, and Keva is at the threshold, signing some paperwork for a man in overalls with the name of the local plumbing company above his left breast pocket. I pass by them and head toward Drago, who's waiting in the middle of the driveway, fiddling with his phone. His thumbs move rapidly as he types. That's got to be a lengthy text or an email. Wouldn't it be easier to just call the person?

When I come to a stop in front of him, he puts the phone away and scans me from head to toe. "Are you serious?"

"Why?" I raise an eyebrow.

"High-heeled boots. And . . . what is that?" He gestures at my chest.

"An oversized sweater dress," I say. It's one of my favorites, yellow with a pattern of big hearts in the same pink shade as my jeans.

I usually pick my outfits based on how I feel. When my mood is low, I tend to go for colorful, silly combinations. Recently, however, I've been choosing my clothes solely because I enjoy Drago's reactions. There's something utterly cute about his grumbling every time he sees my attire for the day. One thing that I've found really surprising, not once has he said "You can't go in public wearing that." Like some of my friends and ex-boyfriends often have. He typically gripes a little or just looks at the heavens and shakes his head, but that's all. He seems to be perfectly fine with me going around in what he calls "chicken jacket" or "yellow eyesore." Some of my outfits are ridiculous, but Drago has never said that I look ridiculous in them.

"Three of you can fit in that thing, Sienna. Go change into something comfy. And put on your sneakers."

"This *is* comfy. And I don't own sneakers."

"You don't own sneakers."

"Nope. Only heels. Sorry." I grin.

"*Isuse*," he mumbles and looks around, zeroing in on Jovan coming out of the garage. "Jovan, keys," he barks.

Jovan looks momentarily confused, but then fishes a set of car keys out of his pocket and throws them to Drago.

"Are we going for a ride instead?" I ask.

"We're going to buy you fucking sneakers, Sienna."

We're walking toward Jovan's car when the plumber passes us. He throws a look at me, then proceeds toward his van. I reach for the passenger door when Drago's fingers wrap around my wrist.

"You're not wearing your wedding ring," he says.

"You said you don't mind."

"I don't," he declares, closes the door after me, and rounds the hood. I expect him to get behind the wheel, but he strides across the driveway toward the van where the plumber is packing away his tools. What's he doing? Maybe he wants to ask the guy someth—*Jesus fuck*!

I dash out of the car and run to the van where my husband is holding the plumber up against the side of the vehicle. Drago's hand is wrapped around the guy's throat and, going by how red in the face the poor man is, he's choking him.

"Drago!" I grab the back of his hoodie and try to pull him off. The guy looks like he's going to pass out any moment. "Hey!"

Drago looks over his shoulder and pins me with his gaze. "What?"

"*What*, what? Are you crazy? Release the guy!"

"We had a deal, Sienna. No wedding ring means men who look at you die." He turns back toward the plumber and resumes strangling the life out of him.

Oh my God, he was serious! I've never seen him be aggressive to anyone. Despite his grumpiness and commanding presence, I don't think that's his nature. Letting go of his hoodie, I check my pockets hysterically. Where, where . . .? Yes! I pull out the wedding ring from my pocket and slide it onto my finger.

"Here!" I lift my hand and wave it in front of Drago's face, trying to contain my panic. "It's back on. Please, stop. Please, please, please."

He looks at my hand, then down at me. "Will it stay on?"

"I'll glue it onto my finger if you want. Just please don't kill the plumber."

Drago's eyes shift back to the hand I'm still holding up in

the air, and he releases his grip on the guy's neck. "All right. Let's go buy those sneakers."

Drago

Sienna is standing in front of the big mirror at the local supermarket, looking at her reflection. It's the only place open this early in the morning that'll have what we're after. I wasn't sure how she'd react about me taking her here instead of her usual shopping grounds, but she didn't even bat an eye—walked in as if she's been doing it every week of her life. It was amusing how excited she got, although she tried to hide it, over finding apparel being sold just a few aisles away from the fresh produce. She insisted we needed to get a box of mandarin oranges as well, and now I get to haul it around while Sienna tries on various athletic clothes.

The outfit she's put on consists of a pale-blue sweatshirt and matching sweatpants, paired with white leather running shoes. I don't know if I've ever seen anyone look so miserable as Sienna does now while she assesses her getup. She's muttering something, so I move my eyes to her lips.

". . . not even a real color. Stupid washed-out blue. It's depressing."

"The color is making you depressed?"

"Yes. Very."

I look around and spot the store attendant standing by a rack of jackets. Leaving my wife to her mumbling, I approach the woman.

"I need you to find me the most ridiculous-looking tracksuit you have in store."

The sales lady's eyes widen in surprise. "The most . . . ridiculous?"

"Yes. Something no sane woman would buy. Screaming fuchsia. Neon-orange. An idiotic animal pattern in a god-awful color. Or something that glitters. Shoes, as well."

"Oh . . . I'll see what I can do."

The attendant rushes away and comes back five minutes later carrying a matching sweatshirt and pants. The set is vibrant lavender and has a wide yellow stripe running along the outside of the pant legs and sleeves. There's no glitter, but the tie string on the pants is made of satin, and it's in the same yellow shade as the stripes.

"That should do it." I nod. "Sneakers?"

She lifts a pair of running shoes. The sole is white, but they do have a colorful pattern on the sides. I take one out of the clerk's raised hand to have a better look. It's a bunch of small multicolored rabbits.

"Perfect." I gather the clothes and the other shoe and return to my wife.

The instant Sienna sees the stuff I'm carrying, she runs over to grab the lot and dashes into the nearby changing room. I lean my shoulder on the sidewall of the fitting room across from Sienna's and watch her feet through the gap between the floor and the door. She is hopping around on one leg while putting on the sweatpants. A small smile pulls at my lips. I don't remember the last time I was so amused by someone. For years, work has been the only exhilarating thing filling my otherwise mundane days. Not anymore. Now, the little hellion with crazy clothes and mischievous grin has been occupying most of my attention.

Fascinated. Yes, I'm completely fascinated with my sparkling wife, and I'll be damned if I know why. She's too young, eccentric, constantly smiling, and sunny to a disturbing level. The thing is, I don't like cheerful people. No one can be happy all the time. If they act that way, they are either stupid or pretending. And if there is one thing I'm one hundred percent certain about, it's that my sparkling little wife is far from stupid. Even if the way she acts can easily convince people otherwise. But it's they who are the fools for not seeing what is so clear to me.

The door creaks open to reveal Sienna in that hideous lavender outfit. I don't understand how she can look so beautiful wearing such idiotic clothes. She grins at me, lifts her phone, and snaps a selfie while pursing her lips at the camera.

"Are you posting that to social media?" I ask.

"Of course. Why?"

"No reason." As soon as I get back home, I'm instructing Mirko to do something with her social media accounts. He hacks government sites on a regular basis, so he must know some way to hide Sienna's images. No one is allowed to salivate over my wife's pictures except me. Yesterday morning, while Sienna was still sleeping, I snapped a quick shot of her in bed with my phone. I'm still not sure why I did that.

On our way to the checkout area, we pass through the home decor section where two long shelves are stacked with different trinkets—dry flowers, glass figurines, photo frames, and other similar items. Sienna stops in front of a bowl filled with marbles in various colors. An excited squeal leaves her lips as she stares at the glass and runs her fingers through the glossy orbs. It's been a long time since I was as thrilled about anything as she seems to be over a handful of stupid glass pearls. I swear, this woman must have been a crow in her past life to be so captivated by shiny things. It's impossible not to be allured by her. A strange warm feeling spreads through my chest as I watch my wife being so happy, and I yearn to see more of that pure joy.

Even though I know she's been lying to me from the start.

"We'll take the path among the trees," I say as I close the car door after Sienna. "Let's go."

"So, you were serious about jogging?"

"I don't joke often, Sienna. Come on. Go ahead of me. Just follow the path."

"Why don't you lead?"

"I want you in my sight so you can't sneak back inside when I'm not looking."

Her shoulders sag, but she turns away and starts jogging toward the trees. I follow a few feet behind, matching her pace while ogling her sweet ass in those snug sports pants. That's one of the reasons why I insisted she goes first down the trail. The other, I wouldn't notice if she says something behind me.

As we are passing by a stretch of lawn where Beli is raking the leaves, Sienna stops and says something to him. Someone should have warned her that the old son of a bitch is antisocial and never talks to people. I linger a few steps to the side, making it look like I'm stretching my hamstrings as I watch the exchange between my wife and the gardener. I have never witnessed him crack a smile, so seeing him burst out laughing and hold up a thumb is incredible. Sienna waves at him and carries on.

"What did she say?" I ask when I approach the old grump.

"Your wife found me a new spot."

"A spot? For what?"

"For my lilies." He smiles and resumes raking the leaves.

I shake my head and continue on my run to catch up with my ray-of-sunshine wife, who is jogging in place thirty yards down the path. She's chatting with Relja. Who should be on the guard shift right now and doing his rounds, damn it! He sees me coming, turns on his heel, and rushes off in the direction of the gate.

"Don't distract my men while they're on duty."

Sienna tilts her head up and narrows her eyes at me. "You're really grumpy, you know. It's kind of . . . cute."

"I've been called a lot of names, Sienna"—I wrap my arm around her waist and pull her into my body—"but cute is not one of them."

I can feel her every breath as her chest rises and falls. Her lips are slightly parted, taunting me. I don't have much restraint left, and the need to make her mine is driving me crazy. Even despite her constant lies since the moment she set foot in my house, and probably before that, too. I let a spy into my home, but the most fucked up thing about this whole situation is—I don't regret it.

I wonder . . . Where did she learn Serbian?

Though I've been closely observing her from the moment she arrived, it took me more than a week to realize that little fact. It happened by accident during dinner a few days ago. Everyone was laughing at a joke while Keva was running around placing bowls of food on the table. Milo, one of the soldiers, stretched out his hand, asking someone to pass him the mashed potatoes. My wife smiled and handed him the bowl while still giggling over the punch line. And Milo doesn't speak English. I don't think she even noticed her mistake.

Ajello obviously knew Sienna could speak Serbian or he wouldn't have picked her. That scheming son of a bitch. No wonder half of the criminal underworld wants him dead. The question is, what should I do with my sparkling little Cosa Nostra spy? Should I kill her quickly, or should I make her suffer?

As I look at her, I realize one extremely inconvenient thing. Even if I wanted to, I wouldn't be able to hurt her. And worse, the mere idea of anyone putting a finger on my wife elicits a murderous rage within me.

"Let's head back." I release her from my embrace and begin walking, suddenly angry as hell.

But it's not her I'm angry at. I'm furious with myself. Because even knowing that my wife is a spy, she's all I can think about. All the. Damn. Time.

I've been spending the bulk of my days away from home so I don't succumb to the urge to put her over my shoulder, take her to the bedroom, and fuck her senseless. I want to keep my distance until I find out what Ajello's game is, but I can't. For over a week now I've been living for the moment when I can climb into bed next to her and hold her close. And every morning, I wake up with such an epic hard-on that I spend thirty minutes in the shower trying to find release while thinking about the little liar sleeping soundly in my bed. This morning, I had to jerk off twice. After my initial round, I left the bathroom only to see her lying there with her top ridden up to under her breasts and ass cheeks peeking out from the green sleeping shorts. I got hard instantly. So, I headed back inside the shower and imagined slamming my cock into her from behind until I came all over the tiled wall.

Sienna follows me as we head back toward the house, and I keep throwing glances over my shoulder. Her high ponytail swings left and right as she hops over the small rain puddles along the path, tempting me to pull her close and run my fingers through the brown strands. Iliya steps through the front door just as we get there, and Sienna rushes toward him, thrusting her phone in his hands. She's babbling something as she stands before him, but I can't understand what she's saying or read her lips. With a wide smile, she runs off to stand next to the fountain and strikes a pose. I pin Iliya with my glare.

"She wants me to take a few shots of her," he mouths. "For her social media."

I instantly snatch the phone out of his hand.

"You're free to go," I snap and turn toward my wife. "If you need anyone to take a photo of you, it's going to be me, Sienna."

"You were sulking, giving off these really grouchy vibes. It seems to be your preferred mood and I didn't want to interfere."

I narrow my eyes. If I catch any of my men taking photos of her, they'll get an up close and personal experience with my grouchy mood. "Get in position," I grumble.

Sienna leans toward the water, extending her hand to touch the stream. The stretchy fabric of her lavender pants accentuates the perfect curve of her pretty round ass.

"Done."

"Thank you," she chirps as she lifts the phone from my hand. "I'm uploading it right away. Love that fountain! The posts of me in front of it always get at least a few thousand likes."

Thousands? I fume as I watch her dance into the house, then head straight to Mirko's office. Fucking thousands!

CHAPTER
nine

I OPEN MY LAPTOP AND CLICK THE EMAIL ICON IN THE upper right corner of the screen. Calling the don would be easier, but with so many people in the house, I can't risk that someone will overhear. I start a new message, enter the email address the don gave me, and move to the subject line, typing: *The Alpha's Chosen Mate, Episode One.*

I shift my attention to the email body, my fingers flying over the keys.

Dear Silvia,

I hope you're well. As agreed, I'm sending you the first episode of my new paranormal romance that you'll be publishing in your online magazine. Please take a look and let me know your thoughts and suggestions for improvement.
Sienna

I add a few blank lines, then resume typing.

It was a cold, starless night when Georgina first set foot on the land owned by Darius, the Alpha of the Black River Wolves pack. Her heart was beating wildly, easily at double its usual rate, as she passed by her new mate and walked inside the den carved into a mountainside. Footsteps echoed off the walls along the narrow hallway as it wound deeper and deeper, broken up periodically by the offshoots leading to many smaller caves set all around her. The den was brimming with members of the pack. She tried to count them, but couldn't get the exact number. It seemed like they all lived within the den.

I stop for a moment, my fingers hovering over the keys. It's been almost three weeks since I arrived at Drago's home, and I kept finding reasons not to call the don. At first, I told myself that I had nothing meaningful to share, then there was always someone around or it was too late to make the call. But an hour ago, I received a one-word message from Don Ajello: SIENNA! It flashed across my screen in all caps, and I couldn't delay checking in any longer.

My fingers lower onto the keyboard once more, but my eyes wander to the big vase on the dresser that's filled with beautiful sparking crystals. I found it on the nightstand when I woke up this morning. Drago must have noticed that I like the multicolored glass when we were at the store the other day and bought these for me. The colors of the crystals are not as intense as those of the marbles at the supermarket, but these are cut into shapes of little diamonds which makes them so pretty. I moved the vase to the dresser where I can see it as soon as I enter the room and stuck my collection of pens and pencils into it.

I take a deep breath and look back at the email, but it's as if a heavy weight has settled over my chest. Putting the laptop aside, I get up from the bed and walk to the window that faces the driveway.

Keva is standing at the edge of the lawn with her hands on her hips, arguing with Jovan. I smile. He probably forgot to call the repairman to come out and take a look at the fridge, which has been humming strangely for the past few days. A bit to the right, Filip and Drago are getting into Drago's car. Both are wearing suits, so they're probably headed to a meeting. I haven't seen my husband in a suit too often, maybe twice so far. It looks good on him.

Just before he gets behind the wheel, Drago looks up toward my window, and our gazes connect for a brief moment. A wave of guilt overwhelms me as the reality of what I'm about to do hits me again. My eyes follow Drago's car as it pulls away. I stay rooted in place until it's out of sight, only then do I head back to my laptop.

I resume my typing, but the sour taste in my mouth refuses to dissipate.

Shortly after Georgina's arrival, it seemed like the pack was facing new challenges. She wasn't certain about the reasons, but from the hushed conversations she managed to overhear, it appeared that the Black River Wolves started a feud with the Transylvania Hills Bears. The Bears lived in the same territory as the Wolves, and both claimed ownership over the specific hunting ground.

Georgina's stay with the Black River Wolves pack was bound to be much more interesting than she originally thought.

To be continued . . .

My mind is still racing as I hold the mouse over the send button for almost a minute before finally hitting it.

The phone rings ten minutes later. Don Ajello's number lights up the screen.

"Silvia," I say as I answer the call, "you got my submission, I assume?"

"Pack?" Ajello's grim voice comes across the line. "Transylvania Bears?"

"It's a code," I whisper into the phone. "Transylvania Bears stands for the Romanians."

"I can't decipher your nonsense, Sienna. Start speaking."

I slump down on the edge of the bed and sigh. "Drago is handling everything around here. Filip, his second-in-command, oversees the execution of things. They launder the money through the club."

"I already knew all that. What else?"

"They have some problems with the Romanians. I didn't catch much, only that Drago upped the security."

"Your husband had a big deal go down the week you two got married. Did it have anything to do with the Romanians?"

"I haven't heard any details."

"And what was that garbage about caves?"

"Many of his men are living here, in Drago's house."

"How many?"

I grind my teeth together and bury my hand in my hair. It feels wrong to tell him all this.

"How many, Sienna?"

"Forty-eight," I mutter.

"And how many men does he have overall?"

"I don't know."

"Well, find out. Fast," he orders and cuts the call.

I look down at the phone in my hand, then throw it on the bed and dash out of the room.

"Sienna!" Jelena calls after me as I'm heading across the foyer "Would you . . ."

I ignore her and burst through the front door. It's a bit chilly outside but I don't head back to get my jacket.

There are several men loitering in front of the huge garage building that houses multiple bays for over a dozen cars situated to the left of the mansion, so I turn right and run toward the trees, away from everyone. The sour taste in my mouth won't leave me and only becomes worse with each passing minute. What will Ajello do with the information I provided? When I agreed to this stupid plan, it didn't sound too bad. But now . . .

I gave him the number of people who live here, in the house. That has to be one of the least meaningful pieces of information. It's not as if the don is planning on invading

Drago's home, but still, divulging that detail makes me feel so dirty.

I like the people here, and it feels like I'm betraying them. Most days, Drago is already gone by the time I wake up, except for the mornings when he drags me out jogging with him. But that only happens three times a week, and we spend about an hour pounding the dirt around the estate grounds. After that, he leaves, and I rarely see him again until dinner time. I've already read all the books I brought with me, which leaves me to spend my days writing in my new notebook or helping Keva in the kitchen.

If Asya saw me now, she would die laughing. At home, I don't think I've fried eggs on my own more than a handful of times. Here, though, I find it surprisingly fulfilling to be involved in the kitchen. The house is always teeming with people. Yes, it can get insane with everyone speaking at the same time and bumping into each other, but it's fun. Before, when it was just Arturo, Asya, and me, it was nice, too. But here . . . It's one big, strange family and, despite my obvious inexperience, I enjoy the mayhem even more. It's hard to feel alone with so many people around.

They hardly know me, but among them, I don't feel like an outsider. When I went into the kitchen the other day, still shaken after meeting Drago's dogs, Keva made me a hot chocolate and demanded I tell her who had upset me so she could whip their butts. And yesterday, when I was complaining that the shoes I wanted were sold out online, Mirko heard me and told me to email him the link so he could "handle it." The shoes arrived the same evening.

And then, there is my husband. Sometimes, I catch him nearby when I thought he wasn't even home. He watches me when he thinks I'm not looking, but I can feel his eyes on me every single time. The sweep of his gaze is like a light brush of a feather tickling the back of my neck. Every nerve in my system ignites with awareness.

I keep up my charade, pretending I don't notice his looks. But I'm fairly sure he knows he's not fooling me and sees through my bluff.

Even so, Drago continues to observe me as if he's trying to figure me out. At times, he reminds me of a gargoyle perched atop a great stone wall. Always watching. And waiting. I'm not sure what he's waiting for, but one thing I do know is, I like it. I like the excitement that stirs within me when he's near. And I love sleeping in his bed.

But what would he do if he found out I'm ratting him out to Ajello? I don't think he would kill me. He might be the head of a criminal organization, but excluding the incident with the plumber, he doesn't strike me as a violent person. So far, I haven't seen him hit or even yell at any of his people. Perhaps that's what he has the priest guy for—to dispose of those who oppose him rather than killing them himself.

I spend half an hour meandering the grounds around the mansion, no particular destination in mind. Eventually, I end up in the backyard. Drago's dogs are running inside their enclosure, but when they notice my approach, they stop playing and focus their attention on me. Whenever I've stopped here previously, I've always expected them to bark, but they never do. They don't do it now, either. They simply regard me. Just like their owner.

Usually, I leave after observing them for a few minutes, but this time, I take one tentative step forward. Then another one. The largest of the three props himself on his hind legs, pressing his front paws onto the iron fence. Cautiously, I approach the barrier and raise my hand to the dog's snout. He sniffs my fingers for a bit, then licks them. I crouch next to the fence and offer my left hand to the other dog smelling my pants.

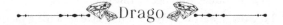 Drago

"When can we expect payment from the Russians?" Keva asks and turns the page of her thick old ledger.

"In two days," I say as I approach the dining table and take a seat across from her. "Why the fuck won't you let Mirko get you a laptop? You can't keep our financial records in that."

She looks at me over the rim of her glasses. "I'm not leaving sensitive information in some electronic box where anyone can access it."

"There are things called firewalls, Zivka. No one can access your stuff with one of those installed."

"Oh, yeah? Tell that to Yahoo."

I rub my temples and sigh.

"Sienna came down to breakfast looking super cheerful this morning," Keva says while a small smile pulls at her lips. "When I asked the reason for her good mood, she said you left her a present. A vase of multicolored glass crystals, which sparkle adorably, apparently."

"So, she liked it?"

"So much that I dropped by your room to see this 'glass' that got her so excited." She takes off her glasses and grins. "Do you know that your wife uses half a million dollars worth of precious gems as a pen holder?"

"She likes them. As far as I'm concerned, she can use them any way she wants," I say. "You didn't send me any pictures today."

"I haven't?" she feigns surprise. "I probably forgot. But you should have seen her this morning when Jovan drove her to the mall. She was wearing neon-green jeans and a yellow blouse with ruffles."

"She paired them with the chicken jacket?"

"But of course. And her yellow heels."

I furrow my brows. "You should have sent me a picture."

"Or you could have been here in person to see for yourself." She points her glasses at me. "You need to stop stalking her around the house, Drago."

"She's my wife. I can stalk her as much as I want."

Keva snorts. "Kovac called earlier. He's getting married on Sunday and has invited you and Sienna to attend."

"I don't do weddings, as you very well know. Especially not Serbian weddings." Going to a party with live music and several hundred guests, all of them yammering and singing in constant glee, is the personification of fucking hell for me. Two minutes of that shit is enough to turn my brain to mush.

"Maybe you could make an exception? Just a quick drop-in?"

"No."

"Shame." She lets out an exaggerated sigh. "Sienna would love it."

I lean back in the chair and imagine my wife in the middle of that madness. Yup, she would be thrilled. "Kovac did mention a new investment opportunity the last time we talked. Maybe we could stop by for a bit. Maintaining good relationships is beneficial for business."

"Perfect. Make sure you take Sienna to buy a dress for the occasion."

I raise an eyebrow. "Have you seen all the clothes that woman owns?"

"There is never 'enough' when it comes to ladies' outfits, Drago."

I roll my eyes and nod toward a small fish tank set on the corner shelf. Several orange fish zigzag among the water plants and other aquarium decorations. "What's that doing here?"

"Sienna bought it today at the mall."

"I don't like fish."

"I know." Keva is already reaching for her phone. "Sienna was very excited about them, but I'll tell Jovan to return the fish tank back to the store."

I clench my jaw. "Just leave the damn thing."

"Are you sure? I can have him do it right away."

"No one touches her fish," I say through gritted teeth. "And where is my sunny wife?"

"I don't know. She didn't come down for dinner, so I assumed she wasn't hungry."

Nodding, I stand up and leave the dining room, on a mission to find my wife. I was half an hour late for a meeting with a business associate this morning because I was waiting for Sienna to wake up so I could see her reaction to my gift. Eventually, I had to leave and it put me in a really bad mood. It got worse as the hours dragged on because I had too much work and couldn't drop by the house to see her, as I try to do at least twice a day. Keva not sending me photos was the icing on the cake of a shitty day, and I'm certain her lack of texts was purposeful.

The great rec room on the east side of the ground floor is packed with people, but Sienna isn't there.

"Anyone seen Sienna?" I ask.

More than thirty heads swivel in my direction. A bunch of noes and shaking follows.

I head to the top floor next, but she's not in the bedroom, either. Closing the door behind me, I return downstairs. Keva gapes at me as I sprint past her and shove the kitchen door open with enough force that it hits the adjacent wall.

"Where is my wife?!"

Four heads snap in my direction.

"She's not here," one of the girls cleaning the countertop says.

"I'm not fucking blind. When was the last time anyone saw her?"

"Maybe she's still outside?" Jelena says. "I saw her go out earlier, but that was about three hours ago."

I turn on my heel and run.

"I can't find Sienna," I bark at Iliya, who's standing by the front door, and grab my jacket. "Jelena says she saw her going outside. You and Relja take the front yard. I'll take the back."

When I burst outside, I head to the garage first in case she's wandered in there. She hasn't.

"Fuck!" I hit the wall with my palm and run back out.

What if Bogdan discovered our location and his guys somehow got to her? She could be gone. Off the grounds. Gone! Or they're still here, biding their time to slip away under the cover of darkness. Our security is tight, so they can't be too far.

I change course and take off toward the other part of the backyard. That's where the dogs are, so I doubt they'll be there, but I need to check just in case.

Something yellow by the fence attracts my attention. Dusk has fallen so I don't realize it's Sienna until I'm halfway to her. She's kneeling on the ground next to the dogs' enclosure with her arms pushed through the gaps, petting Zeus's head. The other two dogs are lying close by with their paws pressed to her legs.

"Jesus fuck." I take off my jacket and put it around her shoulders. She's still dressed in her outfit from earlier, and that ruffly shirt is way too thin for the rapidly dropping temperature. "What the fuck is wrong with you? Are you trying to freeze to death?"

Carefully, I pull her away from the fence and guide her arms inside the sleeves of my jacket. She doesn't even look at me, just keeps her gaze glued to the dogs. I lift her into my arms and run toward the house.

"Sienna?"

Her arms come around my neck, squeezing as she buries

her face against my shoulder. Why isn't she saying anything? Where are those snarky remarks? Mischievous grins?

I reach the front door and kick it open. Keva is hurrying across the foyer toward us, but I barrel straight to the stairway. "Bring me something hot," I yell. "Tea or cocoa. Now!"

When I get inside our bedroom, I place Sienna on the recliner by the balcony and wrap the blanket off the bed around her, then crouch at her feet and start removing her four-inch heels. They have little flowers on the toe part—a perfect choice for traipsing around the wet lawn and mud.

"*Moya blesava mila.*" Shaking my head, I rub her cold feet with my palms.

A few moments later the door behind me opens, and Jelena sets a tray with a big mug of tea and some cookies on the side table.

"Thank you. Now, leave," I say without looking at her. My gaze is focused on Sienna's face, which is absolutely expressionless. The only time I've seen her like this was at the club just before we met.

"Sienna?"

She blinks, pulls her feet out of my hands, and places them on the edge of the seat, wrapping her arms around her legs.

"I had a dog, you know?"

"Had?"

"Yes. His name was Bonbon."

I can't understand the actual words, but I do hear the tone of her voice. It's strangely flat.

"What happened?"

"He died because of me." She leans forward and sets her chin on her bent knees, looking somewhere over my shoulder. "He had kidney failure, but I was too distracted with my sister being missing to notice the signs. When I did, it was too late."

I knew that Arturo's sister disappeared a couple of years back, because he was inaccessible during that time, searching for her. That was when the whole shitshow with Pisano happened. I'm not aware of the specifics about what happened to the girl, aside from that she was missing for months and then ended up marrying a guy from the Bratva's inner circle. But, I can well imagine the hell both Sienna and her brother must have gone through not knowing if their sister was alive.

"But your sister is okay?" I ask as the old wound in my heart reopens and aches.

Sienna's eyes move to meet mine. "Yes. Asya almost died because of me, but she's okay now."

"What do you mean?"

"It doesn't matter." She quickly looks away. "What are their names? The dogs?"

I adjust the blanket around her shoulders and, not being able to resist the urge to soothe her somehow, brush the back of my palm down her cheek. "The big one is Zeus. The one with tan legs is Jupiter. And the third is Perun."

"Named after the gods," she says, surprising me. Zeus and Jupiter are more or less common knowledge, but not many know of the old Slavic god Perun. "I think I'll go to sleep now if that's okay with you."

"Drink your tea first."

Sienna takes the mug I hand her, and after she's done with the tea, she disappears into the bathroom. Fifteen minutes later, she climbs into bed, clutches the pillow to her chest, and pulls the covers all the way up to her chin.

I take a seat on the recliner and watch as she lies there, unmoving, while contemplating what I just witnessed. It appears my wife is neither maniacally happy nor shallow like she pretends to be. But I'm sure that once she awakes, she'll act as if nothing happened and continue with her carefree charade.

Sienna turns on her side, keeping a pillow tightly squeezed to her chest, as she usually does. I thought it was a habit, but now that I think about it, I realize that she only does that when I leave the bed in the morning.

I berate myself and shake my head. No woman could be so blasé about being torn away from her normal life and made to live in a house with people she doesn't know. Married to a man who's a complete stranger. Especially someone as young as Sienna, who has already experienced heartache in her life. Her parents were killed when she was just a little girl, and I know what kind of trauma that leaves. Then, her sister was kidnapped. And now this.

Drago, you idiot. I let her carefree act fool me. And on top of it, I tried to keep her at arm's length because I knew she was spying on me for Ajello. God only knows what's going on in her head and what's hidden behind those smiles that reach her eyes only on rare occasions.

After getting up from the recliner, I strip my clothes and approach the bed. Gently, I pull away the pillow my wife is clinging to, then climb under the covers and wrap my arms around Sienna, pressing her to my body. Immediately, she buries her face in the crook of my neck. Something in her hair scratches my chin. I lean back a bit and look down to see a big yellow butterfly-shaped hairpin at the top of her head. Sighing, I carefully remove the pin from her hair and toss it onto the nightstand. She stirs, grumbling something.

"You can't sleep with that crap in your hair, Sienna," I say and pull her closer to me.

CHAPTER
Ten

Sienna

"I'M TAKING YOU TO A WEDDING THIS WEEKEND," Drago's voice comes from somewhere in the bedroom.

A wedding? I open the bathroom door to see Drago standing on the other side of the room, looking sexy as hell in gray jeans and a black shirt with sleeves rolled up to his elbows.

"I have nothing to wear," I mumble with the toothbrush still in my mouth.

"What?"

I roll my eyes and pull the toothbrush out. "I said, I have nothing to wear."

Drago raises his eyebrows. "Are you fucking with me?"

"I can't go in my old clothes. I'll ask Jovan to drive me over to the store."

Drago finishes buttoning his shirt and comes to stand in front of me. "I'll drive you."

I bite my lower lip to prevent an idiotic grin from spreading across my face. When I woke up, I was afraid he'd start asking me questions about what happened last night, so I bolted for the bathroom. Looks like he forgot all about it, thank God.

"And how come everyone gets to have a wedding, and I only got a five-minute ceremony at the city hall?"

Drago braces his hands on the doorframe on either side of me and leans in close to my face. "Because those people are marrying for love. And you married for money, didn't you?"

I force a smile. "I did."

He dips his head even more, our mouths are almost touching. There's that analyzing look in his eyes again, like he's trying to figure me out.

"There's your answer," he says. "Get dressed. You have fifteen minutes."

I watch his broad back as he exits the room. Once he's gone, I turn around and stomp to the closet to rummage through the mess of clothes I stuffed inside when I unpacked. The space is rather large, but I have way too much stuff. One tear escapes my eye, and I quickly brush it away with the back of my hand.

I don't understand why Drago's words hit me so hard. It's not like I was delusional about our motives. He married me because it was a lucrative business opportunity. And I married him because . . . I'm an idiot. It's the truth. I shouldn't have let my fear of being alone lead me into this disaster. Asya was right. I should have waited to meet someone I would like, maybe love, and only then think about marrying the guy. A shudder races down my spine.

Nope. I would never let myself fall in love. People whom I love have ended up dead because of me. Like my parents. Like my sister almost did. All because of me. This is a much better setup. Drago gets the connection to Cosa Nostra, the don gets his intel on the Serbian organization, and I get to not be alone. Zero emotions involved.

When I step outside fourteen minutes later, Drago is standing by the car, leaning on the hood with his arms crossed over his chest. His eyes scan my pink-and-blue striped wide-leg pants then move up to my pink coat, and for a fleeting moment, a slight smile ghosts his face.

"Did that thing shrink in the wash?" he asks, giving my sleeves a quizzical once-over.

"Coats need to be dry-cleaned, not washed. And these are three-quarter sleeves."

"Will you enlighten me on the purpose of a coat with short sleeves?"

I bat my eyelashes at him "To make me look pretty."

Drago raises his hand and traces the back of his palm down my cheek. Those green eyes capture and hold mine. "If that's the case, I'm afraid it doesn't serve its purpose, *mila moya.*"

I gasp, shocked and hurt. I know I'm not the type of woman who could make men fall to their knees in front of me. And I'm certainly not in the same league as the woman I saw with him in that picture Ajello sent me. But to imply I'm ugly?

I start to step away from him but his free arm wraps around my waist, keeping me pressed to his body. His eyes are glued to mine, glistening dangerously. Taunting me. Daring me. Daring me to do what? To spit into his face? To start crying? No, that's not like him.

The hold around my waist tightens. His other hand is still on my face, caressing my cheek. I squeeze a handful of his shirt in my fist and narrow my eyes at him, trying to decipher what this silent game is about. Drago bends until his mouth is just next to my ear.

"Your coat doesn't serve its purpose," he whispers in Serbian, his voice is husky and glides over me like liquid honey, "because you're fucking perfect, Sienna. More beautiful than anyone I've ever known."

My heart stops. And then leaps as if wanting to burst from my chest, beating at a frantic pace. What if he hears it and realizes I understood?

"What did you say?" I quickly ask.

Drago releases his hold on me and opens the car door for me.

"Time to go." He switches back to English, ignoring my question. "Hurry up. I have a meeting this afternoon I need to attend."

Plastering a carefree little smile on my face, I take hold of the sides of my coat and lower myself onto the passenger seat. While Drago walks around the car, I purposely adjust the rearview mirror toward me instead of flipping down my sun visor, take out the makeup pouch from my purse, and start applying my lipstick. What was that just a moment ago? Some kind of a test?

"I need that, Sienna." My husband grumbles and readjusts the mirror back.

"I claimed it first," I chirp, hoping it'll help cover up how shaken I feel.

Drago moves his gaze from my lips to my eyes and keeps them there for a few long moments. Then, he starts the car.

Drago

The curtain of the changing room slides to the side, and Sienna walks out wearing a Barbie-pink dress with a frill on the hem. I watch her from the sofa situated opposite the tall mirror as she scrutinizes her reflection, turning left and right, checking out the outfit. She looks drop-dead gorgeous in it, as she has in all the previous dresses I've made her try on. I think this is the twelfth one.

She turns around and sticks out her hip. "And this one?"

I move my gaze down from her delicate chest and along her shapely legs, then back up. "No."

"No? What do you mean, 'no'? I've tried on every damn dress here. How is it possible you don't like any of them?"

I lean back and sprawl my arms along the back of the sofa, regarding her. I never said I didn't like them.

"Drago!"

I close my eyes for a second, letting the sound sink in. My name is one of the rare few words which I can fully hear when she speaks.

"Try on a few more," I say.

Sienna gives me an exasperated look and disappears into the changing room. The moment the curtain draws behind her, I get up and head to the other end of the boutique where two men are standing by the entrance. I noticed them in the mirror, ogling Sienna when she came out of the changing room the last couple of times. I grab the jacket of the one closest to me and get in his face.

"You enjoy watching my wife?"

"Take it easy, man. I just had a glance." The idiot grins. "She's a smokeshow. Hard not to look, you know."

"Oh. All right then." I headbutt him.

The other guy grabs my shoulder, so I let go of the man now pressing his hands over his bloody nose, and bury my elbow in his buddy's stomach. He folds in half, gasping for breath.

"Get lost. Before I throw you out myself." I turn on my heel and go back to the changing rooms.

Sienna emerges just as I take a seat, saying something about the belt and the waistline being too tight, but I don't catch all of it because my gaze was focused on the mirror to make sure the two idiots left the store.

When I look at my wife, she's standing with her hands on her hips, glaring at me.

"So?"

I eat her up with my eyes. The new dress is blue and has

a tight bodice that flares from the waist. It fits her beautifully. "You should try on another one."

"Seriously? You're just screwing with me, aren't you?"

She's fucking adorable when she's irritated. The thing is, I don't really care what she wears. I find my wife equally stunning in that idiotic blue and pink monstrosity she's put on this morning as she looks in this elegant dress. But I do enjoy getting glimpses of the various parts of her body each dress exposes. Her bare back. Cleavage. Those amazing legs.

"Next one, Sienna."

She squints her eyes at me and walks back inside the partition. A minute later she walks out wearing only a sky-blue lacy bra and matching panties. "Is this more to your liking?"

I spring off the sofa and reach her in three quick strides. Wrapping my arm around her waist, I carry her inside the changing room and pull the curtain closed behind us with my other hand. Sienna tries her best to wriggle free of my hold, but I grab her under her thigh and prop her against the wall.

"What the fuck was that?" I bark.

"You seem indifferent to the dresses." She tilts her stubborn chin at me. "I was trying to get a reaction."

"Is that so?" I lean into her so my hard cock presses to her core. "Is this the reaction you were trying to achieve?"

"Maybe." Sienna bites her lower lip and hooks her legs behind my back. The hold she has on my neck tightens.

I lower my head and whisper in her ear. "I see you, Sienna." She stiffens in my embrace, but I continue. "I see you hiding something with your chipper acts and those ridiculous clothes. And I'm going to find out what it is."

Her nails dig into the skin of my neck, the sensation making my already hard cock swell even more. She tilts her head to the side, her lips brush my earlobe.

"Never," she says.

"We'll see about that." I place a light kiss on her bare shoulder and let her slide down my body. "Put your clothes on."

"What about the dress?"

I bend and take the colorful heap of satin and lace in my arms. "We're taking them all."

I observe my wife as she picks at the pork chop on her plate. She's been mostly moving the food around and has barely taken a few bites. I reach out with my fork, stab one of the pieces, and lift it to her mouth.

She looks at my fork. "What are you doing?"

"Making sure you eat something."

"I'm not hungry."

"You haven't eaten anything since this morning. I won't have you faint on me. Open your mouth."

Her lips widen slightly. "Fuck you, Drago," she says with a smile.

"So, she isn't as sweet as she wants people to believe." I lean forward. "Open. Your. Mouth."

Sienna grabs the fork from my hand and stuffs the meat into her mouth while staring daggers at me. I take the fork back, poke a floret of broccoli, and raise it.

"We could have eaten back at the house." Her lips wrap around the vegetable as she slides it off the utensil.

"Lunch is served at two. We missed it."

"Missed it? It's your house. Don't you have a say when lunch will be served?"

"I do. And I set the lunch hour for two. If you miss it due to business obligations, you have to fend for yourself."

Sienna looks down at the next bite of pork I'm holding in front of her. "Why?"

"Can you imagine the chaos that would ensue if fifty people all had meals at random times?"

"Yeah, I guess so." She laughs and takes the meat. "I haven't seen any kids in your home."

"My men and women with families don't reside at the house."

"Why?"

The memory of my childhood home engulfed in flames flashes before my eyes. It's been twenty years, but I can still taste the smoke as it choked my lungs, and feel the heat of the fire on my burning shirt as it scorched my skin while I was trying to shield Dina with my body.

"Drago?" Sienna places her hand on my forearm.

"Because I don't allow kids at the mansion. It's too dangerous," I say and take out my phone that's been vibrating in my pocket.

> **14:20 Filip:** We lost contact with the driver. Mirko is trying to locate the shipment through GPS.

"We need to go." I throw money on the table and grab Sienna's hand to leave.

As I'm ushering my wife toward the closest elevator, Sienna is speaking beside me. With all the people around and the noise they are making, I only catch the tone of her voice, not the words.

Another message from Filip arrives as we are exiting the elevator, telling me that we have only a general location for the truck because the GPS signal is weak, and that he's already headed in that direction with a few men to search for the vehicle. The text contains a screenshot of a map with a one-mile radius circle over the area close to our warehouse.

When we reach the car, I place my finger over Sienna's lips. "Stop talking and listen. Someone intercepted one of our trucks. The driver is not responding."

She blinks at me and nods.

"I need you to stay on the line with Filip and wait for him to give you the coordinates after he finds the truck. When you have them, enter the location on the map app and show me the screen with our destination marked. Okay?"

"Okay."

"Keep the line open and listen for any information Filip might have since he'll reach the truck before we do. All clear?"

She nods again.

"Good. Let's go."

Sienna

Voices speaking Serbian come through the phone. Filip must have put it on hands-free mode because I can hear both him and another male. Their speech is rather quick, but I still understand some of what is being said. Nasty curse words, then something about the Romanians not being happy about the weapons business. I throw a sideways look at my husband. He's been driving for twenty minutes in absolute silence. Weapons? I thought the Serbian syndicate only worked with drugs. I try to catch more of the conversation, but it's mostly cussing again. Someone's phone rings. The other guy, I think it's Jovan, hollers something.

"Sienna," Filip says, "we have the location. I'm sending you the coordinates."

The phone in my hands vibrates. I put it on speaker, then copy and paste two large numbers into the navigation app, and a big red dot appears on the map. We're about ten minutes away.

"Take the next right," I say while looking at the phone screen. I can still hear Filip's voice since I left the call open.

Drago's hand enters my field of vision. He grabs the phone and looks at the screen, but while he's doing so, he misses the turn he should have taken.

"*A u kurac.*" He throws the phone on the dash, cranks the steering wheel until the car does a one-eighty, and gets into the lane heading in the opposite direction. The turn is so sudden and sharp that I hit the side of my head on the window.

"Shit!" Drago barks, and without looking away from the road, wraps his right arm around my shoulders and pulls me toward him. "I'm so sorry, baby." He kisses my forehead and releases me. "Ask Filip if they've reached the driver."

I'm still so stunned by his unexpected act that I don't even ask why he doesn't ask Filip himself. The speakerphone is still on.

"Filip? Drago asks—"

"The truck is parked in the back alley," Filip throws in. "We're just pulling up behind it. Stay on the line."

The sounds of car doors opening and closing fill the otherwise dead air, and a few minutes later, a stream of Serbian curses flows across the line.

"The driver is dead," Filip shouts. "A bullet through the temple. The cargo is still in the truck. Untouched."

My husband continues to drive, white-knuckling the wheel, his gaze fixed on the road. "Dead?" he asks and glances at me.

"Yes." I nod.

"When we get there, stay in the car. Filip will take you home."

"Okay." I nod again.

Drago keeps driving, and I keep staring at his profile. Thinking.

We reach the truck, and Drago parks a few yards in front of it, then exits the car. I watch him through the back window as he takes a look in the cabin of the truck before he jumps down and faces Filip, telling him something. Jovan comes up behind Drago and places his hand on Drago's shoulder. The act seems out of place, but I've noticed his men doing it often when they approach him from the rear. It almost seems as if it's to get his attention.

The three of them spend a few minutes in a heated discussion. Filip walks away from the group a few minutes later and gets in the car with me while dialing a number on his phone. He switches to hands-free and starts the car. I listen as he relays Drago's orders to Adam first, and then to Mirko.

My eyes stare blindly at a ribbon of road beyond the windshield as I dig through my brain, trying to recall if I've ever seen my husband talking on the phone.

And I can't remember one instance.

Chapter
eleven

 Sienna

I'VE ATTENDED AT LEAST TEN COSA NOSTRA WEDDINGS over the years. Most receptions were held in restaurants, fancy hotel banquet rooms, or luxury country clubs. The more expensive the venue and the production, the better. There is no grander way to show off your wealth and importance within the Family. So, I'm rather confused when Drago parks the car some distance from a three-story gray stone house.

I heard the music long before we reached the place, but this close-up, it's so loud that it takes me several moments to adjust. An enormous white tent is standing in the middle of the big lawn behind the house. Drago must have missed a turn, because I think we've ended up in the wrong place.

"Why are we at a fair?" I ask.

"This is not a fairground. It's *svadba*. A wedding."

I widen my eyes and look back toward the rectangular tent in front of us. Its sides have been removed, leaving a great canopy to drape over long tables set within. Each table runs the length of the tent and could easily sit about eighty. There are five tables. That's four hundred guests, minimum. I don't think I even know that many people.

At one end, a platform has been set up where a band is playing while a blonde-haired woman in a red dress walks among the tables, singing. Most of the guests are standing next to their chairs, dancing and singing along, but some have gathered around the singer and are putting money into her hands.

Kids—boys in cute suits and girls in pretty dresses—are chasing a dog around, running in and out of the tent through the open side panels. There are no grim-faced men talking business in the corners, no stiff-looking women sitting with their backs straight, worrying over moving a muscle for fear that their hair will come undone while they gossip about those not close enough to overhear them. Everyone seems genuinely happy. So different from the Cosa Nostra weddings.

It's joyful, positive madness. I love it!

"Let's go congratulate the newlyweds." Drago wraps his arm around me, tucking me closer to his side as we walk through the crowd toward the head table on the far side of the tent pavilion. It's set perpendicular to the rest, and more people are milling around it.

The bride is wearing an amazing white lace dress that features a voluminous, full skirt, and the groom is dressed in an elegant gray suit and white shirt. There are two more people at the table—a man next to the groom and a woman next to the bride. All four, however, have pushed back their chairs, and are dancing and singing at the top of their lungs right on the spot.

When the groom notices our approach, he rushes to meet us. Drago and the man exchange a few words, but their conversation is drowned out by all the noise, so I can't hear what was said. The groom moves his gaze from my husband to me, his eyes as wide as saucers, then he composes himself and offers me his hand. I expect us to head elsewhere to sit down, but the groom starts waving at someone and shouts, "Drago's wife!"

A moment later, I find myself surrounded by people—men coming to shake my hand and women kissing my cheeks three times—right, left, right. Everyone talks simultaneously. The whole thing would be a little overwhelming if Drago's body wasn't pressed to my back, and his arm wasn't tightly wrapped around my middle.

"The bride's grandmother," he says next to my ear as the older woman approaches. He continues whispering small details to me about each person who comes forward. "The aunt from her father's side . . . Aunt's lover . . . The groom's younger brother . . . And the older one . . . The bride's mother . . ."

I can't remember half of the names. It continues for ten minutes until my cheeks are tingling from all the kisses, and my hand feels like mush, but I don't mind. In fact, I'm smiling so wide my face hurts. I never would have expected such a warm welcome from people who just met me. It feels like . . . I belong. It's the same feeling I have in Drago's home, like I'm part of a big family.

Once done with all the greetings, we head toward two vacant chairs at the end of one of the long tables. People previously occupying the spots have just left, taking their plates with them. Drago takes one of the seats and pulls me onto his lap.

"So, what do you think?" he asks.

I grin. "It's crazy."

The corner of his mouth curves upward. "I figured you'd like it."

"Let's take some photos." I fish the phone out of my purse and lift it in front of us.

"Do we have to?"

"What kind of question is that?"

I snap a selfie, then look at the picture. "No. You need to wipe that glaring look off your face. Insta will censor my post for disturbing content. Again."

I wrap my arm around his neck, press my cheek to his, and raise the phone.

Click.

"One more," I say and smile into the camera. When I take a look at the new photo, Drago is brooding in this one, too.

"You're not taking this seriously." I reach out and take his chin between my fingers, then tilt his head so he's looking at the phone. His gaze meets mine on the screen. "Now, smile."

He rolls his eyes but smiles. It's kind of sour, but I guess it's the best I'm going to get.

Click.

I let go of his chin and lower the phone. That's when I notice people looking at me strangely. Maybe you're not supposed to take photos at Serbian weddings? I quickly put the phone away.

One song ends and another starts. Obviously, although I don't know it, it's a popular tune because people start yelling and singing along with the first note. I try listening to the lyrics, but it's much harder to understand sung Serbian words than spoken ones. Something about mixing black and gold, then mentioning a . . . frame? Is it about art? A painting, perhaps?

A woman a few seats away abruptly stands and climbs onto the table. I stare, open-mouthed, as she starts dancing, her heels clicking on the linen-clad tabletop, just missing the plates and cutlery. People around her are cheering, clapping their hands. Another woman, further down, climbs onto the table. Then, the bride takes off her shoes and does the same. The crowd goes crazy, and I laugh amid the excitement. Never in my life have I witnessed such a joyous celebration.

I look at my husband and bite my lip. "Can I try?"

"Try what?" he raises an eyebrow.

"The table thing."

His arm around my waist tightens. "No."

"What? Why?"

Drago leans forward. "I won't have my wife mounting a table and shaking her hips with over four hundred people watching."

I narrow my eyes at him. "And what if I dance only for you? Pretty please?"

A low rumble comes from his throat. "All right. But you make sure I keep my eyes on you—only you—because if my gaze wanders, and I notice other men looking at you, the next song playing will be a funeral march, *mila moya*."

I squeal in delight and start unstrapping my heels.

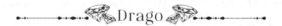

Drago

Transfixed. Hypnotized. Absolutely mind fucked. That's how I feel as I watch my wife dance on the tabletop in front of me. I'm not sure what I like more—her perfect little body, which sways slowly and sensually as she moves, her ridiculously sunny personality, or the brilliant intellect that hides behind her sparkling shell.

Last weekend, I walked in on her and Keva sitting at the kitchen table, discussing money laundering. I leaned my shoulder on the wall and observed my wife as she explained in great detail how it's possible to launder money through renovation work of real estate properties. In the five minutes I spent watching, she gave Keva a step-by-step strategy—starting with the purchase of a derelict building and moving on to the remodeling activities that would allow for the optimum amount of money to exchange hands, and not missing any of the steps in between. And then, she finished by highlighting the estimated timeframe for the whole ordeal. When she was done, she took out her phone and snapped a picture of the pile of carrots she'd finished peeling while she spoke.

But the way she dances now is something else altogether, sending all the blood rushing straight to my cock. I lean back in my chair and let my gaze glide over the long-sleeved blue silk dress. A rather tame choice, given her fashion taste. Well, if you disregard all the sequins and the huge gold heart-shaped earrings.

Sienna places her hands on her waist and, looking straight into my eyes, starts rotating her hips. She's smiling mischievously, and that smile is doing strange things to my insides. So fucking beautiful. The sight of her almost makes me forget the throbbing migraine that started the moment we approached the wedding venue and exponentially worsened the closer we got to the noise.

My enchanting wife is attempting a pirouette without tripping over a plate when a gunshot pierces the air.

She stops in midmotion, her eyes going wide with panic. Shit. I forgot to give her a heads-up about the celebratory shots.

Sienna

Bang!

In an instant, I freeze, my heartbeat skyrocketing, and stare at Drago as he slowly rises from his chair. A few more gunshots ring out somewhere outside the tent. A strangled cry escapes me, and I jump into my husband's arms, wrapping my shaking limbs tightly around his neck.

"It's okay," he coos next to my ear. "That was the best man, shooting into the air. It's a tradition."

"Tradition?" I look up. "Your people are a bit crazy."

"I know."

I should probably get down since people are starting to give us curious looks. Apparently, I'm the only one who wasn't expecting intentional gunfire in the middle of a wedding. I really should try to regain some sort of decorum, but I like being held by Drago. Maybe he feels the same, because he lowers himself back onto the chair without letting go of me.

"So, shooting into the air happens often at weddings?" I trace the length of his jaw with the tip of my finger.

Drago's eyes widen slightly in surprise, but other than that, he pretends he doesn't notice my caress. "Every damn time. And at most of the other celebrations held outside. I should have warned you."

"It's okay." I shrug and lean forward a little bit. His eyes are so gorgeous. As is his nose, even though it is slightly crooked. "Thank you for bringing me here."

Heat races along my spine as Drago's rough palms slide up my back. "You're welcome."

The sensual melody I was dancing to transitions to a fast beat. A new wave of cheers erupts from everyone around us as the band kicks it into high gear with a drum and bass pattern that reverberates through the massive tent. Drago tenses and squeezes his eyes shut. His face twists into a grimace, his lips tightly pursed.

"Drago?" I cup his face in my palms. "What's wrong?"

"Nothing." His eyes flutter open, and he resumes stroking my back.

Doesn't seem like "nothing" to me. His body is rigid and there is a strain in the tone of his voice. I stroke the furrows in his brow, trailing the lines that aren't usually there.

"You look like you're in pain, Drago. What's going on?"

"I'm fine, Sienna."

A few hundred guests belt out the chorus of the song, each refrain louder than the last. Drago lets out a nasty Serbian curse and pinches the bridge of his nose, tightly squeezing his eyes shut.

"Drago?"

He curses again and lowers his hand, but the strain is plainly visible on his face.

"Is it the music?"

"Yes," he says through grinding teeth. "It's too fucking loud."

His hair is so soft as I rake my fingers through the dark strands. I haven't even realized that I've been stroking it. "Let's go home."

My husband tilts his head to the side and looks at me as if he's trying to parse me out. "I thought you were having fun."

"I was. Not anymore."

"Why not?"

Because you're obviously in pain and I can't have fun knowing you are hurting. But I don't say it, of course.

"I promised Asya I'd phone her at five tonight," I lie. "We should get going right away so I don't miss making that call on time."

The corner of Drago's lips lifts just a smidge. "But you have your phone with you. You can make a call from here. Or while we're driving back."

"Um ... I prefer making my phone calls in private." I shoot him a beaming smile. "It's about girls' stuff."

"Mm-hmm. Or maybe it's not your sister you need to call?"

My hand stills midstroke. Had someone overheard me calling the don yesterday and told Drago? I always make sure I call Ajello only when I'm alone in the bedroom or strolling through the grounds where no one is around. No, it's not possible. "Of course not. Why would I lie?"

Drago keeps his eyes glued to mine, a dangerous glint sparks within them, as if he can see right through my lies and defenses, down to my soul. My heartbeat picks up while I stare into those two pools of green with brown flecks. *Run!* Screams the part of me that's terrified of baring my secrets to anyone. *Run, now, while you still can.*

He takes hold of my chin, tilting it up as he slowly caresses my lower lip with his thumb. "*Tako lepa usta, a toliko laži.*"

I blink and try to concentrate on what he said amid all the distractions, but there is too much noise and activity around us so I only understand half of the sentence. I think he said he likes my mouth. My lips part, anticipating a kiss, but Drago releases my chin and leans away.

"Let's head home."

Swallowing the disappointment, I smile and get down off his lap. "Sure."

CHAPTER Twelve

Drago

I WAVE AT THE WAITER TO BRING ME ANOTHER CUP OF coffee and resume watching Sienna and her brother.

Saying that Arturo DeVille isn't happy with his sister being married to me is an understatement. He's also livid as hell because I wouldn't let Sienna meet with him without my supervision. I told Arturo it's a security precaution, but the truth is, I'm afraid he might tell her things I don't want my wife to know.

There are a lot of skeletons in my closet, and Arturo is aware of a few. These past weeks, I've gotten to know my wife rather well. Sienna might have been born into a Mafia Family, but she has no love for violence or bloodshed. She'd fool you with her bravado, but my wife is much more sensitive than she lets people around her believe. She's like a lone dandelion flower in a sea of thorned roses. It would take only a single gust of wind to hurt her delicate seeds. So, I'm not risking Arturio telling Sienna anything that would make her fearful of me.

They are sitting on the other side of the restaurant. Arturo's meal is getting cold on his plate. He hasn't even touched it because he's too busy listing all of my deplorable qualities to my wife.

"—*scheming son of a bitch who won't even let me see you without him present!*"

I don't see Sienna's reply since she's sitting with her back to me, but Arturo's part of the conversation is enough for me to get the gist.

"*Yes, but doing business and having my sister wed the bastard are two different things! And don't give me that crap about you wanting to get married. I don't buy that bullshit. Did Ajello threaten you to make you marry Popov?*"

Yes, Sienna. Did the don threaten you?

My wife's shoulders drop in what appears to be a sigh, then she leans over the table and takes her brother's hand. She's saying something, but I can't see what it is, damn it! Arturo listens with wide eyes and a clenched jaw, then throws a look in my direction.

"*There are things you don't know about him. Things I didn't know when this marriage deal hit the table, or I never would have let you near him. He's dangerous, and I want you out of his clutches.*"

Sienna cocks her head to the side. Probably asking for an explanation of what those "things" are. I stand up and head across the restaurant. It's time to cut this meeting short.

"We're leaving," I say when I reach their table. Whether to torture myself or Arturo, I'm not sure, I trace the tip of my finger over Sienna's bare skin where her fuchsia sweater has slipped down her shoulder. "I need to be at Naos in two hours. Do you want to come?"

Sienna looks up at me and grins. "Can some of the girls tag along, too?"

"Yes." I nod. "I need to have a word with your brother. Wait here."

Arturo gets up, glaring at me the entire time we walk through the restaurant to his car which is parked out front.

"I don't know what you've dug up on me," I say and lean on the hood, "but you'll keep your mouth shut."

A look of surprise crosses his face, but it's quickly replaced with an angry stare. "If you hurt my sister, I'm going to kill you."

"Does your sister seem to be hurt in any way?" I cast a glance through the window to where Sienna is positioning Arturo's untouched plate so she can take a photo of it.

"I'll be watching you," he barks and gets inside his car.

Once Arturo pulls out of the parking lot, I head back inside the restaurant and take a seat next to my wife.

"What did Arturo want?" I ask.

"Nothing much. He was just checking up on me." She leans over the table and smirks. "I think my brother is afraid you're going to eat me."

"I might." I reach out and place my hand over hers. "Do you think I'm dangerous, *mila moya*?"

Sienna's lips part in surprise, and I need all my self-restraint not to slam my mouth to them. It's becoming too hard to resist my young wife, even though I know she's a spy.

"Do you have this place bugged?" She lifts an eyebrow.

"Maybe I do." I place my free hand on the back of her neck. "Do you think I pose a danger to you, as your brother had said?"

"Yes." Sienna's eyes hold mine, unblinking. "Not in the way my brother believes, though."

Her expression is completely serious, but for a fleeting moment, I glimpse a speck of vulnerability behind her willful stare. In a flash, it's gone, and her lips widen into a smile.

"We should get going, Drago. I need to get ready for tonight."

Keeping her hand in mine, I usher her toward the exit.

She may believe that she's successfully avoided the subject, but we'll get back to it soon enough.

I lift the glass of Macallan to my lips and take a sip, observing my wife. Sienna is standing at the bar, laughing with Jelena and three other girls. She's picked out another sparkling outfit for tonight. It's a dress this time, covered in vibrant blue-green sparkly bits. Whenever she moves and the lights reflect off her dress, it looks like she's covered in peacock feathers. She simply glows. I don't understand how she can wear stuff like this and still look like a million bucks. On anyone else, it would look ridiculous. It's also way too short.

Scanning the room, my eyes sweep over every man sitting or standing in the vicinity to make sure no asshole is checking out my wife's legs. Just the thought unleashes my feral impulses.

The moment I saw her after she had gotten dressed for tonight, I sent a word to Misha, my club manager, to relay a message to every male guest before allowing them entry. Any man caught ogling my wife will leave the club with his eyeballs in a wine glass. The people who visit my club are regular clientele, so they know I'm serious. Naos might be neutral ground as far as business is concerned, but that rule doesn't extend to private dealings. The only way anyone can look at my wife is with respect. All other "looks" will garner consequences.

I spot a man leaning on the bar some distance from Sienna, ordering a drink. He's the owner of the local fleet management company. I've worked with him a few times when we had a shortage of available trucks. He came across as a smart guy, but it appears I was wrong, because he seems to be very interested in my wife's ass. The barman passes him a bottle of beer, and the moron heads toward the end of the bar where Sienna is standing. Without moving my eyes off him, I beckon the security guard to approach.

"Drag that idiot to my office," I say and nod toward the guy who now has planted himself next to Sienna and is trying to start a conversation. "Make sure my wife doesn't notice."

Sienna ignores the creep and continues chatting with Jelena. The guy finally leaves, heading toward the restrooms, but my guard intercepts him halfway and not so gently "persuades" the shit-for-brains to visit the back of the club. Time to face those consequences.

"I need to take care of something," I tell Filip in passing. "Keep my wife in your sights."

Before going to my office, I make a detour to the bar to pick up a spoon and a glass, then turn around and head across the dance floor.

When I get back from handling the issue inside the office, a man approaches my booth and stops across from the sofa I'm sitting on. Late sixties, receding gray hairline, thin gold glasses. Endri Dushku. The Albanian leader.

"Endri." I gesture toward the armchair beside him. "What brings you to New York?"

The older man takes the offered seat and waves off the waiter. "Bogdan called me the other day. He had some . . . concerning information to share."

"Oh? And what exactly is causing your concerns?"

"What's prompted your interest in the arms business, Drago?"

"Money," I say and take a sip of my drink. "But you shouldn't be worried. I have no plans to encroach on your territory. "

"You delivered a large shipment to Bratva."

"Yes. But Petrov won't deal with you anymore, so I don't see a problem. And after the clusterfuck with the Irish, you're banned from doing business in New York." I throw my arm over the back of the sofa. "Supplying guns to people who kidnapped the don's wife? To be honest, I'm surprised to see you still breathing. So, I don't see any conflict of interest between the two of us."

Dushku adjusts his glasses. He always does that when he's angry.

"And it'll stay that way?" he asks.

"I'm not looking for a fight, Endri. You have your buyers. I have mine. The market is big enough for the both of us."

"And what about the Romanians?"

"They'll soon be out of the picture," I say. "Once I locate Bogdan."

"You think getting rid of Bogdan will solve your problem?"

"Remove the head, and the rest will scatter like rats. And I mean that literally."

"Well . . . I wouldn't want to be in Bogdan's shoes, then," Dushku says. "I hear you got married. Happened a bit suddenly, it seems. Was that a business decision?"

"Of course."

"Interesting. I noticed your security staff throwing out a man as I was coming in. He was pressing a bloody towel to his face and holding a glass in his free hand. I'm not sure, but I think there was an eyeball inside."

"So?"

"Does that have anything to do with the warning I received upon entry?" He has a calculating smile on his face.

"Yes. But I'm in a good mood, so I decided to let him keep the other eye."

"Well, that's rather . . . out of character for you, if I may say so. Someone might get the idea that the girl is more than a mere business arrangement."

I squeeze the glass in my hand. There are three things to stay away from in my line of work: False loyalties. Deals that sound too good to be true. And any sort of weaknesses.

I trust very few people in my life. Those who have my loyalty, deserve it. I'd die for them, and I know they would not hesitate to do the same for me. Anyone stupid enough to betray me and think they can get away with it, I make sure they don't live long enough to regret their decision.

I don't make any deals unless I'm one hundred percent confident they are solid. Money and power don't sway me, and I'm not here to be anyone's fool.

And I certainly don't have any weaknesses. Or didn't. However, as I look at Dushku's self-satisfied smile, I realize I have one now. And she's currently taking selfies with a martini she isn't old enough to drink.

"Sienna gave me a direct connection to Cosa Nostra and also Bratva. Two birds, one stone," I say, watching his face for the smallest reaction. "It's a matter of principle. I'm simply taking care of my asset."

"So you don't like her?"

"She's barely out of her teens, Endri. Why would I like a spoiled girl who dresses like a clown and spends almost all her time shopping and posting selfies on social media? Sacrifices need to be made for the sake of business."

"I hear she's a pretty little thing. Don't tell me you aren't at least attracted to her."

"I like my women to use their heads for something other than a fancy haircut, Endri."

Dushku laughs and stands up. "Yeah, I see your point. Well, if it doesn't work out, I have a daughter who's just finishing her doctorate program, so she might be more up your alley."

"I'll keep that in mind."

As I watch the Albanian leave, my eyes shift to the spot at the bar where my wife was sitting a moment ago. She's not there. I turn around and find Sienna standing with her back pressed to a column that has our coats hanging on its side, just behind the sofa where I'm sitting. Staring at me with wide eyes.

Shit.

Sienna

"I like my women to use their head for something other than a fancy haircut, Endri."

I plaster my back to the wide rectangular column behind me and close my eyes. It's slightly rough, but the cool concrete finish is a welcome relief to my overheating flesh.

Everything he said is true. People see what you show them. So why does it bother me that Drago actually believes I'm shallow and stupid?

When I open my eyes, the gray-haired man is getting up, offering his daughter as my replacement while he does so. And my husband, the bastard that he is, doesn't seem opposed to it. I should leave and pretend I didn't hear anything, but my legs are rooted to the floor.

Drago turns around and our gazes connect. It takes all my willpower, but I smile and keep that fake grin on my face as he walks around the sofa to stand before me.

"Making plans to replace me? I might not have a doctorate, but I'm pretty sure I'm a more valuable chess piece than that guy's daughter."

Drago lowers his head so our faces are at the same level. The sconce above our jackets on the other side of the column is casting its soft light around us, allowing me to see the pulsing vein at his temple as he stares into my eyes. He places his left palm on the surface next to my head and cups my cheek with his right.

"Do you know what could happen if Dushku figures out you are not just a chess piece?" His tone is low and menacing. "He would make sure everyone who has any beef with me knows about it."

"So?"

"So, I'd have to kill all of them." This time, his words are as lighthearted as if he's planning a summer picnic. He tilts his head slightly. "That's a lot of dead people, *mila moya.*"

"You don't kill people. You have your pet assassin for that. That priest guy," I blurt out without thinking, and only after the words are out of my mouth do I realize what I've said.

He blinks, his dark lashes sweeping languidly down and back up until his eyes are fixated on me again. "My . . . 'pet assassin'?"

Crap. Think! "Yes. Keva mentioned something the other day, and I figured it out."

"Mmm, did she?" He narrows his eyes at me. "Yes. I guess I would need to send . . . *my pet assassin* after them. To take care of that problem for me."

"Why?"

He drops his chin just a little, leaving him looking at me from under his hooded lids. "To make sure they won't be coming after you."

"Why would anyone come after me?" I ask in my most sugary voice. "I'm just a spoiled girl who dresses like a clown."

Drago's nostrils flare. He clenches his jaw, and his gaze is glued to my lips with such intensity that I expect flames to burst forth.

"You are the very opposite of shallow, Sienna. We both know that. I'm fairly certain you're one of the most intelligent people I've ever met."

I suck in a breath, taken aback by his words. But my

momentary shock is quickly replaced with mirthless laughter as I recall the rest of the conversation I'd overheard.

"That's not enough, though, is it? You talked about replacing me," I spit out. "Maybe that'd be the right thing to do. Your buddy's daughter might be a better match for you. You'll probably do more than just sleep in the same bed with her."

Drago closes his eyes, a stream of extremely foul Serbian curses leaving his mouth. Then, he crashes his lips to mine.

I shudder from the ferocity of his kiss—if it can even be called a kiss. This is an onslaught. A hungry, furious claiming. Fisting the front of his shirt, I pull him closer, needing more. His hand comes to grab me under my thigh, and he lifts me. My legs are around his waist, and I marvel at the sensation of being pinned between his hard body and the solid column behind me as his cock presses directly on my core. Drago's mouth glides along my chin to the side of my neck, and when he bites the tender skin there, I feel myself getting wet. I grab his hair, my fingers tangling in dark strands. His hold on my face disappears, and a moment later, he shoves the phone up to his ear.

"I want everyone out," he barks, then licks my neck. "Now, Misha."

The person on the other end of the line is responding, but I don't hear what he says because Drago throws the phone over his shoulder. The sharp clack of it landing on the floor barely registers as Drago's mouth finds mine again. Sucking. Biting.

My fingers are shaking as I rake them through his hair. I've never felt this way. This urge to get closer to him, even though we couldn't be closer than we already are. The sounds of voices and hurried feet are all around us as people leave, but I ignore them, intoxicated by Drago's presence. Nothing else matters. Just him. His body. His lips. His scent. It's the same scent I've been waking up to for weeks.

"Hold tight," he says into my lips and takes a step back.

My arms encircle his neck as his palms move up my legs

and over my ass, under my dress. The lace of my thong rubs over my aching pussy when he tugs on it. The delicate fabric tears. He pulls it away, purposely dragging the lacy material so it brushes over my throbbing clit.

I gasp as my thighs are suddenly slick with my wetness. Drago grabs the underside of my leg again while he unbuttons his pants with his free hand. Oh God, I'm going to have sex—at a club, with people still around. Why don't I care? The cold surface at my back chills the bare skin of my ass as Drago holds me against the column once more. The tip of his cock presses at my entrance.

"Please go slow," I choke out. "It's my first time."

Drago lifts his head and looks at me. "Your what?"

"My first time," I repeat when he lowers his eyes to my mouth. "I'm a virgin."

Green eyes, so focused on my lips, widen, then lift to meet mine. "Do you want to stop?"

I tug on the hair at the back of his head. "No."

Without breaking eye contact, he shifts me slightly in his hold, aligning our hips. A mix of excitement and panic overcomes me. When the tip enters me, I close my eyes and stiffen.

"Sienna." A kiss lands on the side of my chin. "Look at me, *mila.*"

"Will it hurt?" I whisper.

"A little. If you want me to stop, tap my arm. Okay?"

"Okay."

Drago leans forward, whispering hushed, soothing words just next to my ear. He's speaking Serbian, but I catch only random phrases. Something about glitter and the name of a bird, but I'm not certain which one. Maybe a peacock. It doesn't actually matter because the timbre of his voice and his hot breath fanning my neck are melting my insides. This man could read a grocery list and I would come undone just from listening to him.

The tingling in my core is making me crazy. I tilt my head and lick his neck. A low growl leaves his lips and, in the next heartbeat, his cock slides partway inside me. I gasp and grip his hair, reveling in the feel of him stretching my inner walls. There's some discomfort, but I'm too far gone for it to matter. I tighten my legs around him, needing to get him even closer, deeper.

"Say my name," he rasps next to my ear.

"Drago," I moan as he thrusts into me until he's fully sheathed.

"I love hearing your voice." He lifts me, then impales me once more. "Again."

I can't utter a word because I'm too absorbed in the way my pussy clenches around his cock as my whole body shakes. Never in my life have I experienced anything like this. His touch alone is sending shockwaves through my system, lifting me to soar on the currents of sheer pleasure.

"Again, Sienna!" Drago roars as he pumps into me.

I close my eyes and press my cheek to his. "Drago."

A deep rumble leaves the back of his throat. It's guttural and rough. In the next breath, his teeth scrape the skin on my shoulder. More whispered Serbian words. Something about witchcraft, then he curses again. His lips crash against mine once more.

My mind doesn't seem like mine anymore because I can't think. I can only feel—him, claiming me with both his mouth and his cock. I grab his hair and bite his lower lip until I taste the metallic tang of blood. It's punishment for hurting me with his words.

"Not only does she have claws, but sharp teeth, too," he says into my mouth and buries himself to the hilt. "I see you, *mila moya*. And I hate that you hide your real self from me."

"I'm not," I pant, breath leaving me in short bursts as he pounds into me. Faster. Deeper.

My hair has come undone, the tangled strands plaster to my face. It's as if I'm superheating and swelling on the inside as I clutch at Drago's shoulders. A scream builds within my chest while my vision blurs. Like my mind has decided to tune out everything except the sensation of our bodies connecting. Drago's hands squeeze at my ass cheeks, and his next thrust sends me right into oblivion. Whiteness explodes behind my closed eyelids, and I scream, riding the amazing wave and shattering into the tiniest little pieces.

You should have run while you still had the chance, Sienna, the voice in the back of my mind whispers. You really, really should have.

CHAPTER Thirteen

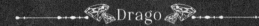

Drago

THE HEAVY DRAPERY IS PULLED OVER THE BALCONY door, keeping the morning light off Sienna who is curled up in bed, hugging a pillow with her arms. She spent the entire night clutching at my forearm while clinging tightly to my side. It was a struggle to wriggle my arm free so I could take a shower and get ready for work.

I move my gaze from her sleeping face down her body, skimming over my T-shirt and pajama pants I put on her last night. She fell asleep in the car on the way home from the club and didn't wake up as I carried her inside and up the stairs to our bedroom. I expected her to rouse when I started removing her jacket and dress, but nope. She just mumbled something and climbed into bed naked. I went through her clothes but couldn't decide what were pajamas and what weren't, so I just clad her in mine. Sienna slumbered through the whole ordeal. This woman could probably sleep through an earthquake. Zero self-preservation instincts.

Some strange primal need stirs inside me at the sight of her in my clothes, urging me to forbid her from wearing anything else when she sleeps. It's stupid. Still, I can't shake it off.

And I don't like it. I don't like these caveman tendencies I've developed, such as the compulsion to strangle every man who comes within ten feet of my wife. Another thing I find hard to process is the satisfaction I felt upon realizing I was her first. No other man has touched her before me. And no other will. Ever.

I lean my back on the wall, rubbing my thumb over a small mark on my bottom lip where she bit me last night. My fierce, sparkling beguiler. From the moment I first saw her, I knew there's so much more to Sienna than she lets others see. It's as if she has shrouded her real self for some reason, and her guise has been eating at me from the start. I quite enjoy small glimpses of her true nature whenever her mask slips away. But the fact she's been lying to me all this time is making me furious. It's been a month, and she still hasn't tried to come clean to me. I can understand her being wary at the beginning, but it should be clear to her by now that I would never harm her. After all the time we've spent together—granted, it hasn't been a lot, but there were enough opportunities—and yet, she still hasn't confessed the truth of why she accepted this marriage.

My eyes wander to the nightstand where three thick notebooks with glittery covers are stacked one atop the other. As I stalked her over the past weeks I've often caught her scribbling in one of them. The leather sofa in the great rec room seems to be her favorite spot, and I spent a lot of time watching her from the doorway. She would write a few sentences, then giggle to herself before resuming. At first, I thought she was keeping a diary, but when I inadvertently glanced inside one of her notebooks, I realized she was writing stories.

The room suddenly fills with light pouring in through the opened door behind me. I spin around and find Filip standing at the threshold, prattling on about who knows what. I pay no attention to his words and lunge at him.

"Never," I spit out as I grab his shirtfront and push him

into the hallway, "fucking never come into the room where my wife is sleeping."

"You weren't answering your messages."

"I. Don't. Care." I pin him with my murderous gaze. "What is it?"

"There's been a fire at the Syracuse warehouse."

"When?"

"An hour ago. One of the security guards reported it, but the connection was lost before he could say more."

"The damage?"

"I don't know. Adam took Relja, and they went to check what's happening."

I let go of his shirt. "Call Adam. Tell him that if it's bad, and if the fire department got called, he's to turn around and head back right away."

"So, we'll just leave it?"

"Yes. If the firemen are there, the police will be, as well. There was almost half a ton of Ajello's cocaine in that building. Unless the blaze can be contained by our men, the warehouse and the product are lost."

"You think it was Bogdan?" he asks.

"Or Dushku. He came to Naos last night. To test the waters, no doubt. But I'm betting it was Bogdan. Did anyone locate him?"

"No. I've had our men searching for him since our driver was killed. So far, nothing. Most of his regular guys have gone to ground. We picked up a few low-level pissants, but they knew nothing of value."

"Well, that's enough proof for me that he orchestrated that, too. Send Iliya to have a chat with our informants. Maybe someone has heard something about Bogdan's whereabouts. Jovan and I will check out the other warehouses."

"Okay. I'll message you when Adam reports in with an update."

"Don't bother. I left my phone at Naos last night. Have one of the men pick it up and bring it here. I'll come back as soon as I'm done."

On my way downstairs, I notice Keva giving an earful to a girl who is dusting one of the paintings in the foyer. I wave her over and nod toward the front door. She follows me outside, and we set off on a path that encircles the house and leads to the garage off to the side.

"Sienna is still asleep. Have one of the girls bring her breakfast upstairs."

"Food?" She widens her eyes at me. "In your room?"

"Yes. And I don't want Sienna leaving the compound until I'm back."

"Why? Did something happen?"

"Looks like the Romanians may have gone on a rampage. I'll alert the guards not to let her pass if she tries to leave, but I'm afraid she'll manage to sweet-talk them."

"No one will dare go against your orders. You know that."

"Where my wife is concerned, I've learned to expect anything. She already has the whole of my crew eating out of her hand." I step over a garden hose strung across the walkway. "Including my dogs."

"You're exaggerating."

"Am I?" I stop in front of the garage and wave my arm at the mansion. "Did you know that Mirko hacked into a website for some sort of boutique and changed someone's existing order for a pair of shoes to have them sent to Sienna via same-day rush delivery?"

"So what?" Keva shrugs as she says, "He was just being nice."

"He's my logistics and surveillance specialist. Not her shopping assistant," I bark. "And the other day, she made Adam play an idiotic PlayStation game with her. She said it was more enjoyable in co-op mode. I thought I was imagining things when I saw my head enforcer leading a scarecrow on the TV screen, blasting giant chickens with pink sparkly magic."

Keva grins. "Oooh, someone is jealous. Does it bother you that she didn't ask you to play?"

"I'm serious." I throw a quick look over her head toward the mansion. "Cosa Nostra killed one of our men. When I brought Sienna here, everyone hated her. Well, except you. And now everyone seems to be besotted by her."

"*She* didn't kill anyone, Drago. And she shouldn't be blamed for something she had no say in. Besides, no one really hated her." Keva furrows her brows, then gives a little knowing smile. "Well, maybe a little."

"I don't know what it is about her." I shake my head. "It's as if no matter how hard people try not to like her, they still end up bewitched by her."

"Speaking from experience?"

"Yes, damn it." I grit my teeth. "She's been providing info to Ajello."

"Well, you would expect the same if one of our girls married into Cosa Nostra. It's how things work."

"Has she been asking around about our business? Fishing for information? Snooping about?"

"No. She mostly chats with me and the girls, and it's usually about books and clothes. We rarely mention business."

"It's not just that." I sigh. "She understands Serbian."

Keva quickly looks away.

"You knew?" I snap. "You knew, and you haven't told me?"

"I suspected."

"Jesus fuck. Why didn't you say something?"

"Do you know that your eyes light up when she enters a room?" She takes a step forward. "For years, I've watched you bury yourself in work, becoming more and more closed-off. I lost hope that something . . . *someone* will be able to pull you out of the dark pit you've resigned yourself to. You've been half-dead, going through the motions, until Sienna moved into this house. And now, it's like you're finally coming back to the world of the living."

"World of madness would be more accurate." I drag my hand through my hair. "She's absolutely oblivious to how dangerous the games we play are. If she ended up with someone else, and they caught her spying . . ."

"But she didn't." Keva places her hand on my forearm. "Why haven't you told her about your hearing, Drago?"

"So that she can inform her don of that, too?"

"You think she would?"

"Without a doubt." I nod and turn to head inside the garage. "I have to go."

Sienna

I stare at the enormous bowl, filled to the top with green pods. "I didn't know peas grew like that."

"And how did you think they grow?" Keva asks as she peels pea pods from her own bowl.

"I don't know. I never actually thought about it." I take a pod and crack it, extracting small green legumes. "So how much do we need to shell for lunch?"

"Oh, these are just to top a salad, so we can stop once we have a cup or two. If it was for a side dish, I would have used the frozen ones because we'd need at least ten pounds."

My eyes widen. "I don't know how you cook for almost fifty people every day."

"The girls help." She tilts her head to the side, looking thoughtful. "I always wanted a big family but didn't get the chance. I guess this is the next best thing."

"How did you end up here, with Drago?"

"I had a friend in New York," she says but keeps her gaze fixed on her hands. "So, I brought Drago and Tara with me. He was seventeen. Tara was four at the time."

"What about their parents?"

"They were in the Mafia. A bomb was planted in their house in retaliation for Drago's father killing some people. Both of them died in the explosion. Drago and Tara survived." Her voice is strained as she brushes away a tear. "Dina, their sister, died as well."

My stomach drops, and I press my hand over my mouth but a shocked gasp still escapes me.

"There were some relatives who could have taken in Drago and Tara, but I couldn't let them stay in Serbia. It was a blood feud, and I didn't want to risk the killers coming after them. I had their passports forged to say they were mine, and we came here."

I stare at her. Moving to a strange country on her own with two kids that weren't even hers? I don't know anyone who would have done something like that. "But, you were once married to their father?"

Keva lifts her eyes to mine. "Sometimes, love doesn't end with the end of the marriage, Sienna. Or life. The man I loved was dead, but his kids weren't. And they were in danger. I did what needed to be done."

I look down at the bowl in my hands. Drago's relationship with Keva makes so much more sense now.

"Did Drago get you more of those . . . glass crystals?" she asks.

I shrug. "Nope. Why?"

"You should ask him for more. I love what you did with them."

"Do you know where Drago is? I haven't seen him this morning."

"He left early. Something about work." She side-eyes me. "Missing him already?"

"I most certainly don't miss that hypocritical boar." I grab the next pod and crumble it between my fingers.

The man referred to our marriage as a necessary sacrifice, making it very clear that he doesn't give a damn about me. And what did I do? I let him fuck me against a wall, enjoying every second of it. And, as if that wasn't enough to show how pathetic I am, I woke up this morning yearning for more, only to find him gone. I still can't decide if I'm mad at *him* for not being there, or at *myself* for feeling disappointed.

"Hypocritical boar?" Keva reaches for the cup of coffee on the table and raises an eyebrow at me.

"Yeah. He discussed my replacement with some guy, and then told me that he's going to send his hitman to kill anyone who may wish me harm."

Keva bursts out laughing. "It looks like the two of you are getting along just fine."

The kitchen door opens and one of Drago's men, Iliya, walks inside. "Drago's phone. He left it at Naos last night." He places the device on the table in front of Keva and leaves. A big crack has split the screen diagonally, a myriad of small lines like a delicate spider web over the rest.

"Drago never leaves his phone behind." Keva wipes her hand on a towel and reaches for it. "Especially when we're expecting a new shipment to arrive, and there's one coming today. Drivers always send updates to him, so if there are problems, we can . . ." She gapes at something on the screen.

"Is there a problem?" I ask because the expression on her face is really strange.

"No. Not at all. It's just, I didn't know his phone was broken." She puts the device back down and takes a sip of her coffee.

"Drago threw it away so he could grab my ass," I mumble.

"I lost my virginity pressed to a wall at his club while people were still traipsing around us."

Keva spits out her coffee, dark-brown drops spraying all over the wooden tabletop. "What?" She wheezes amid a coughing fit.

"Yup. And then, when I woke up this morning, he wasn't there." I glance down at the bowl of peas so she can't spot the tears in my eyes. "I'm done with my batch. Do you need me for anything else?"

"I can take it from here."

I stand up and turn to head toward the door, taking a couple of steps before Keva calls after me. "Sienna. Can you take Drago's phone upstairs and leave it in your bedroom?"

"Sure." I take the device from her outstretched hand and rush out of the kitchen.

When I get to the bedroom, I throw the phone on the bed and turn to leave again, but then halt at the threshold. *Don't do it.* I take a deep breath and peek down the hallway. The fourth floor appears to be deserted, so I close the bedroom door. There's no lock, unfortunately.

Don't do it. My consciousness yells at me as I walk back toward the bed. *You're better than that.*

I climb on the bed and sit in the center with my legs crossed, staring at my husband's phone. Does he have photos of his exes on it? What do the women he's attracted to look like? Tall and sophisticated, dressed in those god-awful boring-colored pantsuits? Drago doesn't strike me as a man who'd keep images of his girlfriends on his phone, but there have to be at least a few. Breaching someone's privacy is something I normally would never do, but this thing is taunting me so badly. What if I only take a quick look? Just go into his gallery and scroll through the last few photos. No. I'm not doing it.

I resist the temptation for a whole five minutes. Then, I grab the phone and hit the power button. The screen lights up.

And it's unlocked. I close my eyes for just a moment and take another deep breath.

His background is a photo of someone, but I can't see the image clearly. The entire home screen is covered with app icons, but I can tell it's a woman. Lying in bed! I didn't even need to go into the damn gallery. I can't believe he still has an ex-lover's picture as his phone background! I swipe at the screen maniacally, trying to find a window with fewer icons so I can see what the bitch looks like. The first three screens are all cluttered, but the fourth is icon-free, and the photo is fully visible. My heart skips a beat.

The bitch . . . is me.

I'm wearing my favorite zebra-striped pajamas, tangled up in the sheets, lying on my side and clutching a pillow to my chest. He keeps *my* picture on his phone.

I swipe back to the home screen and click on the gallery icon. More pictures of me—some of me sleeping, but most are taken from afar, without me knowing. Me—standing in front of a changing room, trying on a dress. Me—taking a selfie next to a rose shrub behind the house. Me—crouching next to a doghouse while Zeus licks at my face. There are more than fifty photos and—

"What the fuck are you doing?"

I jump, startled. My husband is standing in the doorway, staring at the phone in my hands.

"I . . . I . . . I was just checking on the screen," I mumble and quickly click the power button to put the phone to sleep. "It's broken."

Drago reaches the bed in a few long, powerful strides and snatches the phone from my hand.

"Were you reading my messages so you could report to Ajello?" he barks into my face.

"What? No!"

"Really? Why not? From what I've gathered, you can understand Serbian rather well."

My heart sinks to the pit of my stomach. Oh my God, he knows.

"Tell me, *mila moya*, did you know Serbian before? Or did you learn it specifically for this marriage?"

I close my eyes and drop my head. "I learned it," I whisper.

"Fucking look at me when you're speaking to me!" he yells and my head snaps up.

"The don ordered me to learn it!" I scream into his face.

"So it wasn't a coincidence. It was planned well in advance. How long did it take you to prep for your spying mission? Six months?"

I take a deep breath, trying to keep the tears from spilling. "Two."

Drago's eyes flare in surprise. "Two fucking months. How the fuck did you manage to accomplish that?"

"I have a thing for languages," I whisper. "That's why the don chose me."

"Did he threaten you? Because if he had, I'm going to gut that motherfucker."

I grip the bedcover between my fingers, squeezing it with all my might, and close my eyes. Ajello did threaten my brother, but I never believed he would ever actually hurt Arturo. All things considered, I accepted to be a part of this scheme for my own reasons.

"No one threatened me." I meet my husband's piercing gaze. "It was my decision."

Drago's body goes stone-still. His eyes hold mine as anger brews in their green depths. "I want to know what you have told Ajello so far."

"I . . . I told him that you have some problems with the Romanians. He asked about some deal you've made, but I said I don't know anything."

He leans in, getting in my face. "What else?"

"That most of your people live here, in your house."

"How dare you put my family at risk." His voice is dangerously low as he says it, infused with so much disgust that I cringe. It's so much worse than yelling. "Gather your stuff and get the hell out of my room."

I watch Drago's retreating form as he crosses the bedroom and slams the door shut behind him. My body jerks at the sound. After getting off the bed, I pull the duvet down to the floor and spread it in front of the closet. With numb limbs, I start throwing my clothes on top of it. One of the guys took my suitcases to the storeroom on the ground level, and there is no way I'm going there, no way I'm going to risk facing Drago again.

Once I've gathered a good part of my clothes on the duvet, I pull the corners together and drag my load toward the room at the end of the hallway. I repeat the ordeal twice more until I have everything moved out of my husband's suite.

Drago

I can't believe how absolutely unperturbed my wife is. She's sitting next to me, chatting about some nonsense with Jelena with a wide smile on her face. Mirko throws in something, and she laughs. Not a care in the world. In fact, she seems to be enjoying her dinner.

I, on the other hand, spent the whole afternoon berating myself for snapping at her and ordering her out of our bedroom. It's not like I didn't already suspect she's been providing info to her don. Confidential business matters are rarely discussed in the house, so she could have only learned and relayed inconsequential things, most of which, Ajello can easily obtain by other means. Seeing her snoop through my phone, however, made me lose my shit. It's one thing if she passed some of the info she's gathered along the way. It's a completely different matter to purposely dig for more details. And the fact that she wasn't even coerced into spying on me, made the bitter taste of betrayal ten times worse. What makes me even more pissed off is that she probably also saw the photos of her on my phone. Fuck!

Without saying a word, I rise from the table intending to head outside when my gaze falls on the fish tank in the corner. Three of the four orange fish are zooming inside the bowl, but the remaining one seems to be floating on the surface. I cross the distance and look inside the aquarium. The fish is dead, bobbing upside down.

Sienna already lost a pet once and she will probably be distressed when she sees it. *It's a fucking fish! They die all the time. She's not a child to be seriously upset over a dead fish!* Yes, but I can't stomach the idea of having my wife unsettled over anything, even just a little. Even while I'm fucking furious at her.

Throwing a glance over my shoulder to confirm that Sienna is still occupied by the conversation with Jelena, I take out the slippery body and, keeping it hidden inside my fist, leave the dining room.

"Take a picture of this," I say to Iliya, who's on guard duty at the front door, and hand him the dead fish. "Send someone to find an identical one and put it into the fish tank."

Iliya takes the fish by the tail and looks it over. "I'm not sure pet stores are still open."

"I don't fucking care. Make sure it's done," I spit out and make my way outside to clear my head.

The fifteen-minute walk I planned to take ends up being an hour-long drive across town to where my sister rented a studio apartment in a six-story walk-up. I give a slight chin lift to

Tara's security detail. The guys are keeping an eye on her place from a car parked on the other side of the street. I slip inside the building and climb the stairs to the top floor.

"If I knew it was you, I would have pretended not to be home," Tara snaps when she opens the door. "What do you want?"

"I've decided you had enough time to cool off and came to check on you." I walk in, taking a look around. It's a nice, modern place, decorated in tones of white and dark brown.

Tara shuts the door and comes to stand before me with her hands on her hips. Her voice hasn't changed much since she was a kid, retaining its high pitch. I always need to read her lips when we talk.

"I'm fine, as you can very well see. Now, feel free to go back home to your Italian wife."

"This animosity you have toward Sienna is unfounded. She had nothing to do with Petar's death."

"Oh, you're defending her now?"

"Stop acting like a brat." I sigh. "Did you check the rocks?"

Tara's eyes twinkle as they always do whenever we talk about work. Nothing has ever kept my sister's focus for long. She transferred colleges a couple of times and couldn't settle on a major, eventually dropping out altogether. Four years ago, after watching her waste her days, I decided she needed to do something with her life, and brought her in to handle the logistics for my business dealing in precious gems.

"Yes, everything is good except for the tanzanite. It should have been dark blue, but we only got pale ones. Absolutely unprofessional." She shakes her head. "The emeralds we got for the Arabian Prince are fine, thank God."

I nod, step around my sister, and approach the dresser against a nearby wall. On top of it is a picture set into a small silver frame. It's a photo of Tara and Dina, holding hands on their first day of kindergarten. I take the frame and trace the tip of my finger over Dina's smiling face.

Tara lays her hand on my arm. "Are you okay with me taking it? It's the only photo we have."

"Yeah," I say.

It hurts too much to look at it, anyway. Every time I see this photo, I spiral into self-doubt and can't stop reexamining that night, wondering what I did wrong. Would Dina be alive today if I tried to break the window in their room instead? Or if I had been faster?

I put the frame back on the dresser. "Come over to the mansion and meet my wife. Lunch or dinner. You can pick the day."

"I'm not setting a foot in that house while that woman is there."

"I wasn't asking, Tara." I pin her with my gaze. "You'll come. And you'll be polite. End of discussion."

Tara grits her teeth. "Fine."

I turn to leave when my eyes snag on the bookshelf in the corner. One of the books has been left leaning against the back of the shelf. On the cover, a woman in a white vintage dress is embracing a shirtless, long-haired guy, who seems to be suffering from constipation. I'm pretty sure I saw that exact book on Sienna's nightstand, right next to another one with a half-naked guy howling at the moon.

"I have a feeling you and my wife will get along beautifully," I throw over my shoulder.

When I return home, I head directly to my bedroom. A small part of me hopes I'll find Sienna there after all, but when I open the door, my bed is empty.

I take a quick shower and then lie awake for nearly an hour, resisting the urge to seek out my wife and bring her back to my bed. Eventually, I lose the fight and leave my room, making my way down the hallway to the room at the far end of the floor.

Sienna is asleep, curled up into a ball, clutching a pillow to her chest. This bed is too small for both of us, so I slide my arms under my spellbinding wife and carry her back to my own.

Yes, her sole reason for coming into my home was to spy on me. Yes, she went as far as snooping on my phone to read my messages. And yes, I'm still angry as hell.

But I'm not spending a night without her in my bed. Not a single night. I lower her onto the bed, then lie down behind her and wrap my arms around her sleeping form. She might be a sneaky, scheming little spy, but she's my spy.

CHAPTER
fourteen

❦ Sienna ❦

I PRETEND TO BE IMMERSED IN EATING THE PIE SERVED at dinner, while secretly observing my husband. He's wearing jeans and a white dress shirt. The top two buttons are undone and his sleeves are rolled up to his elbows. I still find it unusual that the men here wear such casual attire. The Cosa Nostra members' everyday clothes consist almost exclusively of suits. The only time I've seen Ajello's men dressed casually was on the day of Asya's wedding, and only because Pasha warned that no one in a suit would be allowed at the venue. I've seen Drago decked out in a full suit several times so far, but he typically wears just a button-down shirt and jeans.

He hasn't said a word to me since he caught me with his phone five days ago. Mostly, he acts as if I'm not even present. Except at night.

Every evening, an hour or so after I go to sleep, he comes into my bedroom at the end of the hall and carries me back to his own. The first time, I didn't realize it happened until his arms wrapped around my body as he pulled me against his chest. I pretended I was still asleep while sinking into the comfort of his bed and the warmth of his body. The following morning, however, I woke up in my new room.

At first, I thought I dreamed it all, but then I smelled his scent on me. I wasn't sleeping when he showed up the following night, but I acted like I was. And in the morning, when he carried me back, I did the same. I'm not actually sure if he knows I'm faking being asleep, but he can't expect I wouldn't notice him carrying me around five nights in a row. Maybe he's pretending, too.

I don't know what to think of his actions. But one thing I do know is that keeping up this farce is becoming unbearable. I want to be able to touch him and to freely snuggle into his side. And I want us to have sex again so much that it feels like my pussy weeps with need. I could tell him the truth. Explain my reasons for accepting the marriage, even though he would probably just laugh at me. Who in their right mind marries a stranger because of the fear of being alone? No. I can't bare myself to him like that.

Drago is nodding at whatever Filip is saying, his eyes focused on his second-in-command's mouth. Not at the ground as I initially thought. He's completely ignoring me sitting at his side.

Feigning indifference, I pick up my phone off the table and, pursing my lips, take a selfie. Drago doesn't turn around. It's as if he doesn't give a fuck about me. Only, he does.

After I saw my pictures on his phone, I started paying more attention and noticed things I missed before. How he frequently comes into the kitchen while I'm there, asks Keva a nonsensical question, and then leaves. Each time this happens, I can feel his eyes on me while I pretend to be engrossed in whatever I'm doing at that moment. Or, whenever he stumbles upon me playing video games with Adam, he barks orders and sends him on an errand, even when it seems rather trivial. And, yesterday, when I was playing with the dogs outside, I saw my husband standing by the garage, watching me. The instant he realized I'd spotted him, he turned away and left.

I'm done being ignored.

"Hey, Filip." I prop my chin on my hand and smile. "Can I ask for a favor?"

Both Drago and his right-hand man look at me.

"Um, sure," Filip says, throwing a quick look at Drago whose eyes are glued to my lips. "What do you need?"

"Do you have some free time tomorrow?" I chirp.

"He doesn't," Drago snaps.

I tilt my head and look at him, keeping the smile plastered on my face. "I was asking Filip."

"And I responded. What do you need him for?"

"I wanted to ask Filip to teach me to drive a car. But if he's busy, I'll ask someone else." I shrug. "Is Adam available?"

"No."

"Oh. How about—"

"He's not available, either."

I raise an eyebrow. "I haven't said who."

"Doesn't matter. None of my men are free. Contain your sunny attitude, it won't do any good around here." Drago's jaw is set in a tight line, and his nostrils are flaring.

"Why?"

He grabs the back of my chair and leans forward until his cheek brushes mine. "Because I'm the only man who's going to bathe in your sunshine, Sienna," he says next to my ear. "No one else."

He pulls back and glares at me. Someone is jealous, it seems, and trying very hard not to show it.

"And are *you* available tomorrow?" I ask.

He clenches his jaw even more. "No."

"Too bad. I'll have to try to find someone else then." I take my plate and stand up from the table. "Good night."

The weight of Drago's eyes on me is heavy as I make my way to the kitchen, and then again when I return and leave the dining room. Once I reach my bedroom, I take a quick shower and head to the mountain of stuff I keep on top of the dresser. There's only one small closet in this room, and it doesn't fit all of my clothes. I'm rummaging through the pile in search of pajamas when the door behind me bursts open.

Startled, I yelp and spin around. Drago is standing at the threshold, his eyes locked on the towel I'm clutching around myself. It's a rather small towel. I wait until his gaze moves to my face and innocently bat my eyelashes at him. "You're early. I'm still awake, so please come back in an hour."

He covers the distance between us in several long steps and places his hands on the dresser, caging me. His breathing is labored and the muscles on his neck are taut. He's angry.

I loosen my grip on the towel and let it fall to the floor, but Drago's stare stays fixed on my face. I reach out and slowly undo a button on his shirt. And then another. He doesn't say anything, doesn't even flinch as I work through the rest. Next, I lower my hands to undo the button and zipper of his jeans, then hook my thumbs on the waistband and tug his pants, along with his boxer briefs, down, releasing his hard cock.

A low growling sound leaves his lips, but he remains still even when I lick his exposed chest. The self-restraint this man has is unmatched. Circling my arms around his neck, I lift onto my tiptoes.

"I miss you, Drago."

With a swipe of his arm, clothes from the dresser behind me fly to the side. Drago grabs my thighs, lifts me, and slams my ass down on the cleared-off top.

Wetness pools between my legs as he slides his hands behind my knees, jerking me forward. His cock enters me in

162

one swift thrust. I suck in a breath. Like I've been underwater and just broke the surface, gasping for air.

He stands perfectly still, not moving a muscle, while I revel in the sensation of his cock lodged within me. I tighten my arms and legs around him and take another deep breath. My pussy muscles contract around his thickness as it swells even more.

I look up and meet his gaze. He's not just mad. Based on the look in his eyes, he's consumed with fury. Leaning forward, I place a light kiss on the edge of his clenched jaw. Then one more, closer to his lips which are tightly pressed together. Other than our breathing, the ticking of a clock somewhere in the room is the only sound that breaks the silence.

I hook my feet together behind his back, but Drago remains motionless. It's a punishment. Or that's what he probably believes. Nine beats. Ten. He tilts his head slightly to the side and inhales. My legs are shaking. I'm going to come just from the feel of his cock inside me. Fifteen beats. Not even his hands move, they are still clutching the back of my knees. It's a duel—his need to fuck me versus his will to have me punished. Eighteen. Nineteen.

"Drago," I say next to his ear.

He sucks in a breath. The next second, he pulls out and slams inside of me again. And again. I let go of his neck and grip the edge of the dresser, clinging to the wooden surface as he pounds into me. Each thrust is harder, and faster.

The lights are on, so I can see anger war with satisfaction on his face as he plows into me like a madman. Breath leaves me in short bursts. He pulls my leg up with his left hand while the other slips around my nape, squeezing my hair. My whole body trembles, and I pant, staring into his lust-filled eyes. The dresser bangs against the wall behind me with each thrust of his hips. There are fifty people in this house, and I'm pretty sure every one of them can hear us. And I don't give a damn.

"Say my name again!" Drago bites out as he keeps up his thrusts.

I tilt my chin up, lips tightly pressed together. His temporal vein is pulsing, and his muscles strain. The grip on my hair intensifies, canting my head back.

"Fucking say it, Sienna."

He's pounding me so hard that I probably won't be able to walk tomorrow. There is no sign of indifference now. He's losing it completely. I fucking love it.

"Drago!" I scream as my orgasm erupts while I'm lost in his eyes.

They look almost feral as he buries himself fully and explodes. He keeps his tight clasp on my hair and holds my gaze as his warm cum fills me.

Silence reigns again, fractured only by the sounds of our heavy breathing and the ticking clock.

Drago

I've been awake for almost an hour, gazing at the morning sky visible beyond the balcony door. Holding my wife tightly in my arms. She usually sleeps on her side, her face buried against my chest, but at some point during the night, she climbed on top of me. Sienna is now plastered to my chest, her arms wrapped around my torso and her legs straddling my waist.

I should get up and go find Filip so we can discuss where to obtain enough product to cover the losses suffered in the

Syracuse warehouse fire, but I can't make myself leave this bed. It is so damn good to have my little spy back in my arms.

The past few days have been a fucking nightmare filled with frustration. I tried my best to ignore her but couldn't stay completely away. During the day, it was somewhat manageable. I kept finding stupid reasons to chance upon her. It helped quell the need to have her near, but most of the time, it led to me getting even more agitated when I found her having fun in the rec room with my men. I almost lost it when I saw her playing a video game with Adam again.

I've never been a jealous man. The idea of losing my shit just because some guy talked to my woman seemed idiotic.

Seemed. Past tense.

Last evening, after Sienna asked Filip to teach her to drive, I sent a text to all of my crew, letting them know that if I catch any man socializing with my wife while I'm not present, I'll snap his neck.

Sienna stirs, her naked pussy gliding over my hard cock. When I carried her into my bedroom last night, I threw her onto the bed and fucked her again. It wasn't enough. Not even close. Tightening my hold around her waist, I roll us over and brace myself so I don't crush her. After sliding my free hand between our bodies, it takes less than a minute of teasing her clit to make her wet. She's still half-asleep when I push my cock inside her. I expect her to tense from the sudden intrusion, but she just smiles and opens her legs wider, watching me with veiled eyes.

I pound into her, my thrusts hard and fast, the ferocity meant as punishment for her betrayal. When Ajello proposed this marriage deal, I suspected there was more to his plans than simply reviving our collaboration. I anticipated that she would be an informant for her don. As Keva said, I would have contrived the same if I was in Ajello's place, so her spying didn't feel like treachery in the beginning. I wasn't in love with her then. But I am now. So fucking in love that I couldn't even handle spending a single night without her in my bed.

Sliding my palm up her stomach, I drop a kiss on her shoulder. Then, I bite the sensitive skin in the hollow between her neck and collarbone. Even her scent is intoxicating. I'm drawn to her like some distant cold planet is pulled toward the sun, needing to feel her warmth. I need more of it. Each ridiculous outfit, all the sparks lighting up her vivacious eyes, and every teasing smile has pulled me deeper into madness. I should have sent her back to Cosa Nostra the moment I realized her deception, but I didn't. I can't imagine my life without her sunshine anymore.

I take her leg and put it over my shoulder, sinking deeper inside her. Sienna moans beneath me and grabs my forearms, her fingernails scraping my skin as her eyes bore into mine.

Her body trembles as she comes, throwing her head back in ecstasy. My little traitor. I should have finished first, denied her an orgasm, taken a small measure of revenge for what she's doing to me, but I couldn't. Only once she sags in bed and I'm certain she's done, I let go of my restraint and find my own release.

My wife's dark-brown eyes find mine, capturing me. They remind me of a cat's—large and hypnotic, warm and so impossibly sweet. She lifts her hand as if to place it on my face, but I move away.

"Breakfast is in ten minutes." I slip out of her and head toward the closet to get a change of clothes. "Be in front of the garage in half an hour if you want that driving lesson."

When I turn around, Sienna is still sprawled out in the middle of the bed, my cum dripping from her pussy.

"Leave some hot water for me." She smiles, completely ignoring my antagonistic tone.

I grip the closet door with all my strength, trying to

suppress the need to go back over there and kiss that lying mouth.

"Use the shower in your room." I slam the closet door shut and walk into the bathroom.

Sienna

He left.

I wrap my arms around myself and stare at the empty spot in the garage where Drago's car had been parked. It's only eight. I haven't even gone to breakfast. I just showered and ran downstairs. When I glanced out of the window five minutes ago as I got dressed, he was speaking with Filip outside of the main garage door. I bite my lower lip in frustration and head back toward the house, dialing the don along the way. I received another "SIENNA" all-caps message on my way down here.

"It's been ten days since your last check-in, Sienna," he barks without preamble.

"There are too many people around here. I'll try to be more prompt going forward."

"Update. Now."

"Well, we had a situation here on Friday, which left everyone feeling on edge for the rest of the day."

"Details, Sienna. Was it something at the club?"

"Nope. The fridge broke down."

A few beats of silence follow. "The fridge?"

"Yeah. It was after business hours, and it's one of those large industrial types. It took hours to find—"

"I don't give a fuck about Popov's damn fridge!"

"But nothing happens here that's related to Drago's dealings. The fridge was the highlight of the entire week and—"

The line goes dead. I cringe. It looks like he's not happy with my report. I stuff the phone into the back pocket of my jeans and resume walking toward the mansion.

People are eating in the huge dining room, their chatter can be heard from the foyer. I smile, saying good morning as I walk by the long table, and enter the kitchen. Keva and four other girls are rushing around, pulling out plates from the cupboards and filling cups with coffee on big round trays. It's quite a feat to feed so many people three meals a day.

Keva runs over to one of the six ovens to take out a cheese pie, a traditional Serbian breakfast dish, yelling at the same time to only serve Mirko tea because he is not allowed to have coffee. One of her helpers dashes inside the kitchen to say that Beli is whining that he is still hungry; his piece of pie was apparently smaller than usual.

"You can tell that ogre that if he has an issue, he can take it up with the complaints department!" Keva shouts, slamming the oven door closed, and turns to me. "There are plates with extras on the counter. Take a few to the food-devouring horde."

I grab the two huge, oval plates and carry them into the dining room. When I get back to the kitchen, I end up with a tray filled with coffee cups thrust into my hands. I take these out to the dining room, too, and grab a piece of the pie for myself on my way back.

When everyone finishes breakfast, there is a mile-high stack of dirty dishes in the sink, and all three dishwashers are full. I turn around, intending to ask someone to show me how to turn them on, but everyone seems busy. Peering down at the closest dishwasher, I ponder what to do. I've never actually turned one of these on before. At home, either the maid or Asya handled the kitchen cleanup. There are program buttons on the dishwasher door, and I know I need to choose one, but I guess I should add the dish detergent first. Is there a specific compartment for that? I don't see one. A big bottle of liquid dish soap sits next to the sink that's overflowing with greasy pots and pans. I unscrew the top of the bottle and pour a good amount inside the nearest machine, then repeat the same process with the other two. With that done, I select the heavy wash cycle for each and turn them on.

"Sienna!" Jelena calls from somewhere behind me. "The meat order arrived. Can you get one of the guys to bring everything in and sign the papers for the delivery guy?"

"Sure."

I run to the dining room and usher Relja to the kitchen's back door that's used for freight. While he unloads the boxes from the van, I go over the order form the delivery guy handed to me. It says the shipment contains one hundred and fifty pounds of pork and two hundred pounds of chicken.

"So, this is a monthly provision?" I ask as I sign.

"Weekly," the guy mumbles.

Weekly? That's three hundred and fifty pounds of meat! I look up from the paper to find the delivery guy staring at my glittery red knee-high boots.

"Just like Dorothy, but more badass, yeah?" I grin and knock my heels together, twice.

He nods, his eyebrows hitting his hairline. "Yes."

"Oliver," Keva yells, "if Drago catches you drooling over his wife's legs, you'll have to consider a career change. It'll be hard to drive with your eyes in your pocket, honey."

The guy's head snaps up. He grabs the form out of my hand and hightails it out the door without saying goodbye.

When Relja leaves after bringing in the boxes of meat, Keva and I are the only ones left in the kitchen.

"This is crazy," I say and jump to sit on top of the counter next to the stove where she's put on the kettle for tea.

"I know." She smirks and looks at me sideways. "But you like it, am I right?"

"Yes, I like it. I like it here."

"We like having you here, too."

I lean my head on the fridge to my right and sigh. "Drago doesn't."

"He does. He just doesn't want to admit it." She lifts the kettle and pours the water into a chipped cup in front of her. "And you know why."

I close my eyes. *He told her.* "Because I'm passing info about Drago's business to Ajello."

"I think it's a bit more complicated than that, Sienna."

"What do you mean?"

She shrugs. "That's not for me to say, dear. You'll have to ask your husband."

"He hasn't been talking to me lately."

"Can you blame him?" Keva asks, looking at me over the rim of her teacup.

"No, I guess not." I sigh. "What's wrong with Drago's hearing?"

Keva's eyes widen. "So, you've noticed." It's not a question.

"It took me a while. I figured something wasn't right when I would ask a question, and it seemed like he didn't hear me. But I also noticed that he didn't appear to have a problem hearing what was being said when he spoke with his men."

"Drago suffers from high-frequency hearing loss. It means, in most cases, he can't perceive high-pitched sounds, or when he can, he can't distinguish what's said." She sets the cup on the counter and takes my hand. "Imagine talking with someone on the phone, but the connection is bad, and you can only hear some of the words, or parts of the words. You can *hear* the person on the other end, but you can't *understand* what they're saying because a big part of the conversation is lost."

"He's reading lips to compensate, isn't he?"

She nods.

"He's really good."

"Well, he's been doing it for a very long time, Sienna."

"How long?"

"Almost twenty years," Keva says. "The bomb blast that destroyed his home, killed his parents and sister, did serious damage to his eardrums."

"Is that when he got the burn scars as well?"

"Yes."

I take a deep breath and bite the inside of my cheek. "Can he hear me? When I speak?"

Keva's hand squeezes mine. "Your voice is rather high, sweetheart. He can hear you, but for Drago, it probably all sounds like mumbling. He'd have a hard time understanding most of what you say without lipreading. But he likely can hear very clearly when you say his name because there are no high-pitched consonants in it."

"Why hasn't he told me?"

"It isn't exactly common knowledge. You know how the Mafia world works, Sienna. People could use that information against him, especially during important meetings."

"He thinks I would tell the don," I choke out.

"He does."

I gape at her. How can he think I would share something that private? "Don't tell Drago I know. Please."

"Why?"

"Just don't."

"One of these days, I'm going to sit you two down and make you fucking talk to each other." She shakes her head and reaches for her cup, but then suddenly yelps. "*Jebem ti lebac!*"

I follow her gaze and my eyes land on the dishwashers on the other side of the kitchen. Sudsy foam is pouring out from around the doors. I jump down off the counter and rush after Keva who's running toward the chaos. When I reach her, she's already stopped all three machines and is in the process of opening the closest one. A stream of white bubbles bursts out of the appliance even before the door is fully down.

"Jesus!" she shouts, looking at the mess that doubles when she opens the second dishwasher. "What on earth happened here? Call the girls and get some rags!"

"Um . . . I think it's my fault," I mumble as I open the drawer to get the kitchen towels.

Drago

I park my car and walk inside the warehouse where we stored the last weapons shipment. Filip and two security guards are standing by a pile of crates, while a third guard is a few feet away, holding a man at gunpoint.

"Is that Bogdan's guy you caught snooping around?" I ask.

"Yes." Filip nods. "He was messing with the lock on the back door. There was someone else with him, but he took off. Adam went after the guy."

I take out my gun and turn toward the would-be saboteur. "Planning on destroying another one of my buildings?"

The man shakes his head and whimpers. I aim at his left thigh and pull the trigger. Clutching his leg, he falls to his side. "Let's try again. What were you doing here?" I ask.

"Checking the security," he wails.

"So the others can come tonight and torch it? Nice." I crouch in front of him. "I know that Bogdan has a substantial shipment coming in next week. I need the date, the route, and the vehicle description. And while we're at it, I need the locations of the two warehouses he uses for storage."

"I don't know any of that."

I press the barrel of my gun to his right thigh and fire. The man screams, rolling to his other side, gripping his newly wounded leg. I grab his shoulder and yank him back to face me.

"Did this help you with your knowledge?" I ask. "Or do you need additional incentive?"

The guy mumbles something that sounds like an address. I throw a look over my shoulder and see Filip typing into his phone. "Locations?"

"Yes." He nods.

"Perfect." I refocus back on the Romanian guy. "When is this shipment arriving?"

"Tuesday, early morning."

"Good. Now, the truck route."

"I don't know. I swear!"

"Who does?"

"Bogdan and his logistics guy. Mircea."

"The short dude with the glasses who always follows Bogdan around?"

"Yes."

"Thank you." I rise, shoot the guy in the head, and turn to my second-in-command. "Is Bogdan still MIA?"

"No one has seen him for weeks. Iliya says his informants believe Bogdan went back to Romania."

I drum my fingers on the wooden surface of a crate. We've been trying to locate the son of a bitch, but no one has set eyes on him in a while. I've known the Romanian leader for years, and he would never leave the country when he has a shipment coming.

"He's not in Romania," I say and nod toward the body. "Throw this one in the fridge, I'll need him next week. Have Adam put a tail on Mircea, but don't touch him for now. I also need our men to check out the locations the dead guy gave us, but make sure they aren't seen."

"All right. What else?"

"Bogdan's trucks are arriving on Tuesday morning, giving us four days to get ready. We'll set up three teams. One team will intercept the truck. The other two will go to the storage locations on Monday night and wait. When we have the truck, they can set those shitholes ablaze."

"Retaliating against Bogdan by stealing his shipment and blowing up his warehouses is one thing, but what are we going to do with the extra weapons?"

"I'll call Belov and see if Bratva wants more guns. That money will cover our losses from Syracuse."

Filip watches me, dragging his hand through his hair. "Bogdan will go ballistic, Drago."

"Yes, he will."

"Should we up the security on the mansion?"

"Double it. I'll go get Tara before this all goes down. I want her at the house until this shit blows over."

"She won't like it."

"I don't give a fuck," I bark. The phone in my pocket vibrates. "Do we have any small pistols somewhere?"

"How small?"

"Really small. Get me a pink one, if possible." My phone vibrates with another notification. "I'm going to teach Sienna how to shoot. Just in case."

Filip's eyes nearly bulge out of his sockets. "Is that . . . wise?"

"Don't let her smiles and silly clothes fool you, Filip. There's much more than meets the eye where my wife is concerned. Honestly, I'd be surprised if she doesn't already know how to fire a gun."

I leave my second-in-command standing with a confused expression on his face and exit the warehouse. When I get behind the wheel, I take out my phone to check the messages. There are two, both from Keva. The first is a photo of my wife crouching in a pool of white foam, collecting it into a bucket with a soup ladle. She's wearing sparkling red high-heeled boots with a matching bow on her head. The second is a text, letting me know that my wife poured liquid soap into the dishwashers.

I open the photo again, zooming in on Sienna's face. Her eyes are huge and intent on what she's doing, and if I paid attention only to them, I'd assume she's panicking. But her lips are drawn into a huge smile. This woman is such a contradiction.

I close the image and type out a message.

> **17:10 Drago:** Ask my wife if she knows how to shoot a gun.

The reply arrives less than a minute later.

> **17:11 Keva:** Sienna? What's wrong with you? Of course she doesn't.

> **17:12 Drago:** Ask her.

The phone vibrates with a new text.

> **17:14 Keva:** Yes. God help us.

I stare at the message for a few moments, then burst out laughing.

CHAPTER
fifteen

I LEAN MY SHOULDER ON THE DOORFRAME AND REGARD my wife. She's at the kitchen island, cautiously cutting up something with measured slides of her knife. Despite being busy with domestic chores, she's wearing another crazy outfit paired with gold faux fur slippers. Her fashion choices are completely ridiculous, but she's beautiful as hell, even when wearing her absurd getups.

When I came home last night, Sienna was already asleep. As I do every night, I carried her to my bed. I ate her perfect pussy while she was still half-asleep, and then I fucked her. Hard. I held her in my arms all night, but still took her back to her room this morning before heading to work. I don't know why I keep doing it. I am so fucking angry, but can't determine the reason behind my rage. Is it her lies, or that she lied to *me*? Maybe I'm angry at myself because, even after everything, I can't make myself hate her.

And *that* is the fucking problem. That is why I'm here now staring at *my wife* like a goddamn creep.

As I watch, Sienna sniffs and brushes her eye with the back

of her hand. I become alert immediately and march across the kitchen.

When I reach her, I grab her around the waist and lift her to sit on the island next to the cutting board.

"Drago?" She blinks at me in confusion as tears slide down her cheeks.

I close my eyes for a second, trying to calm down. Whoever dared to say or do anything that made my wife cry will be leaving this house within ten minutes. In a fucking body bag.

"What. Happened?" I ask through gritted teeth.

"Um . . . I'm helping Keva prepare an onion sauce."

I look down at the cutting board. Fucking onions. "Nevena!" I beckon the girl fumbling with the spices. "Take these away."

"What? Why?" Sienna asks.

There's no way I'm telling her that I nearly went ballistic because she was crying over damn onions. Instead, I reach behind my back to take out the gun Relja got for me and place it on the counter next to Sienna.

"Glock 42," I say. "Relja couldn't find a pink one on short notice."

She arches an eyebrow at me. "Why would I need a gun?"

"Just a precaution. We're expecting some problems."

Sienna takes the gun and looks it over, then releases the magazine. "Only six rounds?"

"You plan on going on a rampage, *mila moya*?"

"Maybe." She snaps the magazine back in with a flourish.

My cock hardens at the sight of her looking so innocent, with her feet dangling off the counter, and, at the same time, handling the gun like a pro.

"Did your brother teach you to shoot?" I ask.

She laughs. I wish I could hear the sound.

"Arturo would never let me touch a gun." She leans forward and waggles her eyebrows. "I told him I was going to a dance class. I even carried a bag with dance shoes and a costume with me, and showed him some moves I learned online so he wouldn't ask questions."

"You're going to keep that gun in your room, but if you are leaving the house, even to go play with the dogs, take it with you."

"My room?" She pauses, eyes twinkling. "Or our room?"

I'm tempted. So fucking tempted, but can't give in. I grab her chin and tilt her head up. "Your room, Sienna. I thought you understood that."

"So we're just fuck buddies who happen to be married?"

"Something like that."

She scrunches her nose at me and swats my hand away. "Go to hell."

I follow her with my eyes as she jumps off the counter and heads toward the door only to stop halfway to the threshold. She stands there for a few seconds, then turns around.

"From this point on, forget the fuck buddies part, Drago. I'm done," she bites out and cocks the gun I gave her. "If I find you in my room again, you'll witness firsthand just how much I've learned in those classes."

And then, my sparkling, innocent, ray-of-sunshine wife raises her gun, aiming at the empty milk jug next to me on the counter. An epic boom echoes through the spacious kitchen as the container flies backward and ricochets off the pantry door. Someone screams. Filip and three other men burst into the room with guns drawn. They don't even pay attention to Sienna, who is still standing in the middle of the kitchen, holding the gun in her hand, and looking cute as a button in her pink sweaterdress and fuzzy slippers. Everyone is yelling, making my head feel like it's going to explode, but all I can see is my wife. She stares daggers at me, a wicked grin gracing her face. Everything else fades away, as usual, when she's in the room.

I saunter up to her and grab the back of her neck. She

narrows her eyes at me and tilts her chin. My little devil who walks the world disguised as an angel. I wrap my free arm around her waist, pulling her up against my chest in the process, and crash my mouth to hers.

Something thuds on the floor, probably the gun. Sienna's arms loop around my neck, holding tightly as she returns the kiss. Our tongues battle for supremacy. But then, she suddenly stops and leans away.

"Put me down."

I loosen my hold, letting her slowly slide down my body.

"Remember—not a foot inside my room," she says, then bends to collect the gun off the floor and sashays out of the kitchen.

When Sienna is out of view, I turn toward my men, who are on the other side of the kitchen, watching and looking confused.

"Back to work," I snap.

They put their guns into their holsters and hurry out, passing Keva where she stands in the doorway with her hands on her hips.

"It's official," she declares. "You two were made for each other."

Sienna

I lay the gun inside the nightstand drawer before shoving it shut.

"That son of a bitch," I mumble as I slide beneath the duvet and pull it over my head.

My hands are still shaking, so I slip them under the pillow and take a deep breath. I've never shot a gun outside of the shooting range before. Dear God, I could have hurt someone. I could have shot my idiot husband by mistake. It's not like he doesn't deserve it, but still, just the thought of Drago getting hurt makes me nauseated.

This is not me. I don't go around threatening people, shooting at stuff, for God's sake, but that man . . . that damn man is making me lose my shit like no one ever has.

"I'm done," I mumble into the pillow.

I'm going to pack my stuff and call Arturo to come and get me. The don will probably go apeshit, but I don't care. I can't handle this anymore.

Throwing the blanket off, I rush to the dresser and start taking out my clothes, only to stop when I get to the workout gear Drago bought for me. The look on my husband's face when I walked out of the dressing room wearing the tracksuit was priceless. I drop down on the bed, clutching the matching sweatpants and sweatshirt to my chest. I don't want to leave. But I don't want to stay, either. I . . . I don't know what I want anymore.

My gaze shifts to the phone on the nightstand. I reach for it and hit my sister's number.

"How is my favorite sister?" I chirp when Asya takes the call.

"Your favorite and only sister is fine. And she knows that tone. It means you did something."

"What?! Of course I didn't! I just wanted to chat."

"We spoke two hours ago. What did you do, Sienna?"

I lie down on the bed and tilt my head up to stare at the ceiling. "I almost shot my husband."

"Shot?" she yelps. "What are you talking about? What happened?"

"He bought me a gun." I shrug even though she can't see me. "I was mad at him."

"So, you shot him?"

"No. I shot a milk jug. An empty one. But if my aim had been off, the bullet could have ended up in his kidney."

"And why are you mad at him?"

"I asked him if all we are is fuck buddies. He said yes. He's mad at me, too." I sigh. "I've been giving intel on the Serbian organization to Ajello. Drago found out and kicked me out of our bedroom. Now he ignores me. Well, when we're not having sex, that is. But he's still mad at me."

"You're sleeping with him?"

"Of course I'm sleeping with him. Don't you sleep with your husband?"

"I'm not spying on my husband! How . . . how can you two be sleeping together when he knows what you've been doing?"

"Very nicely, actually. The sex is amazing, and Drago likes to cuddle afterward." My lips curve up. "I love it when he pulls me into his body and wraps his arms and legs around me. I feel protected, like nothing can touch me when he's there, you know? But then, in the morning, he carries me back to my new bedroom and continues to pretend that I don't exist during the day."

"And it bothers you."

"It doesn't. I'm just saying." I shrug again. "He has the most amazing eyes . . . Light green with brown flecks. But when he's mad, they get darker. It's sexy as hell."

"So, you like him?"

"No, not particularly. He's grumpy most of the time and he doesn't talk much. I wish he did. His voice is sexy, too." I roll onto my stomach and bury my nose in the pillow. A faint smell of Drago's cologne clings to it. He's never spent a night here, so it's probably from my hair. He usually tucks my head into the crook of his neck when we sleep.

"So . . . you don't like him." Not a question, but I can still hear the uncertainty in her tone.

"Nope. I just like being around him?"

"That doesn't make any sense," Asya sighs.

"I miss him when he's not here. I don't like him, but when he's not around, everything seems . . . empty. He made me go for a run with him one morning, and we've been jogging together three times a week ever since. He bought me this amazing lavender—"

"You jog?"

"Yes. Well, until he caught me checking out his phone. He thought I was reading his messages so I can report on his business to the don, but I just wanted to see if he had photos of his exes on there."

"Mm-hmm."

"Oh, I forgot to tell you. He took me to a wedding before the phone incident. It was in this huge tent. At least four hundred people were there. And a band. I danced on a table."

"You what?"

"It seems to be a thing at Serbian weddings." I laugh. "I wish you could have seen it. Even the bride did it. I took a selfie with Drago and posted it on my social media. Didn't you see it?"

"Um . . . not exactly. Your accounts have been set to private for weeks."

"What? I probably clicked something by mistake, I'll switch it back." No wonder no one has been commenting or liking my photos.

"Are you still snitching on your husband to the don, Sienna?"

"A little. The last time Ajello called me, I told him some nonsense about the fridge being broken and, before that, I said that Drago is buying another truck. I need to check in again next week, so I have to come up with other trivial stuff that I can give him."

"Drago's people are not talking about business when you're around?"

"Oh, they do. I'm just not letting Ajello know any of the sensitive info."

"And does your husband know that?"

"No."

"You need to tell him, Sienna."

"Why would I do that? I don't give a fuck what he thinks of me."

Silent seconds stretch before Asya finally replies, "Because you're in love with your husband."

"What?" I burst out laughing. "I'm not in love with him. Don't be ridiculous."

"I know you, Sienna. And I know how your mind works. You *are* in love with Drago, but you'd rather keep lying to yourself than admit it."

My body tenses. A sense of foreboding washes over me, starting in the pit of my stomach and then spreading through the rest of my system until I fear it's going to swallow me whole. "No," I choke out.

"He's not going to die, Sienna."

I bury my face into the pillow to stifle a whimper. She doesn't understand.

"What happened to our parents was never your fault. Neither is what happened to me. You need to stop believing that everyone close to you will end up dead or hurt, sweetie."

"I need to go," I mumble into the pillow. "I'll call you tomorrow."

"Sienna, please—"

I end the call, turn on silent mode, and slide the phone under the pillow.

It's almost time for dinner, but I don't think I can handle food now. Or people. After getting up from the bed, I take my pajamas and underwear and head into the small attached bathroom. I stay in the shower until the water goes from hot to freezing cold. Then, I climb back into bed, but instead of sleeping, I end up staring at the blank wall.

I've probably been staring at it for an hour when I hear the door being opened. I squeeze my eyes shut and listen. A few seconds pass in complete silence before the click of it being closed reaches my ears. He didn't come in. Why does that make me want to cry?

The mattress dips beneath me, and whatever breath was left within me gets lodged in my chest. Held captive like my suddenly still heart. The blanket slides off my body slowly, inch by tiny inch until it's off completely. A touch lands on my hip, right where my top has ridden up. It's so light, no more than the tip of a finger. I can barely feel it as it moves over the skin of my stomach, tracing a line just above the waistband of my pajama bottoms.

"You never asked me how I knew you can understand Serbian," Drago's deep voice fills the stillness in the room.

I tense but keep my mouth and eyes shut. There's no point in replying since the lights are off. His other hand comes to my waist, fingers hooking onto the band as he slowly slides the pajama pants down my legs.

"You are exceptionally good at pretending, *mila moya*. But you slipped up during dinner a while back."

His fingers are stroking the skin on my thighs as he pulls the panties down. A small moan escapes me, so I quickly bite my lower lip, trying to suppress the next. I know he knows I'm awake, but I keep up the guise nevertheless.

"I have to give it to Ajello, choosing you for the job was a magnificent move. If it was anyone else, I would have seen through the deception much earlier. But I was blinded by the innocent, sunny girl with wide smiles and ridiculous outfits, one who came into every room or situation in a whirlwind of color and joy." The panties are off and Drago strokes a path up my legs, higher and higher, until he reaches my pussy. "Was it out of obligation to Cosa Nostra? Or did you simply want to royally fuck up my life, just for the thrill of it?"

His finger starts sliding inside me as his thumb presses onto my clit, circling it.

"I guess it doesn't matter anymore. But know one thing, my beautiful, glittery spy. The choices you make bear consequences. Feel free to keep shooting at me. And I'll keep being mad at you for lying to me. It doesn't change things."

I suck in a breath as he adds another finger, stretching me. My eyes are still closed but I can feel his presence over me, and then his breath between my legs. I take hold of the headboard as tremors rack my body. The slight trembles at his earliest touch have turned bone-shaking as if I'm burning up with fever.

"You're mine now, Sienna. There is no going back!" he growls and buries his face between my legs, sucking on my clit so hard that I scream his name at the top of my lungs.

I let go of the headboard and thread my fingers in Drago's hair while he continues to devour me. I can't take a second more of his onslaught, but at the same time, I will fucking die if he stops. I'm lost, ready to explode when his fingers slide out of me. He takes one slow, long lick up my slit, and then his mouth vanishes. My eyes fly open.

The illumination in the room is scarce, just moonlight coming through the small window, falling on Drago's form. He's standing at the foot of the bed, unbuttoning his shirt as he stares at me. I love watching my husband when he puts on his clothes because he does it slowly and methodically, every movement calculated. But I enjoy seeing him remove them much, much more.

Drago drops his shirt onto the floor and proceeds to unzip his jeans. My eyes feast on his wide shoulders and sculpted chest, my soaked pussy throbbing with need. The moment I see his huge cock, my mind goes blank. A strange growling sound fills the silence, and it takes me a moment to realize that it's coming from me. I leap off the bed, right at my husband.

His large hands grab me under my thighs, gripping tight, and the next second, my back is slammed against the wall by the window. Drago's face hovers before mine, his eyes boring into my own. His breathing is slow. Deep. I wrap my arms around his neck and tangle my fingers in his hair. And then I pull it. Drago's nostrils flare and his breaths quicken.

"Do you tell your don the details of how I fuck you, as well?"

I smile. "Maybe."

Drago grinds his teeth. Even in low light, I can see the muscles in his jaw twitch. I slide one hand toward his neck and the other to trail the line of his chin with the tip of my finger until I reach the corner of his mouth. I wish he would kiss me right now. It's different from sex. Having sex with Drago Popov is an experience that tops everything I've ever encountered. It's raw, angry, and unapologetic. But being kissed by my husband is like having my mind relentlessly seduced and set to smolder by the heat of his lips on mine. And it scares the living shit out of me.

"Sometimes, I wish I could kill you, Sienna."

He crashes his mouth to mine as he thrusts his cock inside me. And both my pussy and my brain combust.

CHAPTER
sixteen

ARTURO DEVILLE'S HOUSE IS SITUATED IN AN upscale neighborhood. Close enough to everything important, but well away from all the craziness of a Saturday night. Or at least as much as living in New York allows. I stop my bike in front of the iron gate and push up my shield visor. Staring directly into the camera, I press the call button. A few moments later, the gate slides to the side.

I park my bike and head toward the front door where Sienna's brother is standing, glaring at me.

"What the fuck are you doing here?" he asks through his teeth.

"Are we going to discuss business on your porch?"

Arturo sizes me up, then turns and heads inside. I follow him across the spacious living room. Despite its size, the room feels unexpectedly cozy, like home. There's a big bookshelf, a comfortable leather sofa, and a piano in a corner. Photographs line the walls, most of them featuring Sienna and her sister.

Arturo steps around the breakfast bar that divides the space and enters the kitchen, heading toward the stove.

"What do you want?" he asks as he adds a bit of seasoning to whatever he has on the grill.

I move to the breakfast bar and take a seat on a barstool furthest to the right, positioning myself so I have his face in my direct line of sight. The underboss has a deep voice I can hear without a problem, but I don't take chances where business is involved.

"One of our warehouses caught fire," I say. "I need more product."

"How much?"

"Half a ton, minimum."

"Six weeks," he says as he flips the steaks.

"That doesn't work for me. I need it here in ten days."

Arturo uses his fork to stab a chunk of cheese off an antipasto platter and puts it into his mouth, observing me as he chews. Power games—Italians sure seem to love them.

"I can get you the drugs next weekend," he says with a smirk, "but I have to add a 30 percent rush fee to the regular price."

"That's rather steep. Are all your family members getting that rate, or am I special?"

Arturo throws the fork in the sink and crosses the kitchen with a furious look on his face. "You are not my fucking family."

"I married your sister. It counts as 'family' where I came from." I tilt my head to the side, holding his gaze. "But then again, where I'm from, no one would have been able to make me give up my sister to a virtual stranger. Tell me, Arturo, do you also let your don tell you when you're allowed to take a piss, or can you make that decision for yourself?"

I don't see the knife until it's halfway to my face. I block his hand, diverting the direct hit to my eye, but end up with a long slash down my cheek. Seizing Arturo's wrist in one hand, I grip the hair at the back of his head with the other and slam his face down onto the wooden bartop between us. He roars and forces the knife toward my head again. I let go of his hair, grab his knife-wielding hand, and twist. I don't hear the snapping sound but, based on Arturo's howl, I broke his wrist.

A powerful hit to my chin makes my head snap to the side. I take a step back and shake my head, trying to rid myself of the ringing sound in my ears. I thought that son of a bitch was right-handed.

Arturo rounds the breakfast bar and charges at me. I avoid the left hook aimed at my face and bury my elbow into his chest, but then, I end up gasping for air when he knees me in my gut. Straightening, I grab the front of his shirt and slam him against the nearest wall. The back of his head hits one of the large picture frames, which falls and shatters into pieces.

"This discussion should have happened before the marriage certificate was signed, you know." I spit blood to the side, then throw a punch into his stomach. "But your sister is mine now. And there is nothing you can do about it."

"If I knew what a sick fuck you are, I never would have let Sienna marry you."

"I'm no worse than other men in our world. Look at your don. Mailing body parts around as a warning."

"Yeah. You just nail people to walls and carve crosses into their chests." Arturo leans forward, his stare burning through me. "Sienna cried for weeks after her dog died. Just imagine what will happen when my sister finds out your little secret. So, I don't have to do anything other than tell her that small detail, and she'll run back home."

"She can run. But I will come for her and get her back."

"You won't be getting her back, Drago. Ajello might be ruthless, but he would never force a woman to go back to a man she's afraid of."

I wrap my free hand around Arturo's throat and squeeze. "Then I'll have to make sure you can't tell Sienna anything."

Arturo's left hand shoots up, grabbing my throat in return. "You can try."

The bang of a door against a wall as it flies open and the thunder of running feet reverberates through the house. A pair of arms wrap around my waist, pulling me away. I try hitting the man holding me with my elbow, but another seizes my limbs. Arturo launches himself from the wall, rushing at me, but two other guys grab and hold him back.

The Cosa Nostra don walks in and comes to stand in the middle of the room. "Family squabble?" he asks, looking at me, then he shifts his gaze to his underboss.

"Yeah. We can't agree on where we'll spend next Christmas. At Arturo's or my place," I say.

"Indeed." The don nods to his men. "Escort Mr. Popov out. They can finish their holiday planning some other time. I need to talk with Arturo."

I shake off the men holding me and take a step toward the don. "I know about your little spying scheme. That shit stops now, Ajello, or I swear to God, things won't end well."

Without waiting for his reply, I turn and head toward the front door. When I reach the threshold, I look over my shoulder and meet Ajello's eyes. "And if your underboss dares to meddle in my private life, I'll have to kill him."

"Sienna loves Arturo. Killing him wouldn't be healthy for your marriage," he says. "And Arturo won't be meddling."

I nod and step outside.

Sienna

Ink from a broken pen on one of my favorite shirts. Perfect. I'm hurrying across the foyer to find Keva and ask her for a stain remover when I hear the roar of a bike. I peer out the window overlooking the driveway as a black motorcycle pulls to the side. Once the engine dies, the driver dismounts and removes his helmet. It's Drago. I had no idea my husband rides a bike.

Drago leaves the helmet on the handle and approaches the front door. A gasp leaves my lips as I stare at the left side of his face. It's covered in blood. I rush toward the entrance and reach it just as he walks inside.

"Oh my God." I press my hand over my mouth, staring at the long cut down his left cheek. It's still oozing.

"Keva!" I yell and take a step forward, reaching my hand toward his chin, but he jerks his head away.

"Are you fucking five?" I snap and try again. "Let me see."

He doesn't move this time, and I take his chin between my fingers, turning his face to the side.

"Jesus, Drago." I sniff, staring at his cheek. The cut is four inches long.

"What's going . . . Oh my God!" Keva runs up behind me. "Get him to the kitchen, Sienna. Right now."

Drago takes a step, and my hand falls from his face. I stare at his back as he walks across the foyer, then trot after him.

"Clean him up." Keva thrusts a kitchen towel and a bowl of warm water into my hands. "I'm going to get a first aid kit."

I look down at the bowl in my hands, then at my husband as he takes a seat on a chair at the kitchen table.

"Give me that," he says as he unzips his jacket. The white shirt underneath is covered in blood stains.

I put the bowl on the table and dip the kitchen towel into the water. Drago reaches to take the cloth from my hand, but I pull it away.

"Stay still," I mumble and step to stand between his legs. Gently, I begin to clean the blood off his face.

I start with his neck and then move to his chin. My hand is shaking, and the trembling only becomes worse as I get closer to the cut. The only other time I've seen this much blood was when Arturo cut his palm while filleting a fish a decade ago. I screamed and fainted.

Drago's fingers wrap around my wrist, pulling my hand away from his face. "You don't seem to be handling the sight of blood very well."

I look into his questioning eyes. "I'm fine."

"Your face is so pale, it's turning green. Give me the towel."

I grit my teeth. "No."

His other hand comes to the small of my back, pulling me even closer until my lips are barely an inch from his. "Give me the fucking towel, Sienna."

"No. You're going to hurt yourself."

"Why do you care?"

"I don't," I say, my lips touching his.

Keva bursts into the kitchen, carrying a box full of medical supplies. "How did you get that?" She slams the container on the table.

Drago lets go of my wrist. "Knife. Do you have a tetanus shot in there?"

"Do I look like an ER to you?" Keva snaps and leans in to look at his cheek. "That will need stitches. What happened?"

"I had a chat with my brother-in-law."

"Arturo did that?" I gape at him in surprise. "Why?"

"A business disagreement."

"Idiots," Keva says as she sprays something on his cheek. "Sienna, there's a sewing kit in there somewhere. Find it."

"Shouldn't he go to a hospital?" I turn and start rummaging through the supplies, acutely aware of Drago's hand that is still at the small of my back, keeping me close.

"This one would rather die from blood loss than set foot in a hospital again."

I pass the sewing kit to Keva, who is using gauze to clean Drago's cut, and slant my eyes to the burn scar visible above the collar of his shirt. When I look up again, Keva is holding the sides of the gash together with two fingers while thrusting a curved needle through his skin, sewing it up right in front of my eyes. I place my shaking hand on Drago's other cheek and hold my breath.

Keva is talking, but her words are muted as if someone has covered my ears. With a quick tug, she ties the thread and cuts it. "One more."

There is a strange thumping sound at the back of my head. It's as if my heart somehow moved there and is now beating at twice its normal rate.

Does it hurt? It must hurt even with the numbing spray. My brother did that? "I'm going to fucking kill him," I whisper and brush the back of my hand down Drago's other cheek.

The needle pierces my husband's skin again. I want to look away but can't lift my eyes. Keva pulls on the thread and Drago winces. It's a minuscule movement of his jaw, but I feel the twitch under my palm. Everything before my eyes dissolves.

"Sienna?"

I hear Drago's voice, but it's far, far away.

"Sienna! Look at me, baby." He's yelling now, but his shouts have never been more distant.

All I can see is the white haze before me, but soon enough, it's replaced with blackness.

Drago

Sienna's eyes roll back, and I catch her as her body sags against mine.

"Sienna!" I cradle her gently in my arms, shaking her slightly to rouse. "Please, baby."

Keva smacks my forearm. "Stop shaking the poor girl. She just fainted."

"What! Why?" I look down at my wife's pale face as panic brews in my chest. "I'm calling a doctor."

"Don't be ridiculous. She'll come around in a minute. Sit back down so I can put a dressing over your wound."

"I'm taking her upstairs," I say and head out of the kitchen. Keva hollers after me, something about infection, but I ignore her.

I carry Sienna to our bedroom, but I can't make myself let her go. Instead of placing her on the bed, I sit down on the edge and continue holding her in my arms. Her head is resting against my chest, and some color is returning to her cheeks already. Sienna's eyes flutter open, but her gaze remains unfocused.

"Baby?" I tighten my grip on her. Can she hear the thunderous beating of my heart?

She mutters something I can't decipher.

"You fainted," I say and lower my head, nearing her face. "Don't you dare do that ever again."

Sienna blinks, then says something else and narrows her eyes at me. I wasn't paying attention to her lips, but I think I heard "Arturo," so I assume she asked about her brother.

"He's in a bit of a worse shape than me, but he'll live," I say and drop my eyes to her mouth.

"Who?"

Fuck. I misunderstood. "What did you just say?"

"I said you can't order me not to faint."

Order. Arturo. Too similar sounding. Shit. "Yes, I can. And I was talking about your brother."

Sienna places her palm on my uninjured cheek. "What did you do to my brother, Drago?"

"I broke his wrist. And maybe a few ribs."

"What?" She straightens so she's sitting upright on my lap. "Because of some business crap?"

"He started it."

She raises her eyebrows and touches my bottom lip with her finger and starts to trace the line of my mouth in a feathery caress. "Arturo would never attack anyone unless he's provoked. Did you provoke him?"

"Maybe a little." I draw her finger between my teeth and nip at it.

"Ouch." She pulls her hand away. "What was that for?"

"For scaring me." I fall back on the bed, pulling her with me. "No more fainting."

Sienna smiles wryly as she straddles me. "I'll try my best."

"Good. Blouse. Off. Slowly."

She starts unbuttoning the silky thing. Lime-green with gold stars. It's supposed to be a piece of clothing, but it reminds me of gift wrap paper instead. I place my hands on her waist, then slide them up her ribcage to her green lace bra.

"Where do you find these things, Sienna?"

"In stores." She throws the blouse to the floor and unclasps the bra, releasing her firm, mouthwatering breasts.

I squeeze them in my palms and watch as she sucks in a breath. "Are you wearing matching panties?"

"I'm not sure. Why don't you check?"

I brush my palms down her chest and stomach and grab the elastic waistband of her skirt. It's gauzy like a ballet tutu, but gold, the color matching the stars on her shirt. With as much care as my big hands allow, I pull it up and over her head.

"Green, as well." I smile and pinch the band at the back of her panties. And then, I pull up.

Sienna arches her back, her mouth half-open in a silent moan. With my free hand, I move the lacy strip to tuck it between her folds. Keeping my thumb over the fabric so it won't slip away, I tug on the waistband once more.

Sienna lowers her head and leans forward. Her quick breaths fan across my face as I loosen the hold on her panties, only to pull on them even harder the next moment.

"So, are we back on speaking terms?" She pants and grabs the two sides of my shirt and yanks, tearing off several buttons. "Or are we still only fucking?"

Letting go of her panties, I wrap my arm around her middle and roll us over so I'm on top. "I haven't decided, yet."

I take off my ruined shirt and the rest of my clothes, and Sienna's gaze locks onto mine while she slips her hand between her legs. There isn't a sexier sight than my wife, in nothing more than her green panties and gold heels, playing with her pussy.

I bend to grab her panties, which are blocking my view, and pull them down her legs.

"Wider," I demand and move to the recliner by the bed, absorbed in her delicate fingers as they tease and massage her clit. "Faster, Sienna."

"You're just going to watch?"

"Yes."

She bites her lip and hastens her movements. Her breaths quicken while her eyes seek my own again. She adds her other hand—circling, pinching. My already straining cock hardens to granite, but I don't make a move to touch it as I watch her.

Have I ever been so enthralled with anything, *anyone*, in my life? I should know the answer to that, but every bit of rational thought has fled as I focus on my sparkling wife. I should be worried about that, but again . . . mental capacity is nonexistent. It seems that this strange little creature has royally fried every brain cell I had. Every smile, every idiotic pair of shoes and glittery dress, and every fucking time she said my name, have sealed my fate.

Sienna arches her back, her body shaking as she comes. I leave the recliner and climb over her, positioning myself between her legs. She's still trembling as I move her hands and thrust my cock into her heat. A sound escapes her lips. It rolls over me on a wisp of her breath. A moan. I can hear it, but it's not enough. I want to hear her scream my name. I want to soak up every resonance my wife makes as I fuck her.

Sliding my palm up, I wrap my fingers around her delicate neck and squeeze it lightly. Not hard enough to harm her, just a slight pressure so I can feel the vibration of her vocal cords.

"Say my name," I order as I retreat and slam into her again.

"Drago," she whispers. Most of the sound is lost to me. There are no vibrations for me to feel.

"No whispering." I rake my other hand in her hair, tilting her head up as I pound into her. She's wet, but so tight, that each thrust threatens to push me over the edge. "Again."

The tendons of her neck tighten under my palm as she throws back her head and moans while her pussy spasms around my length.

"Drago."

Not a whisper this time, and I hear it crystal clear. I crush my mouth to hers, claiming that sound. Claiming her, with my mouth and my seed as it erupts inside her. She's mine, and anyone who dares to take her from me, her brother included, will meet a quick and painful death.

CHAPTER
seventeen

I AWAKE TO BLISSFUL WARMTH AND, FOR A MOMENT, wonder if extra blankets are covering me. Then, I realize the warmth is seeping from the big body cocooning mine. My eyelids lift, feeling light despite the lack of uninterrupted rest.

He let me stay.

I don't dare move and risk waking Drago. Maybe he fell asleep and forgot to take me back to my room? I'm not missing this chance and will enjoy being in his arms for as long as possible.

The hold around my waist tightens as Drago pulls me closer to his body.

"You know, I've been wondering something from the start," Drago's voice drifts from above my head. "Why don't you dye your hair crazy colors, as well?"

I smile and turn around to face him. It's not easy, considering that he's basically keeping me glued to his front. Somehow, I end up with my face plastered to his chest. Untangling one of my legs from his, I throw it over his waist and climb on top of him. I cross my arms over his chest and rest my chin on my hands.

"Brown works best with my wardrobe," I say, looking into his eyes. "I can't have pink hair and wear orange. What would people say?"

"If they are wise, they'd keep their mouths shut."

"Oh? And if they're not wise?"

He takes one strand of my hair and twists it around his finger. "Then, I would . . . send my pet assassin to shut them up. Indefinitely."

"Why would you bother? It's only a little old me. I doubt what people say is worth so much trouble."

"There are always consequences for what people say. Many have been crucified or died because of loose tongues."

"The guilty, or the innocent?"

"Death doesn't discriminate. I do."

I lightly brush his cheek near the cut with the tips of my fingers. "Will I end up nailed to a wall, too?"

Drago releases his hold on my hair and trails his knuckle along my jaw. "You will definitely end up pinned to the wall. Many times, *mila moya*."

"But no nails?" I smirk.

He leans forward and places a kiss on my lips. "No."

"I'm sorry, Drago," I whisper into his mouth, then remember he can't hear it. Leaning away, I make sure he can see my lips and say it again. "I'm sorry for lying to you. I didn't share anything important with the don, I swear."

"Why not?"

I shrug. "It just didn't feel right."

"Because?"

"Because I like it here. I like Keva, the girls, your men . . ."

Drago's jaw clenches. He grabs the back of my neck and squeezes.

"You are not allowed to like my men, Sienna," he bites out. "Nor any other man. Just me."

"Is that an order?"

"Yes."

"You're not exactly likable, Drago," I say and press my lips together, trying to subdue the urge to laugh. The dark look on his face is hilarious. "I mean, I could try to like you if you'd stop glowering all the time. Or stop waking me up at six thirty to run with you."

He narrows his eyes at me but says nothing, so I continue, "Maybe you could try spoiling me with presents. But not guns! Think shoes, or maybe a nice neon-colored jacket. Or more of those pretty crystal pebbles. Green would work great as sea glass rocks in my fish tank."

His hold on my neck loosens, and his hand slowly glides down my back and over my ass, all the way to my pussy. I suck in a breath when his finger teases my entrance.

"Flowers would help, too. As well as—" I gasp when his finger slips inside.

"Please continue, I'm taking notes."

"Notes?" I moan and press my face to his chest. My breaths leave me in short bursts.

"Yes. On courting my wife," he says as he slides in another finger. "But maybe I should try something else now since there aren't any shoes or jackets close by."

Suddenly, his finger withdraws. Drago grabs my waist and pulls me up until I'm crouching just above his head, my pussy weeping over his wicked mouth. One long, leisurely lick, and I'm grabbing onto the headboard and pressing my forehead on my hands. His tongue strokes me—slowly, methodically. Each move is deliberate but bears more pressure, making the throbbing in my core increasingly intense. I'm barely keeping it together when he squeezes my ass cheeks and sucks my clit.

I scream. Tremors rack my body, making my limbs shake as he sucks harder and harder. My eyes roll into the back of my head, and, with another loud cry, I come all over his face.

Yes, this is definitely better than flowers.

"Where is the gun I gave you?"

I slowly lift my tired lids and watch Drago as he buttons his shirt and reaches for the holster on the recliner. He looks mouthwatering in an all-black outfit.

"In the nightstand drawer," I say when his gaze switches to me. "In my room."

"There is no 'your room,' Sienna."

"Oh? Well, I might be sleeping here, but all my stuff is there. You exiled me, in case you forgot."

Drago grinds his teeth and scoops me into his arms. "I exiled your three tons of clothes," he says in a gruff voice.

"Yeah, right." I laugh and bury my hand in his hair. "Say you're sorry, and we're even."

His hold on me tightens, but he stays silent, glaring at me.

"Okay, I'll help you. Repeat after me. Sienna, I'm sorry for throwing you out. And your pretty clothes."

"I'm not sorry for banishing your clothes," he mumbles.

"And me?"

Squinty eyes sear through me, and he crushes his mouth to mine. "I'm sorry," he mumbles into my lips.

"There. It wasn't that hard."

"And your clothes are back here."

"What?" I wriggle until he lowers me to the floor and rush toward the closet. When I open it, I see all of my things returned to neat order on shelves and hangers. Drago's stuff is all tucked away, relegated to a measly two cubbies and a handful of spots on the rod.

"I had Jelena and a couple of other girls bring them here while you were still sleeping. It took me an hour to put it all inside," he says and wraps his arm around my waist. "I envy your kind."

I tilt my head so he can see me speak and raise an eyebrow. "My kind?"

"The kind that could sleep through an earthquake and nuclear disaster combined. An alien invasion, too, probably."

"Hopefully, there won't be one of those. If the house is attacked when I'm asleep"—I laugh—"I'll end up dead before I realize what is happening."

Drago turns me around to face him, his green eyes staring me down. "If there's an attack on the house, you can keep on sleeping, *mila moya*," he bites out, "because I'll make sure the bastards are dead well before they even think about getting close to you."

I bite my lower lip while keeping his gaze. He really means it. "Okay."

"But I still want you to carry the gun when you leave the house. We have some shit going down tomorrow night, and I need to know that you're safe."

"If it makes you feel better, I will, but it won't do any good."

"Why not? From what I saw, you're an excellent shot."

I smile. "When aiming at jugs and range targets, sure. But I could never shoot a person, Drago."

"You would if your life depends on it."

I take his chin between my fingers and tilt his head to the side. His cheek is still swollen and bruised, but it looks a little less raw today.

"I've never even killed a spider. I just let them be." Rising onto my toes, I place a kiss on his chin. "You won't ever see me point a gun and fire at a man."

Drago's hold on my waist tightens, and my feet lift off the ground. He slowly raises me until our faces align.

"If it comes down to you or him, Sienna, you're going to shoot him," he says through gritted teeth. "In the head or in his heart. And as many times as needed. Nod."

"Drago—"

"Nod, Sienna!"

I sigh and nod, even though I know I would never be able to kill a human being. Even if that means my death.

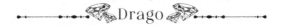

Drago

I cock my head and stare at the thing on a shelf before me. It looks like an ugly child born to high-heeled boots and sandals. I can't believe that sort of thing exists, not to mention, it's violet and made of leather-like material. My phone vibrates with an arriving text while I'm trying to decide where someone would wear footwear like that.

> **11:08 Iliya:** We have Bogdan's logistic guy. I'm bringing him to Naos.

I type a quick reply, ordering Iliya to take the Romanian to the basement, and reach for the violet oddity.

"These, as well," I say to the store attendant who's standing a few paces behind me, holding another two pairs of extremely ugly shoes.

Leaving the store, I send a quick message to Keva to find out what my wife is doing. I don't like the idea of leaving her in the house if I'm not there, but it's not like I can bring her to a torture session with me. I'll just have to make it a quick one.

The reply from Keva arrives and I stop midstep when I look at the screen. It's a photo of my wife crouching on the grass in front of Zeus. She's tying a big red bow around his neck. The other two dogs are sitting on either side of Zeus, wearing the same getup.

> **11:16 Drago:** Tell her to take that crap off my dogs. Right now.

11:18 Keva: Why? They're cute.

11:18 Drago: Those dogs are trained for fucking combat. They're not poodles.

11:20 Keva: They don't seem to mind. But if you do, feel free to tell her yourself.

11:21 Drago: I'm telling you to do it.

11:23 Keva: Because you can't say "no" to your wife?

I curse and put the phone back into my pocket.

Mircea, the Romanians' logistics guy, is sitting on the floor behind the wine crates in the basement. Iliya is standing guard close by, his gun pointed at the man's head.

"Untie his hands and bring him over here." I nod toward the table in the corner. I've got a map spread out on top of it.

The Romanian thrashes about as Iliya drags him across the room. When they reach the table, Iliya pushes him onto a chair and cuts the zip tie binding his wrists.

"Right or left-handed?" I ask.

The guy blinks at me stupidly, then looks around, probably searching for a potential escape route.

"Well, it seems I'll have to guess." I take the knife Iliya holds out.

Grabbing the man's left wrist, I slam his palm onto the table and plunge the blade through the back of his hand, anchoring him to the wooden surface. He screams, staring at the blood pooling around the knife. Ignoring his wailing, I set the permanent marker before him on the table.

"I need you to indicate the exact truck route, final destination, and locations of any planned stops before the shipment gets there. I want the times, too."

When he doesn't reply, I yank him back by pulling his hair and get in his face. "You gonna start losing a finger for every second you remain silent. I'm a busy man, Mircea. All I can spare is five for you. I don't think you want to find out what happens when time runs out, but I can guarantee you'll be holding that pen in your fucking mouth, and I will still get what I need from you."

The Romanian nods and grabs the marker with shaking fingers and draws two wobbly X's on the map.

"What's this?" I ask, pointing at the first mark.

"Plates exchange before they hit the weigh station."

I take out my phone and check the location on the map. It's a big truck stop with a gas station and a restaurant. Too busy for an attack.

"What's this place?" I point at the destination location. It's not one of the two places provided by the guy we caught at our warehouse.

"An abandoned paper factory," he chokes out.

"Security?"

"Four people. Armed. Two more at the gate."

"Your men or contacted personnel?"

"Mercenaries."

I nod and look up at Iliya. "Call Filip and tell him there's been a change of plans. We'll wait until the truck reaches the destination and hit them there."

"How many people do you need?"

"I'm going to head over and have a look at the building. I'll let you know once I have a better idea. Have someone get the body we stashed in the fridge and bring it over there tomorrow."

When Iliya takes out his phone to make the call, I turn back to Mircea, who's staring at his bloody hand with wide eyes.

"Where's your boss hiding?" I ask.

"I don't know. I swear I don't know." He whimpers.

"Too bad." I take out my gun. "Head or heart?"

The man's eyes flare, nearly bugging out of their sockets, and, for a few seconds, he simply gapes at me. Then, he jumps off his chair and starts pulling the lodged knife out of his hand.

"Head it is." I cock the gun, butt it against his temple, and pull the trigger. Mircea jerks and then his body slumps forward.

"That's for our driver."

CHAPTER eighteen

SOMETHING WEIRD IS GOING ON.

My eyes wander over the people sitting around the dining table. Everyone is silent, focused solely on their lunch. There's no chatter, no laughter. That never happens. Meal times are always a cacophony of activity, making it impossible to hear your own thoughts over all the noise. Right now, I bet I could hear a pin drop. Aside from the occasional clutter of utensils, the only sounds breaching the stifling stillness in the room are the voices of the security guards coming through the two-way radio Mirko has set out on the table in front of him. He's been carrying that thing with him since this morning.

"Gate—all clear."

"South wall—all clear."

"Checkpoint A—all clear."

"Naos—all clear."

Keva comes up to Mirko and places a plate of food in front of him. He starts eating without uttering a single complaint. Definitely not normal. Mirko always whines about the low-cholesterol diet Keva has him on, but now doesn't say a word about being served grilled chicken instead of pork chops like the rest of us.

I look at the empty chair to my left. Drago was away most of the day yesterday and returned home well after midnight. I waited for hours, unable to sleep. The images of that stubborn boar—hurt or worse—flooded my mind. My hands were shaking. It started as a tiny tremor in my fingers, but as time passed, it got worse. When the bedroom door finally opened, and he stepped inside, I wanted to run and jump into his arms, hug him as hard as I could to reassure myself that he was safe. I didn't, because it would mean that I care. It would mean yielding to those dangerous feelings that have been brewing inside me for quite some time. So, I stayed in bed, pretended I was asleep. Those feelings that threatened to burst from my chest? I pushed them down. Pushed them deep, deep down, burying them so they wouldn't be able to come out.

A woman's angry yelling explodes in the foyer, pulling me out of my thoughts. All heads snap in that direction, but no one makes a move. I look at Jelena, who's holding a fork in the air, halfway to her mouth.

"Drago went to get Tara," she mumbles. "I guess she's not happy."

The shouting continues. I get up and dash across the dining room. When I reach the foyer, I find Drago heading toward the stairs, holding a screaming black-haired woman over his shoulder in a fireman's carry. She's hitting his back with her fists, but he doesn't seem to notice. He lowers her down at the foot of the stairs and barks something I don't catch.

"I don't give a fuck," she snaps in Serbian and pins me with her gaze. "I'm not spending a minute in the same house with her."

Drago looks over his shoulder at me.

"Italian bitch," Tara spits out at me in English.

I tense. Even knowing she has every right to hate me,

it hurts. I make myself smile while maintaining eye contact. "Hello."

Drago narrows his eyes at me, focusing on my lips. The lower one is trembling slightly, so I pull it between my teeth.

"What did you say to my wife, Tara?" he asks in a calm tone, but I can see the pulsing vein in his neck.

I take a step forward and place my hand on his forearm, make my smile grow wider. "She didn't say anything."

"We've already established that your pretense doesn't work on me, Sienna." He wraps his arm around my waist and pulls me into his body. "She said something that hurt you. No one is allowed to do that. Not even my sister."

Tara huffs, annoyance written all over her face. She leans against the banister and crosses her arms while her glacial glare drifts back to her brother.

"It was nothing, Drago." I squeeze his arm slightly. "I swear."

He searches my eyes and clenches his jaw. "Get to your room. I don't want to see you until you apologize to my wife. Now, Tara."

Tara turns around and runs up the stairs.

"You're overreacting," I mumble.

"Tara needs to learn to show respect. She doesn't have to like you, but she will remember that you're my wife. Especially while she's under our roof."

My breath catches. He said *our*. Not *my*. I reach out and brush my fingers along his jaw. "What's going on, Drago? The extra security. Bringing your sister here. I saw guys carrying crates of ammunition to the storeroom."

"We're going to intercept the Romanians' weapons shipment tonight and blow up two of their storage locations."

"What?" I pinch his chin and pull his head lower. "Have you lost your fucking mind?"

"It can't be avoided, Sienna. But don't worry, you'll be safe."

I stare at him. This house is a fucking fortress. Of course I'm going to be safe. But what about him? He's going to be out there, playing the damn war games with the second-largest criminal organization in New York! He's going to get hurt.

"Sienna?" He tugs on my waist, tightening his embrace, but I'm spiraling into a bottomless void and can't pull myself back to reality.

I'm suddenly cold. My hands are clammy, and numbness is settling over me because I know what's coming.

Someone will enter my room in the middle of the night. They're going to say that something bad has happened and that I need to be strong. Just like Arturo did when our parents were killed. Just like when Nino came to tell me they found Asya's things in the snow while my brother was scouring the city for her. I can't do that again. I can't.

"Sienna." Drago is now holding my shoulders. "Baby, are you okay?"

I press my palms to his chest and shove him. Instantly, his hands release me, and I spin and run up the stairs. I can hear him calling after me, but I just keep running until I reach the fourth floor and stop on the landing. My breaths are shallow and rapid, and my hands are shaking. I can't go into our bedroom. There's too much of his presence there, even when he's not physically in the room. I turn in the opposite direction and flee toward the third door on the right. It's one of the rooms that's unoccupied. However, when I get inside and lean against the back side of the door, I find Drago's sister lounging on the bed.

"What the hell are you doing in my room?" she snaps. "Get the fuck out."

"Sienna!" Drago's voice reaches me from somewhere in the hallway.

I push away from the door, sprint toward the bed, and quickly crawl under it. The sound of heavy footsteps thunders across the floor. Doors are opened and then shut again. The hurried footfalls getting closer. A few moments later, Tara's door swings wide. I tilt my head to the side and spy Drago's feet through the gap under the bedcover fringe.

"Is Sienna here?" My husband's voice fills the room.

I close my eyes. Shit. I thought he wouldn't look for me here. Tara is going to tattle on me any sec—

"What would your wife be doing in my room?"

My eyes fly open. There's a stream of Serbian curses and the door slams shut.

Minutes stretch in silence before Tara speaks. "How long are you planning on staying under my bed?"

"I'm not sure."

The bedframe creaks above me. A hand grabs the hem of the bedcover, pulling it up, and Tara's face materializes in front of mine.

"I asked Keva about you," she says, looking at me upside down. "She called you a volcano of happiness. Always cheerful and smiling. You don't seem very cheerful to me."

"Fuck you, Tara."

She wrinkles her nose, a bit of a sneer taking over her face. "She also said you're super nice. I guess she got that part wrong, too."

"I'm not going to be nice to someone who called me a bitch."

"Fair enough." She shrugs, her hair swaying with the movement.

"So, what did my brother do? Did he threaten to lock you in your room, as well?"

"Nope," I say, staring at the wood frame just over my head. "He's just working on getting himself killed."

"And why do you care? You only married him because your don ordered you to."

"I don't care."

"Oh yeah? Why are you crying, then?"

"It's the dust," I mumble and try to wriggle my arm up to wipe my eyes, but there isn't enough space.

"Sure."

The sound of steps and Drago calling my name still echo through the hall, but they're fading. He's probably moved on to the floor below.

"I think he's gone. You can come out now."

"I'm quite fine here, thank you," I say.

Tara widens her eyes at me and snorts. "Move over."

I watch in confusion as she gets down to the floor and slides under the bed next to me.

"I'm sorry for calling you a bitch," Tara mutters.

"I'm sorry Cosa Nostra killed your boyfriend."

We fall silent for a moment. Just before it starts feeling awkward, Tara takes a deep breath. "He was cheating on me. We broke up a week before he died, but I didn't tell Drago."

I tilt my head to the side to look at her. "Why not?"

"Because I didn't want him to know I also failed at that."

"Failed? The guy cheated on you."

"I cheated on him, too." She shrugs. "It's like I can't do anything right. Drago saved the wrong sister."

"What do you mean?"

Tara closes her eyes. "When the bomb went off in our home, Drago was downstairs. My twin sister and I were sleeping in our bedroom, which was on the second floor."

I suck in a breath. Her *twin*?

"Drago got hurt during the blast, but still managed to get to us, even with the fire raging all around," Tara continues, her voice shaking. "He couldn't carry us both at the same time, though. I remember I was screaming, which is probably why he took me out first. Then, he went back inside for Dina."

"What happened?" I ask, trying to suppress the tears, and failing.

"We had a large propane tank just outside, used for our gas stove. Once the fire from the initial blast spread, it exploded. Drago survived. Barely. Dina didn't. She inhaled too much of the smoke. They couldn't save her." She pauses and sniffs. "Drago still blames himself. He almost got burned alive trying to shield Dina with his body until the firemen got to them, but he still believes it's his fault."

Dear God. I can't even imagine what it was like for either of them.

"He used to grumble about being stuck with two baby sisters, but the truth is, he was the best big brother anyone could ask for," she continues as her voice shakes. "Used to call us sugar and spice because Dina was so sweet, and I'm . . . not so much."

I wiggle my hand a bit to the side and wrap my fingers around Tara's, squeezing. "I'm so sorry."

She looks down at our joined hands. "I don't give a damn that you're from Cosa Nostra, you know. I was just afraid that you're going to somehow steal my brother from me."

"Tara, I would—"

"I know," she interrupts me and smiles. "Did you really put silk ribbons on Drago's dogs?"

"Yes." I grin.

Tara blinks at me and laughs. "I think I might move back into the mansion after all."

"I'd like that."

"Now, spill." She squeezes my hand. "Why are you hiding from Drago under my bed?"

"No reason." I look back up at the wooden bed boards above me.

Drago's yelling and the thumping of multiple feet still can

be heard from somewhere inside the house. I know my behavior is idiotic, but I can't make myself go out there and face him. I'm afraid I'll break down and beg him not to go.

"Sienna?"

"What?" I choke out.

"You're crying again. Are you allergic to dust?"

I close my eyes and mumble. "Yes."

Drago

I slam the final door on the second floor and look down the hallway. Where the fuck is that woman? I've checked every damn room in the house, and it's like she's disappeared from the face of the earth. I take out my phone and call Relja.

"Bring me Zeus," I growl into the phone as soon as I see the call has connected and then I head upstairs.

Just as I reach the landing on the fourth floor, the door to Tara's room opens, and my wife slips out. A strange expression crosses her face when she sees me, but it is quickly replaced with a smile.

"Oh, Drago, were you looking for me?" she chirps as she approaches. "I thought I heard you calling my name."

My eyes capture hers and I take a step forward.

Sienna takes a step back, still smiling. "Drago?"

I advance another step, and one more until I have her trapped against the wall. Her mask is in place, but her eyes are red. I don't think I know anyone who goes to such lengths to hide their real feelings. Bracing my palms on either side of her head, I lean toward her until our noses touch. "Stop."

She raises an eyebrow. "Stop what?"

"Pretending. It may work with other people, *mila*, but not with me." I grab her chin. "I see you, Sienna."

The fake smile disappears. She blinks, and one tear rolls down her cheek. A low growl emanates somewhere behind me.

I look over my shoulder and find my dog a few feet behind me, his teeth bared and eyes fixed on my hand. "Really, Zeus?"

He growls again.

Sienna uses the situation to her advantage, ducks under my arm, and rushes down the hallway. Stopping in front of our bedroom, she throws a quick look at me and winks. "Have fun tonight!"

The door shuts in her wake. Zeus trots toward it and sits down, barring entrance. On guard.

"Traitor." I shake my head and turn to Relja, whose eyes are bouncing between me and the dog. "Make sure no one tries to get inside my bedroom, or they'll end up with missing limbs."

He nods.

"Is everything ready?" I ask as I'm putting on my holster.

"Yes," Filip says. "Adam has teams in position near both of Bogdan's warehouses. They'll be waiting for our signal."

"The guy from the fridge?"

"In Iliya's trunk."

"Good. Let's go."

We leave the house and head toward the SUV parked on the driveway. Iliya and two other men are waiting by the second vehicle. I open the driver's door, but before I get inside, I look up at the window to my bedroom. It's easy to spot since it's the only one lit up on the fourth floor at the moment. Sienna is standing behind the curtain, looking down at me. She hasn't left the bedroom since this afternoon. I tried getting inside twenty minutes ago, but *my* dog almost bit my hand off when I reached for the knob.

"What am I going to do with you, *mila moya*?" I mumble to myself and get behind the wheel.

The paper factory is two hours away, so we don't reach it until well after midnight. I park by the fence next to a small service building, and Iliya pulls up behind me. The gate leading into the factory yard is three hundred feet away, around a corner. I exit the SUV and take a look at my phone. There are five pulsing red dots on the screen, marking the location of each of our vehicles. Two of them are moving—Jovan's and Relja's cars following Bogdan's truck. They are about twelve minutes away.

"We'll seize the opportunity when the gate opens to let the truck through," I say to the men gathered around me. "Filip and I will handle the guards at the gatehouse. Iliya, you and Milo take care of the driver and turn the truck around. Then, head to the north warehouse, but avoid the major roads. I don't want it showing up on any of the traffic cams. Vanja, follow them in my SUV. Tomorrow, I'll see if the Russians are interested in taking the cargo off our hands."

"What about the security guys inside the factory?" Filip asks.

"Both Jovan and Relja have a three-man team with them, they can handle the mercenaries. As soon as Iliya turns the truck around, the guys will drive inside and directly up to the factory entrance. From there onward, it's all about brute force and firepower. Adam is on a lookout down the road, but he can provide backup if needed." I take out my gun and cock it. "We can't hide our approach. There are cameras at the gatehouse, so they'll see us coming. Don't get shot."

The first part of the plan goes without a problem. As soon

as the gate slides to the side, Filip and I use the truck as cover and approach the door on the back side of the gatehouse. We each take out a security guard. By the time we return to the truck, one of my men is already dragging the body of the truck driver away. Iliya jumps up in the cabin and reverses the rig. The moment the gate is unobstructed, two cars shoot past us toward the factory building. A big metal loading door at the front of the structure starts sliding to the side. Bullets rain on Jovan's and Relja's vehicles before the factory door is halfway open, making it blatantly evident that there are more men than we anticipated inside.

"Fuck!" I take off toward the firefight, keeping to the road's edge and away from the line of gunfire, with Filip on my heels.

Bogdan's security seems to be focused on Jovan's team. The guys are returning fire from behind the cars they are using for cover on the other side of the yard. When I'm close enough and have a good angle to see a few of the thugs, I stop and shoot. Filip crouches next to me and fires at the son of a bitch who's been keeping our guys pinned down from the second-story factory window. Above the pop and crack of flying bullets, the roar of an engine coming up behind us is getting closer. A few moments later, Adam zooms past us on his bike, heading toward the factory door. We stop shooting while he makes a sharp turn and throws a smoke bomb through the entrance. White fog fills the doorway and barrels its way inside the facility.

It's hard to see the targets with all the smoke around, so I wait until it starts to clear and shoot as soon as the shape of a person becomes visible. Jovan and the rest of the guys have advanced and resumed firing, too. It takes a few minutes for the smoke to dissipate completely, and when it does, seven bodies are sprawled on the ground in a river of blood.

"Someone go get Iliya's car," I bark and turn to Adam who's checking one of the dead guys. "Warehouses?"

"Already burning. I gave the order the moment we were done with the truck."

"Perfect. Let's leave the message for Bogdan."

Ten minutes later, we get into the cars and head home, leaving the naked body of the fridge guy tied to the big iron gate. A sign of a cross carved into the flesh of his chest.

Sienna

Thirty minutes earlier

"He bought me shoes, you know." I pull the sweater around me tighter. "I found the bags this afternoon. Three pairs. He hid them in the back of the closet, under a pile of his jeans."

Zeus cocks his head to the side and regards me.

"Of course they're for me. Two pairs have rhinestone-covered heels and the third is violet with silver silky ties. I was just kidding when I told him he needed to buy me presents, and he knows it very well. He bought them anyway."

I look down at the driveway visible from the window. Two of Drago's men are standing by the garage, smoking. They both have automatic rifles on their backs, and Perun and Jupiter are with them. Further back, in the greenery around the house, there is another group of three, and more are making rounds along the wall that encircles the property. From what I saw when I took Zeus for a walk, there are at least twenty men on guard duty inside the perimeter. There are likely more on the outside.

"He should have taken more men with him," I continue my one-sided dialogue with the dog. "When I asked Keva why he left so many men here instead of bringing them along, she said Drago didn't want to risk leaving the house unguarded. There are twelve-foot concrete walls around the compound, for crying out loud!"

Shaking my head, I turn away from the window. "Was he always so thick-headed?"

Zeus straightens his ears.

"Yeah, I bet he was."

My eyes fall to the phone in my hand. I've had a death grip on it since the moment Drago left with his men. It's been hours. The edges of the damn thing are imprinted into my palm from squeezing it so hard, waiting for Drago to message me back. But he won't. And I'm left agonizing and worrying if he's okay.

Why would he when only yesterday I told him that I don't even like him? So, I messaged him instead. Eight times. There were no replies. Then, I considered calling him. It would be pointless, though, since he wouldn't be able to clearly hear me, but the sound of his voice would reassure me that he is alive. In the end, I decided against calling because I didn't want to distract him from . . . from whatever they are doing.

"I can't take this anymore," I whisper and run out of the room.

The house is eerily quiet. The thud of my feet and the clicking of Zeus's nails are the only sounds that echo through the hallways while I dash down three flights of stairs. When I reach the ground floor, I turn left and head to the east wing, stopping at the last door. It's the room where Mirko spends most of his time. My hand is shaking as I grab the knob and walk inside.

Mirko is sitting at a desk covered in various electronic equipment, with keyboards, wires, and power cables running every which way. Six big monitors showing the camera feeds from around the grounds are mounted on the wall in front of him. His two-way radio has been jammed onto what little room remains on the desktop. The chatter of people over the airwaves is coming through loud and clear.

"Sienna?" Keva's voice comes from my right.

I turn and find her sitting on a sofa that's been pushed next to a wall. She's holding a big mug in her hands, steam rising above the rim. Tara is snuggled up beside Keva, legs tucked under her.

"Are you guys having a late-night party?" I make myself smile.

Keva cocks her head to the side, giving me a pointed look. Her eyes fall to my hips, and I release the hem of my sweater which I've been fidgeting with, and hide both my hands behind my back so she won't notice the shaking.

"He's going to be okay, Sienna," she says in a calm voice.

"Oh, I know." I shrug and place my hand on Zeus's neck.

"You can join us if you want."

The sound of gunshots explodes from one of the radios. I freeze.

"And listen to people killing each other?" I laugh. "No, thanks. I'm going to go crash now. Lack of sleep isn't good for the health of the skin. See you tomorrow."

I turn on my heel and leave the room, slamming the door closed after me. Despite the barrier, the rat-a-tat of the fire-fight is loud and clear, and each bang reverberates inside my chest. I run down the hallway and across the foyer toward the front door while Zeus trails after me. When I burst outside, the guard on duty at the front of the house looks at me in surprise.

"I'm taking Zeus out to pee," I say and take off toward the grounds on the left.

I run around the mansion's east wing until I reach the last window on this side of the house, then squeeze myself behind the shrubs that grow underneath. Light pours through the open sash, and sounds. Shouting. Gunfire. I can hear it all streaming from the radio in Mirko's office. Leaning my back against the cold exterior wall, I close my eyes.

My mind is spinning, an avalanche of thoughts about

Drago covered in blood barrels through. Overwhelmed, I slouch forward and rock myself back and forth as my insides tie up in knots. I don't realize I've chewed off my nails until there's nothing left of them. I nearly massacred them earlier, when I was waiting for Drago to reply to my texts, and now I've finished the job. It's not pretty, but it helps to stifle the urge to scream.

Suddenly, Mirko starts yelling. I'm too distraught to understand everything he's saying, but I catch Adam's name and something about the number of security guards being greater than expected. The sound of gunfire raging pours from the radio, not just several single gunshots like before, but a full-blown skirmish. The terror that has been brewing in the pit of my stomach grows, spreading through my entire body. I can't breathe. It feels like I'm being attacked by a wild animal. It's pawing at my chest, each resounding shot is a slash to my flesh by vicious claws.

I bury my face between my knees and press my palms over my ears as hard as I can. I should have done something. Anything. Maybe, if I told Drago that I'm terrified something bad will happen to him, he would have stayed here, but I was unable to make the words leave my mouth. I was too scared to confess how fucking worried I am about him.

Something wet brushes the back of my palm. I lift my head, finding Zeus standing in front of me.

"He's not going to die, is he?" I choke out.

The dog leans forward, his big dark eyes regarding me with a question of his own. It's as if he's asking me, "Why do you care?"

"I don't care," I mumble and pick at the brilliant red leaves of the burning bush next to me, striping the branch bare of its beautiful colors. And then another. And another. The vibrant reds that have always brought me joy when I've played

221

outside with the dogs are now mocking me. Reminding me of my nightmarish thoughts.

Drago.

Blood.

Death.

I can't stop. I keep ripping off the leaves with all the vigor I wish I could put into silencing the gunfire still ringing from Mirko's open window. My fingers are cramping, and my palms are raw from pulling at the branches of the bush, but I don't stop until there isn't even a single red leaf left within arms' reach. The low-hanging branches of the shrub are stripped, many broken. But the ruin I've caused is a futile result of my impotent rage.

I wish I could rip out the feelings I have for my husband as easily as the leaves. Just tear them out and throw them away.

People say that loving someone is the most amazing feeling ever. It's not. It is absolutely the worst. The more you love them, the more it'll hurt when they're gone.

The deafening sounds of the gunfight suddenly cease. I look up to see Keva closing the window above my head, cutting off the radio broadcast. It's somehow easier like this, no longer hearing what is happening.

Zeus takes a tentative step toward me and nudges my shoulder with his nose. He's been observing me as I lost my shit this entire time and hasn't interfered. I wrap my arm around his neck and stare at the destruction laid bare at my feet.

The rumble of approaching vehicles brings me out of my thoughts. Several cars, and the distinct roar of a bike, fill the stillness of the night. The men are back. I should run and see if Drago is okay, but I can't make myself move. My foolish idea is that if I stay hidden, bad news can't find me. Have I reverted into a naive child covering my face with my hands, believing that the bogeyman won't come?

"Three hours ago?" Drago's voice reaches me. "If she's not found within the next five minutes, I'm going to gut some-one! Sienna!"

I take a deep breath. He's okay. Angry as hell, judging by all the yelling, but okay.

Crawling from under the branches of the burning bush, I leave my hiding place and rush across the lawn toward the front of the house. My hands and pants are stained with soil and vegetation, and I'm pretty sure I have some twigs and leaves in my hair, as well.

Drago is in the middle of the driveway, holding the guard I passed earlier by the front of his shirt and shouting into the man's face. He notices me as I come closer, and shoves the man away. The ambient light falls on his face, revealing every sharp line. His jaw is clenched, his nostrils flaring, as he glares at me through narrowed eyes. He looks ready to strangle me. I stay rooted to the spot as he approaches. His long but slow strides eat up the ground until his chest almost bumps my face.

"What the fuck are you doing outside in the middle of the night?" His voice is low and strangely steady. A calm be-fore the storm.

I raise my hands and press them to his chest, then slowly glide my palms down across his rock-hard abs. When I'm done with the front of his torso, I trail my fingers up his arms to his shoulders and down again on the other side, checking every part of him. No injuries. His back is next. I press my forehead over his breastbone and slide my hands under his jacket. Nothing at the small of his back. I glide my palms upward and over his shoulder blades, making sure I don't miss a spot. This is as high as I can reach. I think his shirt would be wet if he was shot higher, but I need to be absolutely sure.

I step back, take the front panels of his jacket, and start pulling it off.

"Sienna." His voice is hushed. Soft.

"Shhhh." I throw the jacket on the ground and shuffle around him to scan his other side.

There are no blood stains on his shirt, but I rise onto my toes and pass my palms over the tops of his shoulders, and his upper back just in case. When I'm done, I wrap my arms around his waist and press my cheek on the expanse of his back.

"Satisfied?" he asks, turning around to face me.

I nod and tighten my hold on him.

"You have leaf crap in your hair, Sienna. Care to explain?"

I shake my head. He can think whatever he wants. Maybe he'll decide that I'm nuts.

Rising on my tiptoes, I pull him down for a kiss, then jump into his arms. Drago's lips feast on mine, sucking and biting as he carries me inside the house and up three flights of stairs. Only when we reach our bedroom does he release me from his hold, and only for a moment while we tear off each other's clothes. And then, I'm in his arms again. Trailing a line of kisses along his chin before peppering them all over his face. He's alive. He's okay.

Chapter
nineteen

 Drago

I TRAIL MY HAND ALONG THE SOFT SKIN OF SIENNA'S BACK and thread my fingers into her hair. She stirs a little, pressing her face into the crook of my neck. We had sex three times last night, but having her naked body plastered to mine keeps my cock perpetually semi-hard. Any slight brush of her delectable curves across my groin, and I'm instantly ready to go. For a moment, I consider waking her for another round, but then change my mind and keep massaging her scalp. She needs to rest. Instead, I use my free hand to grab my phone off the nightstand.

Last night, my wife sent me a bunch of messages, but there was too much shit going on, so I read only the first three and never had the chance to respond. At the time, they came across as trivial, but as I scan over the message thread now, I realize it was anything but.

> **22:23 Sienna:** I need to go buy some cosmetics tomorrow.

> **23:39 Sienna:** You should take Zeus to the vet. I think he has an ear infection.

23:48 Sienna: Found the shoes you got me. You need a better hiding place.

23:57 Sienna: I think I'd like to go to your club again.

00:06 Sienna: [Selfie with Zeus. Both are sprawled on the bed.]

00:09 Sienna: What about my driving lessons? You promised!!

00:12 Sienna: Is there another wedding we can crash sometime soon? I could dance on the table for you again.

00:16 Sienna: [Another selfie with Zeus on the bed.]

I notice a peculiar thing when I skim the contents. The first several messages are statements that don't *ask* for a reply. But she probably *did* expect me to text her back. When I didn't, she sent the photo of her and Zeus. And Sienna knows very well I don't allow my dogs in the bedroom. If I had seen that image last night, I would have demanded she get Zeus off the bed and out of the room. She sent that specific photo on purpose, but when I still did not respond, she switched to asking questions.

She knew we were about to get into a confrontation with the Romanians, but none of her messages showed any interest in that. Just seemingly random nonsense. But they weren't nonsense, were they? It's never "what you see is what you get" where my wife is concerned. I have to ignore the shit she says and the way she acts. Dig deeper to find the truth.

Statements, then the photo, and then the questions. Attempts to get a reaction from me?

She was worried about me but didn't want to show it.

I lower my head until my mouth is right next to her ear. "You are like a damn Rubik's Cube, Sienna. I can spend days trying different moves to find the right pattern."

She mumbles something and presses even closer against

my body. Untangling my fingers from her hair, I take her chin and tilt her head up.

"Tell me, my glittery spy, has anyone ever managed to solve the puzzle?"

She blinks sleepily and scrunches her nose at me. "What the hell are you rambling about?"

"I'm talking about your text messages. Your crazy clothes and ridiculous footwear choices. Your smiles."

She raises an eyebrow. "What's wrong with my smiles?"

"The wider they are, the sadder your eyes get."

Her body tenses, but it only lasts for a second. In the next breath, her lips curve into another of those false grins.

"Are you trying to psychoanalyze me, Drago?" She juts her chin at me. "I've had enough shrink sessions to last me a lifetime, so please, kindly fuck off."

Shrink sessions? I wrap my arm around her, keeping her close. "Why?"

"It's personal," she snaps and shoves at my chest. "Let me go."

"Why, Sienna?"

"I tried to kill myself!" she yells into my face. "There. Happy? Now, let me go!"

Dread explodes inside my chest, then spreads, consuming my entire body. I can't move as I stare at my wife while she beats upon my breastbone with her fists, trying to make me release my hold. I should let her go. She obviously wants to be alone, but I can't. The mere idea of her not existing makes me want to set the whole fucking world on fire. There is no world without her in it. Not for me.

"Sienna." I sweep away a lock of hair that has fallen over her face.

Sienna tries to swat at my fingers, but when she fails, she sinks her teeth into the side of my hand.

"Feeling better, now?" I ask.

She glares at me through tangled strands and mumbles something I can't decipher. I doubt anyone could when her mouth is full the way it's now.

"Chomp harder if it'll help."

A tear rolls down her cheek. She lets me go, leaving a sizable indent in my flesh. I cup her face with my palms and wipe away her tears with my thumbs. "What made you do that, baby?" She knows I'm not asking about the bite.

"When my sister was abducted, it was my fault."

"How so?"

"Luna and I planned to go out that night, but she canceled at the last moment. Asya was never into hanging out in bars, but I convinced her to come with me since Luna couldn't. She didn't want to go, but I kept pressing until she caved. We snuck out." She closes her eyes and continues. "Met a guy there. He was funny and made us laugh a lot. When I told Asya we should head home, she said she'd like to stay a while longer."

Sienna's eyes open as more tears stream down her cheeks. I brush them away, but they just keep on coming.

"I had pilates the following morning, you see, so I left my sister alone with a man she didn't know and went home. I climbed into my bed, under the warm covers, and went to sleep while my sister was raped on the cold snow outside of that bar. She suffered while I overslept. I never even went to the damn class."

Her lower lip trembles as she speaks, and her hands shake. I want to tell her that she can stop, that she doesn't have to say anything more if it's hurting her so much. Watching my sunny, sparkling wife break apart in front of my eyes is like a knife through the chest. But I keep silent, knowing she needs to let it all out.

"For months, we didn't know if Asya was alive or dead. Arturo couldn't find her. The whole of Cosa Nostra searched for her, without result. I spent weeks sitting on the porch, hoping she would miraculously come through the gate, until one day, I realized she probably never will."

Sienna takes a deep breath. "I went up to her room, took the sleeping pills the doctor had prescribed me, and climbed into Asya's bed. I just wanted to sleep."

"Jesus, baby." I lean forward and place a kiss on her forehead. The longing to hold her to me and envelop her with all my might is overwhelming, but I wouldn't be able to see her as she speaks. "How many did you take?"

"Whatever was left in the bottle. Arturo found me and rushed me to the ER."

I wrap my arms around Sienna and crush her to my chest, holding her tightly. It doesn't feel like enough. I move my hand to her hair and tuck her face into the crook of my neck.

"Promise me," I choke out.

Sienna mumbles something into my neck, a "what" most likely.

"Promise me you'll never do anything like that again."

Her palm travels up my chest and neck and stops at my jaw. She sits up on my stomach and grips my chin in her fingers as she leans forward.

"I promise. But I want one in return."

"All right."

"You won't get yourself killed, Drago." She squeezes my chin. "Please."

I move a strand of hair off her face and trace the shape of her lips with the tip of my finger. As I do, it dawns on me that she's purposefully facing me with her mouth in line with my eyes. "Why? Just a while ago you told me you don't like me."

Her lips widen into a smile under my touch. "You have exceptional taste in women's shoes."

"Are you ever going to stop this charade, Sienna? You can just tell me the truth. It won't be the end of the world."

"What truth?" She laughs.

"That you're in love with me."

The smile vanishes off her face, and her body goes still. "You're delusional."

"No, I don't think I am."

She lets go of my face and leans away, getting ready to run.

Not happening. I wrap my arm around her and roll us, pinning her on the bed with my body.

"Let me go!" she snaps.

I move my hand along her hip, between her legs, and press my fingers onto her pussy. Sienna's eyes flare.

"I realized something recently," I say as I slowly circle her clit, applying a bit more pressure with every stroke. "It really turns me on when you're angry."

She pins me with a murderous stare. I move my finger between her folds and slide it inside her heat.

"Do you want to know why?" I ask as I add another finger. "Because I know that's the real you, *mila moya.*"

Sienna's breath hitches. I stretch her slightly, then curl my fingers up, finding her hidden spot, and press a little harder. She closes her eyes and moans as her body trembles.

There is nothing more beautiful than seeing her like this. Unguarded. Without pretense. Mine. She might lie with her words, but her body always tells me the truth. I remove my fingers and position myself at her entrance, slipping only the tip of my cock inside. Sienna's eyes snap open, searing into mine. Her green-painted nails dig into the skin of my arms.

"It's okay, baby." I lower my head until our foreheads touch as I slowly slide into her. "I'm in love with you, too."

A strangled gasp leaves her lips as she takes all of me in. Her eyes stare into mine from beneath her dark half-lowered lashes and wisps of hair that have fallen over her face. It's as if she is still trying to hide from me. I reach out and sweep the silky locks away, then caress the satin-like skin of her cheek with the tips of my fingers.

"No more hiding from me," I say as I pull out and immediately slam back into her. "Do we have a deal?"

For a moment, sheer panic crosses Sienna's face. I bury my fingers in her hair and pin her with my gaze. "I love every side of you, *mila moya*. I love you when you laugh, but I also love you when you're sad. I love you angry—pissed off and determined." Dipping my head even lower, I growl, "I even fucking adore when you threaten to shoot me."

"You're crazy." She laughs while a single tear slides down her cheek.

"Trust me, there isn't a sexier sight than my wife pointing a gun at me while wearing a gold tutu and fur slippers."

My next thrust makes her pant. I quicken my pace, pounding into her and making the headboard bang into the wall along with my movements. "Promise me that you'll try."

"I promise."

Sienna

Hard, fast knocking breaks the silence of the night. I open my eyes and sit up in bed. The room is completely engulfed in darkness, not even moonlight pierces the gloom. The door screeches open—the sound so much louder than it should be. A figure of a man stands in the doorway. I can't see his features, only his shape outlined by the light spilling from the hallway.

"Sienna," the man says. My brother's voice.

"Arturo? What are you doing here?"

He opens the door wider, and the strip of yellow light falls onto Drago's side of the bed. It's empty.

"I need to tell you something, Sienna."

My lower lip trembles. No. "Get out!" I scream and leap off the bed, intending to run over and close the door, but my steps are sluggish like I'm treading through water. Everything is happening in slow motion.

"I need you to be strong now," Arturo's voice continues. It's distorted somehow as if it's coming from a deep dark pit. I still can't see his face.

"Shut up! Shut! Up!" I yell as I force myself toward the door. Just a few more feet and I'll reach it.

"I'm so sorry, Sienna."

I freeze with my hand outstretched. My knees buckle and I hit the floor.

"Your husband is dead."

Ringing fills my ears, getting stronger until I can't take it anymore. I press my hands over my ears and scream.

"Sienna! Wake up!"

I blink. Drago is lying on top of me, holding my face between his palms.

"I had a nightmare," I choke out.

"I could see that. What was it?"

There is so much concern in his eyes. I reach out to trace his furrowed eyebrows and stroke the tip of my finger down his nose to his tightly pressed mouth. My hand is trembling and my heart is beating at supersonic speed. I know it was just a dream, but I can't shake off the terror.

"I dreamed that all my clothes and shoes turned white." I tilt my chin and place a kiss on his lips. "It was awful."

Drago narrows his eyes at me. It's clear he doesn't believe me. I thread my fingers through his hair and press my face to his chest, breathing in his scent.

"Sienna."

Shaking my head, I squeeze him tighter. I don't want to talk about it. He's okay. That's all I need.

He rolls us until our positions are reversed, with me atop

him now. Tucking my face into the crook of his neck, he strokes the skin at my nape, just below my hairline.

"Was the dream about your sister?" he asks in a low voice while his fingers continue their soothing path. "I don't dream about mine that often anymore. My . . . other sister. I'm not sure if it's easier, or harder. Sometimes, it feels like I'm betraying her because I don't think about her as often as I once did."

His voice is so strained. It's as if he's forcing himself to actually speak the words aloud. Not wanting to talk about certain things is a very familiar concept to me, and it's painfully clear that he's doing this for my benefit.

I lift my head and look my husband right in his eyes. "It wasn't your fault," I whisper. "Tara told me what happened. You did all you could."

"Did I? My brain says I did. But my heart won't let me accept that truth. It never will." He cups my cheek in his palm. "It doesn't matter what everyone says. Doesn't matter that it was someone else's doing. The heart will always take the blame because it can't understand that the love it feels wasn't enough to save a loved one from harm. And that's okay, as long as the brain understands it."

A tear escapes my eye, sliding down my cheek as his words resonate deep within me. He gets it. I'm not sure if anyone else could.

"My brain understands," I mutter, but then realize that his eyes are still focused on mine.

Tilting my head up a bit, I wait for his gaze to move lower, then repeat my reply.

Tiny wrinkles appear in the corners of Drago's eyes as he smiles. He wipes my tear away with his thumb, then traces the outline of my lips. "Who told you?"

"I figured it out a few weeks ago." I glide my fingers through his hair. "Why don't you wear hearing aids?"

"I did. They helped when there was no background noise.

But with sounds all around or several people speaking at the same time, every single thing got amplified. I thought my fucking head was going to explode. It's the same when I'm surrounded by very loud sounds now."

"But, you run a club. It doesn't get any louder than that." I stare at him, completely dumbfounded by the realization of what he experiences every day. "And the meals here, with everyone always speaking at the same time? How do you manage?"

"I guess, I have a really thick head." He smirks.

My God, the level of concentration and focus he needs to maintain every single day is unfathomable. I bite my lower lip.

"Can you . . . hear me?"

Drago's eyes slide to mine, our gazes clashing. From what Keva told me, he probably can't, but I'm still hopeful.

"Only when you're next to me. But at a distance, even at just a few feet away, then no," he says, his smile vanishing. "I'm sorry, baby."

"It's okay." I lean in to kiss him just as a loud knock sounds at the door.

"It's probably Filip. I have to go." Drago takes a nip of my lower lip, then reaches inside his nightstand drawer and pulls out a velvet pouch. "For your fish tank."

I undo the thin string and empty the contents on the bed. A bunch of green-colored crystals, in a multitude of shapes and sizes, spill onto the white sheet. They glisten in the overhead light as it reflects off the brilliant surface of the glass stones.

"Oh my God! I have notebook stickers that look just like that, only smaller. These are so pretty! Like little green diamonds." I squeal in delight and take one in my palm. "Did you get them at that crystal shop in Brooklyn?"

"Not exactly."

"Will the color wash out if I put them in the fish tank?"

A deep rumbling sound of Drago's laughter fills the room. "I'm pretty sure it won't."

CHAPTER Twenty

Sienna

"I THINK WE SHOULD TAKE LOLLIPOP TO A VET," I mumble, following the orange fish with my eyes as it dashes this way and that between the water plants.

"Lollipop?" Tara raises an eyebrow.

"I like candy names," I say and point my finger at the fish in question. "See that stripe on his right side? It wasn't there before. Maybe he developed a skin condition."

Tara leans forward, pressing her nose to the glass. "It looks normal to me. Just a part of the pattern on the scales."

"No, I'm sure it wasn't there before."

"Then, it's got to be dermatitis. Or should I say 'scaletitis'?" she giggles. "Oh, there's Adam, he had an aquarium once. Hey, Adam! Come here."

Drago's head enforcer steps into the dining room, somehow shrinking the space with his huge presence. He crosses his arms over his chest, making his biceps bulge and the artwork on his full-sleeve tattoo pop. "What is it?"

"Sienna thinks one of her fish is sick. The one with the stripe on its side."

Adam crouches next to Tara, his head tilting askew as he observes his "patient."

"I see nothing wrong with it."

"He didn't have that mark before." I point at the fish. "See?"

"No, it's just a patt—" He snaps his mouth closed. "Oh, yes, it can happen sometimes with that specific species. They change their coloring all the time. Nothing to worry about."

"Really?" I look back at the fish. The pet store salesperson never mentioned it.

"Of course. Don't worry if it happens again," Adam quickly adds.

"And what about its fin?"

He glances at the fish tank nervously. "What about it?"

"His left fin was torn. And now it's full again."

"Yes, they have amazing healing abilities and can regrow fins and tails."

I narrow my eyes at him. "It's not the fish that I bought, is it?"

"Um, not exactly." Adam raises his hand and brushes the back of his head, guilt written all over his face. "The previous one kind of . . . died. The boss had Iliya send us all a photo of it with an order to find one that looked the same and swap it."

Tara falls into a fit of laughter.

I look back at the fish tank and imagine Drago instructing his men to comb the city, looking for a specific fish for me. A warm tingling feeling floods me as it does each time I think about my husband. It threatens to drown me.

I close my eyes, and my mind instantly drifts to two nights ago when Drago pinned me under him, claiming that I'm in love with him. Panic explodes in the pit of my stomach. It's not true. I like him. When he's away the entire day because of work, like today, I feel empty somehow. But I'm not in love with him. And he's most definitely not in love with me, regardless of what he said. Our marriage is just a business agreement that worked out well. Nothing more. Nothing less.

"Um, Sienna . . . Can you pretend you don't know about the fish?" Adam asks, pulling me out of my thoughts.

"Sure." I nod and make myself smile.

"Thank God." Adam lets out a sigh of relief.

Once he leaves, I untie the string on the pouch with my new glass pebbles and take a handful of stones. My hand hovers over the water as I let the crystals fall. I'm watching them sink to the bottom of the tank when Tara shrieks beside me.

"Sienna! Are you crazy?"

I look at her, confused. "What?"

"Where did you get these?"

"The rocks? It's colored glass Drago got for me. Aren't they pretty?"

Tara opens her mouth, then closes it, only to open it again as if unable to form words.

"He . . . he knew they would be used in a fish tank?" Her voice sounds kind of strained.

"Yes. He even asked what color I wanted. Why?"

"Um . . . because it's not glass." She picks up one of the crystals from my palm and looks it over. "That, my dear, is a ten-carat emerald, worth at least fifteen grand."

I blink, bewildered, and look at the fish tank where at least twenty similar stones grace the sandy depths.

"But, he told me . . . He told me it was just glass. Why would he do that?" I gape at my "decorations."

"Yeah, I wonder why." Tara snickers. "Prince Saeed won't be happy."

"Who's Prince Saeed?"

"The billionaire who ordered those months ago."

I look back at the emeralds in my palm, and the familiar feeling of panic surfaces again. Letting the rest of the green stones fall into the fish tank, I watch as they make a small splash before settling down next to the others.

"I think I'm getting a headache," I say, avoiding looking at Tara. "I'm going up to crash for a bit."

"Don't be sad about the fish. It happens."

"I know."

Reaching our bedroom, I head straight to the dresser and grab the vase filled with "glass crystals" Drago gifted me, then take a seat on the edge of the bed. Dozens of colored rocks scatter onto the bedcover when I tilt the container. I slide my pens to the side and pick up the nearest stone. It's fiery red and shaped like an oval, with many facets that reflect the light spilling through the window. A ruby, most likely.

There are a few more red stones among the others of various hues. I don't know much about precious gems, but based on the colors alone, there are sapphires, amethysts, and many others I don't recognize.

"Silly man," I choke out as I collect the stones back into their vase.

When I have my "pen holder" back on the dresser, I walk to the closet to get my notebook from its hiding place between my sweaters and take a pen from the nightstand drawer.

Georgina had a secret, I write, as my hand shakes slightly. A huge, horrible secret. It was so bad, that she would rather die than confess it to anyone. Especially to herself. She's fallen in love with her grumpy wolf man.

Drago

The door to my office opens and a short, almost gaunt man in a charcoal three-piece suit walks inside. His white hair is slicked back, contrasting with his thick black eyebrows visible above the rim of his black-framed glasses.

"Mr. Dubois." I motion toward the chair on the other side of my desk.

When the Frenchman takes a seat, I pull out a big velvet box from the drawer and set it before him.

Most jewelers purchase precious stones exclusively through regular channels because they want to assure their customers of gemstone authenticity by delivering certified products. Some buyers, however, are not interested in paperwork. They just want the best rocks. Mr. Dubois caters to that kind of clientele. Arabian princes. Business moguls. Oligarchs from all over the world. They don't give a fuck about certificates as long as their wives or lovers can wear the most expensive piece of jewelry in the room.

"This isn't what we agreed on, Mr. Popov," Dubois says.

"I know."

He takes off his glasses and points them at the box. "Prince Saeed was very clear in his request. Emeralds, not sapphires."

"I'm afraid the emeralds are no longer available. The sapphires I'm offering are worth 20 percent more," I say and reach into the drawer. "And I have a gift, as an apology."

"His Highness has specifically asked for emeralds. It's absolutely unacceptable to—" He stops midsentence, staring at the gem on my palm. "Is that . . ."

"Yes. A G SI1 five-carat round diamond." I place the diamond on his outstretched hand and lean back. "Call the prince. Ask if my gift is enough to compensate for his disappointment about receiving sapphires instead of emeralds."

The jeweler takes out a small magnifying glass from his pocket and inspects the rock from every angle. Once done, he pulls out his phone and makes a call. I assume he's speaking French since I can't read his lips and I'm having difficulty understanding what he is saying. But, based on Dubois's excited tone, he must be conversing with Prince Saeed.

"The money will be wired within the next five minutes," Dubois says after ending the call. He carefully returns the diamond to me. "His Highness asked me to convey his gratitude for the gift, and he confirmed that sapphires are an adequate substitute."

I nod and place the diamond inside the box. "As soon as I get a confirmation about the receipt of the money, our business is concluded."

Dubois closes the box but keeps his hands on it as if he's concerned the thing may disappear. "If I may ask, what happened with the emeralds?"

"My wife needed them."

"Oh? Would she like them used for a beautiful bracelet? I have an amazing new designer back in Paris, I'm sure we can come up with a magnificent custom piece—"

"They weren't for her jewelry. She needed them for her aquarium."

My phone vibrates with an incoming message. I glance down at the screen, seeing a notification from my bank that the payment has come through.

"Excuse me? A what?"

"The glass thing with water and fish inside," I clarify and offer him my hand. "Thank you for your business, Mr. Dubois. Pass along my best wishes to the prince."

The Frenchman slowly rises and shakes my hand, gaping at me from behind his thick-rimmed glasses. Holding the box under his right arm, he heads toward the door but then stops at the threshold.

"Why didn't you keep the diamond for your wife?" he asks over his shoulder.

The corner of my lips curl up. "It's colorless."

Filip walks inside my office just as the jeweler leaves.

"Any activity?" I ask.

"No. No one's spotted Bogdan's men near any of our locations."

"Good. They'll need some time to organize before they hit us back. Did Roman Petrov confirm the meeting?"

"Yes. He will be here in half an hour," Filip says and clasps his hands in front of him. "Tara just called."

"What did she want?"

"To let me know she and your wife are on their way here. They should arrive any moment."

"What?" I spring out of my chair. "I gave a specific order that neither of them is allowed to leave the grounds."

"It looks like Mrs. Popov was very persuasive with the guards at the gate." He takes his phone out of his pocket, holds it up to his ear, and listens to the person on the line. "They just arrived at the back entrance."

I slam my palm on the desk and sprint across the office into the narrow hallway. It's unlikely that the Romanians will retaliate today, but I don't want either my wife or sister at the club—the most probable target. Kicking the back door open, I step outside just in time to see Sienna exiting a car, wearing a green dress with feathers all over the bodice.

I march across the parking lot until I'm standing right in front of my wife and pin her with my hard gaze. "What the fuck, Sienna?"

"Drago." She smiles. "Tara and I decided to pay you a visit."

I grit my teeth and look over the women's heads to glare at Relja and Iliya, who dared to bring them here against my orders. They are hanging back on the other side of the car, fidgeting.

"Explain!" I roar.

Both men cringe and take a retreating step.

"Drago." Sienna wraps her fingers around my wrist. "It's my fault. I insisted."

"Why?"

"I just wanted to see you." She shrugs. "And I am carrying the gun you got me."

Some of my rage dissipates. I reach out and stroke her chin with the back of my hand, then look at my sister. "You should have known better."

"I wanted to cheer up Sienna," Tara says, but then mouths the next sentence. "*She knows the fish had died.*"

The rest of my anger disappears. I drop a quick kiss on the top of Sienna's head and look at Iliya. "I want twenty men positioned around the club while the women are here."

Iliya nods and reaches for his phone. I take another glance at my wife's short dress.

"And, Iliya, make sure the same warning as last time is delivered to all male guests upon entry."

The Russian pakhan narrows his eyes at me, then looks at the older man sitting next to him, saying something in Russian. I place my palm on Sienna's knee. A small smirk breaks across her lips as I slowly stroke her skin while she continues to mess around with her phone.

"I'll take an entire load of the Romanians' ammunition," the pakhan states, "but I want an additional five percent discount for getting rid of the truck for you."

"I'm already selling you the goods way under the market value, Roman."

"That's my offer. Take it or leave it."

I give him a pointed stare and nod. This transaction is more about the principle. I want Bogdan's shit gone.

"The word around is that you also have another type of product to offer," he adds. "I'd like to pick something out for my wife."

"You won't get any discount on that."

"I'm not concerned about the price when I buy things for my wife," he barks, visibly offended.

"Let's go to my office, then." I kiss Sienna's bare shoulder. "I'll be back in ten minutes."

"I'll go check if Tara needs help." She turns toward the other side of the club where my sister is standing with two guys, both seem to be trying to get her to the dance floor.

"All right."

I follow Sienna with my eyes as she leaves the booth and heads toward the group. The men standing with Tara notice Sienna's approach, their heads snapping in my direction a moment later. I let them see in my eyes what will happen if either is still there when my wife reaches them. Both men mumble something and hightail it out of there. Good.

Sienna

"The vibe here is super weird tonight," I mumble.

Tara casually takes a sip of her sangria. "How so?"

"Your friends ran away the moment they saw me approaching." I glance at the waiter carrying drinks, and his head turns to the side as soon as he sets his eyes on me. People seem to be trying really hard not to meet my gaze. In fact, it's like everyone is purposely avoiding looking at me. Or, men at least. "Is my dress that awful?"

Tara sizes me up, her eyes halting for a few moments on the feathered bodice. "It's the most outrageous piece of clothing I've ever seen. But nope, it's not the dress."

"Then, why?"

"They received Drago's warning at the entrance."

"A warning? Oh my God, did he tell people I brought a gun? It's not even loaded! I only took it because Drago insisted. I'd never shoot at anyone, well, except your brother."

Tara chokes on her drink, her eyes bulging. "You shot at Drago?"

"Long story." I wave my hand. "I should have left the gun with the bouncers like everyone else."

"The gun is not the problem. It's the spoon that terrifies them."

"The spoon?"

She smiles into her glass. "Yup. They're extremely worried about that spoon."

"Are you drunk?"

Tara doesn't get a chance to reply because a blond man in his late twenties wraps his arm around her waist from behind.

"I knew it was you, Tara darling," he slurs. "How long has it been? Three years?"

She rolls her eyes and removes his hand from her middle. "Leave, Gary. You know I don't mess around with my brother's business associates."

"Always a party pooper." The guy laughs and switches his gaze to me. "Maybe your friend has a more positive attitude."

Before I can offer a response, Tara grabs the guy by the front of his white dress shirt. "That's Drago's wife, you idiot! Leave!"

"You don't say. Maybe the lady would like to try out something different." He reaches his hand toward me, staring at my boobs.

"She wouldn't." I take a step back, but he still manages to brush his fingers down my arm.

"Gary, please. Drago will come any moment," my sister-in-law whispers nervously and glances somewhere behind me. "Oh shit."

I turn around and see my husband standing in the

passageway leading to his office, a murderous glare focused on Tara's friend.

"I'll be off, then." Gary's somewhat frantic voice comes from behind my back.

Drago watches the guy retreat to his booth, then heads across the dance floor toward the bar.

"Fuck, Sienna, he's going for a spoon," Tara squeals, grabbing my arm. "You need to go there and distract him while I get someone from security to throw Gary outta here."

"Why?"

"Because Gary is our investment banker, and Drago is planning on taking out his eyes."

"Yeah, right." I laugh.

"I'm not kidding, Sienna!" She shakes my arm. "Men are avoiding looking at you because they all got warned that if they do, they will lose their eyes. Go there and stop him!"

I watch Tara as she rushes toward one of the bouncers by the exit, then glance to the bar where Drago is taking a spoon from a drawer. This is ridiculous. He is not going to take a man's eyes out because he ogled my boobs.

Behind the bar, Drago raises the spoon in front of his face, feeling the edge with his thumb, then heads toward the booth where Gary is sitting. His jaw is clenched and his mouth is set in a hard line. He's staring at the banker with murder in his eyes. Shit.

I dash across the dance floor, bumping a few people with my elbows along the way. When I reach Drago, I leap into his arms, clutching his neck and wrapping my legs around his waist.

"Hello there." I grin and kiss his tightly pressed lips.

Drago's hand slides under my thigh to support me, but his eyes are still focused over my shoulder.

"Hey." I take his chin between my fingers, tilting his head

so he'll look at me. "Any chance you can get me more of those pretty crystals?"

"What color?" he asks through gritted teeth.

"Red. They will look nice in the flower pots on the kitchen window. Do you think that shop has some?"

"It does."

I smile, stroking his cheek while a warm feeling spreads through my chest. "So you consider rubies suitable as flower pot decorations?"

His hand squeezes my thigh. "I was thinking red beryl, but it can be rubies if you prefer those. Was it Tara who spilled the beans?"

"Yes. She was very distressed when she saw me throwing a handful of emeralds into the fish tank." I smile. "Why, Drago?"

"You love sparkly things, just like I do."

"So, why give them to me?"

"Because the most sparkling one is already in my possession, and her glow can't compare to any rock."

It shouldn't feel so good, to hear him calling me his possession. It shouldn't make me this wet. But it does. It makes my core ache with the need to feel him inside me, to have him cement that statement with action.

I tangle my fingers in his hair. "Yeah, I do like my clothes to glitter."

A waiter passes by us, carrying a tray of drinks. Drago throws the spoon he's been holding this whole time, and it clatters on the surface, hitting one of the glasses.

"I'm not speaking about your ridiculous clothes, Sienna."

His gaze holds mine, piercing and serious, somehow primal in its intensity. Sometimes, I believe he can devour me with his eyes alone.

Out of the corner of my eye, I can see people throwing curious looks at us. My dress has ridden all the way up my thighs, providing everyone a full view of my legs and, probably half my ass, but I don't give a single fuck. My whole being is attuned to Drago, to being in his arms. He's all I see. All I feel. Even with all the scents filling the air around us, the only one I smell is his subtle mint fragrance. I've never been so mesmerized by a person.

"Were you really going to take that guy's eyes out?" I whisper when Drago's gaze shifts to my lips.

His jaw clenches, and he turns around, carrying me toward his private booth "Tara talks too much."

I glance over Drago's shoulder at the exit where two security men are pushing the banker outside, Tara overseeing their efforts. She looks up and, with a wink, raises her thumb.

When we reach the big leather sofa, my legs untangle from behind Drago's back, but instead of letting me down, he takes a seat with me straddling his lap. I release my hold on his hair and trail my fingers along his chin to his mouth. He parts his lips, his teeth nipping the tip of my index finger.

"What was that for?" I ask.

"A punishment for distracting me from my mission."

"Do you often have an urge to take people's eyeballs out?" I ask, even though I'm still expecting him to say that Tara was simply fucking with me.

A small smirk forms on his face. "No. It's a rather new development."

I let my thumb stroke the curve of his lips, then slide my palm along his jaw. The music blasting from the speakers changes to a slow melody—"The Sound of Silence." This song was playing when we met, and I remember how his mere presence affected me at the time.

There was wonder and instant attraction, and I felt a strange pull toward him without even knowing who he was. But, simultaneously, there was another sensation that I couldn't identify, too overwhelmed by his essence.

I recall it now. A subtle tendril of fear, a primal instinct, as if my subconscious was trying to warn me that a very dangerous man was standing before me. I ignored it.

"There is no pet assassin, is there? When I heard Adam talking about the priest, he was talking about you."

Drago's gaze leaves my lips, moving it up to meet mine. He's not smiling anymore, and his answer is just there, clearly visible in his eyes. I think that deep down, I always knew the truth.

"Pop is an old nickname from when we were young punks, back in Serbia. Adam is the only one who still calls me that sometimes."

His rough voice reverberates through my being, straight to my heart, each word falling like a boulder on my soul. I was born into Cosa Nostra, and the ways of the Mafia are not unknown to me. Every man I've ever met has probably taken a life at least once, but other than our don, none are so vicious in meting out their brand of justice. I wait for my consciousness to rebel, for the feeling of dread to rise, suffocate me. It doesn't come.

Ever since I can remember, I've felt like a circus performer—standing on a ball, trying to keep my balance, the fear of crashing down always present in my mind. No real aim or purpose, other than keeping myself upright while even the tiniest movement of the ball under my feet made me flail my hands in the air, trying to regain my equilibrium.

As I stare at my husband's somber face, I realize I haven't felt like that for quite some time. For the first time in my life, I feel as if I'm standing on solid ground, in the arms of a man who nails the bodies of his enemies to the walls.

"Say something, Sienna." Drago's eyes are glued to my lips, waiting for my reaction. His teeth are clenched tight, mouth pressed into a thin line.

"Why the cross?" I ask, my voice barely audible.

"It's a signature. A play on my old nickname. A way to

send a message to those who might get an idea about coming at me or mine."

"And what's the message?"

"That I will absolve them of their sins. Personally. And in blood. The same way I did to the people who killed my family."

"You found them?"

"Every single one. No one touches my family and remains breathing." His hand travels along my jaw toward my chin and then back to squeeze my nape. "And no one gets to ogle my sparkling wife. Whoever dares, I'll make sure it's the last thing they'll ever see."

I suck in a breath and lean forward a bit. With my dress around my hips, Drago's hard dick is pressing directly onto my pussy. He tilts his head to the side and reaches for a small remote lying on the sofa's arm. A moment later, the two lamps on either side of the booth turn off, shrouding our immediate space in semidarkness. All around us, the lights above the dance floor, other booths, as well as at the bar are still on, but we're left in the shadows, mostly hidden from prying eyes.

Drago's hands land on my thighs, then slowly push the fabric of my dress higher. I can't hear his ragged breaths with the music blasting overhead, but I can feel his warm exhales on my face.

"Do you remember the wedding I took you to? Where you danced for me?" he asks and captures my lips with his. His hands have reached the elastic of my panties, his fingers tangling with the lacy straps on my hips.

Nodding, I grab a fistful of his shirt and bite his lower lip while my body buzzes with electricity. No matter how close we are to each other, it's never enough. I feel a tug, and then a tear on the left side of my panties.

"I wanted to pull you off that table and fuck you in front of everyone there. To claim you as mine. And make sure everyone knows it."

The right side of my panties gets torn, too, and then he slides his palm between our bodies, circling my clit with his finger while unzipping his pants with his other hand. The moment his cock springs free, he grabs me under my ass, positioning me above his solid length.

"Do you have anything to confess, Sienna?"

It's too dim to clearly see the expression on his face, but every so often, a strobe of light over the dance floor reflects off his light-green eyes. Eyes that are boring into mine. A whirlwind of feelings twists in my stomach, demanding to be let out. I bury my hands in his hair and, staring into his depths, slowly slide onto his cock.

A gasp leaves me as he fills me, lodging himself deep. I squeeze his dark strands between my fingers and rock my hips, taking even more of him in. My gaze holds his captive as I ride him, but no words leave my lips.

I know what he's asking for. He wants me to tell him that I love him. I can't. I'm too afraid to voice the truth, to say out loud what we both already know. Each time I even think about it, panic rises within me, gripping me in its claws, squeezing. I'm aware that my fear is irrational. You can't seal a person's fate with three simple words. Still, I can't make myself do it, too scared that I might lose him.

The pressure in my core builds as I rotate my hips, needing to feel even more of him. Drago's hand squeezes my ass cheek, then moves along my hip to my pussy and pinches my clit. I gasp, my breathing fast and shallow. The brilliant piercing eyes of my husband are still pinned to my own when he leans forward and touches his forehead to mine.

"It's okay, *mila moya*," he whispers, pressing his thumb to my bud. "You don't have to say it. I know you will, when you're ready."

His lips seize mine—biting, claiming. I squeeze my eyes shut and kiss him back as I reach for the remote control he left on the cushion beside us. A slight press of a button, and the elegant column lamps on either side of the sofa come back to life, bathing us in the pale-blue glow and restoring the ambient awareness around us. Over a hundred people are in the club tonight, and each one of them can now clearly see me riding my husband's cock.

Drago's eyes widen in surprise, and a corner of his lips curves up. "Why?" he asks.

Throwing the remote to the side, I press my palms on my husband's face, devouring him with my eyes while I continue to slowly ride him. I inhale his scent, drink in his essence, and embrace the very darkness I once feared when we met. This man. The only one who's ever understood me. The man I can't imagine my life without anymore.

"Because I want everyone to know, too," I say.

"Know what?"

"That you're mine." I lean forward so he can feel my rapid heartbeat. "And that I'm yours."

Chapter
Twenty-one

 Drago

Pumpkin-orange. Of course.

I lean my elbow on the bathroom doorframe and continue towel-drying my hair as I watch my wife. Sitting on the edge of the bed, her right foot propped on the nearby recliner, she's painting her toenails. The brush in her hand is held by the tips of only two fingers, the other three extended outward, making me think that the polish on her fingernails isn't yet dry. Her outfit today consists of shiny turquoise leggings paired with an orange sweater. The pants have a pattern of fish scales, making them look like a mermaid tail in a way. I smile and push away from the jamb, heading across the room.

"Hey, what are you doing?" she says as I wrap my hand around her ankle and pull her leg up so I can take a seat on the recliner.

I place her foot on my knee and take the nail polish brush out of her grasp. The confusion on Sienna's face becomes a surprise when I dip the applicator into the bottle on the nightstand and resume the work she started.

She reaches out and places her finger under my chin,

tilting my head up. "What would your men say if they saw you painting my toenails? It's not a very manly thing, you know?"

I raise an eyebrow. "Should I go kick someone's ass after I'm done? Would that maintain my alpha male status?"

"I don't think that's necessary." She laughs. "But I'd love to see the look on their faces."

"No one would ever make a comment on it because if they did, it would mean they were looking at your legs. And it wouldn't end well for them," I say and continue with my task. "Stop wriggling your toes."

"Sorry." She snorts. "Don't forget the glitter dust."

"Should I know what that is?"

"Glitter dust. Here." She places a small round container in my hand. It's filled with a shimmering powder of some kind. "Just take a little pinch and sprinkle on the nails. Quickly now, or the nail polish will dry and the glitter won't stick."

I scrutinize the tiny thing on my palm. It's smaller than my thumb, so there's no way I can "pinch" anything from inside. It takes me a few tries just to open it. I spill a bit of the glitter on my palm, take some between my fingers, and carefully let it fall over Sienna's toenails.

"Enough?" I ask and look up to find my wife staring at me, her eyes glistening.

"It will never be enough, Drago."

I don't hear a sound, so she must have whispered it.

"Of glitter?" I ask.

Sienna's knuckles gently brush my cheek, her lips spreading into a smile. "Of you."

The smile is *real*, and it makes her entire face glow. Her gaze falls to my palm where I'm still holding the rest of that damn glittery powder, and that smile transforms into a mischievous grin.

I frown. "Don't you dar—"

Her warm breath blows on my hand, sending a cloud of gold particles all over me. A million shimmering specks float through the air like tiny gems while my wife laughs, watching them land on my head, face, and even stick to my chest.

There was a time in my life when I would have found this stunt immature. Silly. But from my wife—the most valuable jewel I've ever held in my hands? I'm having a hard time hiding the grin that's threatening to split across my face. All the pretty rocks on which I built my empire are used to make a person shine on the outside. My Sienna lights up every corner of my soul.

"Remember what I do to people who cross me, *mila moya*?"

"Gold looks good on you, Drago." Another fit of giggles. "Something about the wall, wasn't it?"

"Exactly." I leap from the recliner, grab her around the waist, and carry her across the room.

"I'll be back in a few hours," I tell Relja, who's on guard duty by the front door, and put on my coat. "If anyone allows my wife to set a foot outside the compound walls, I'm going to snap their neck."

"Sure, boss." He nods, eyes focused over my head.

"If anyone reports anything even remotely suspicious, contact me immediately."

"I will."

I turn to leave when I feel a tap on my shoulder and look back. "What?"

"There's something on your head," he mumbles.

I rake my fingers through my hair. My hand comes back

with several specks of sparkling gold dust. I squeeze the bridge of my nose and curse.

Heading to a meeting with Boston Cosa Nostra faction. With fucking glitter in my hair. I stride toward the garage, smirking at the absurdity of it all.

We arranged to meet an hour out of the city. I would have preferred for it to happen in my club, but Nera Leone wanted to stay off Ajello's radar.

I pull up my car next to a black sedan with blacked-out windows, killing the engine, and Filip parks next to me. The only other vehicle in the diner's parking lot is another pricey car, tinted windows included. Looks like Don Leone's wife decided to drive up here instead of flying because these don't look like a rental.

A *closed* sign hangs on the diner's door, but the lights are on, and even though there are no servers anywhere, a woman is seated at a table on the far right. Two men in black suits are standing behind her, hands clasped behind their backs.

"Only two bodyguards," I say as I exit my car.

Filip follows my gaze and shrugs. "Maybe she wants to be clear that it's a peaceful meeting."

"Or, maybe she wants us to know that she's not scared of us." I push open the door and head toward the woman who has been running Boston Cosa Nostra while her husband has been ill.

I've never met Nera Leone in person, but I know that she's much younger than her husband who's in his late sixties. I expected a woman of around forty, perhaps, not one in her midtwenties. If that. With her dark-blonde hair spilling over her long red coat, I would never have pegged her for the cunning opponent I'd heard much about.

I may not conduct business in the Boston area, but I keep tabs on what's going on up there. Knowing all the big players in the field, and uncovering whatever secrets they are trying to hide, is a must in my line of work. It's not common knowledge that Don Leone has been unwell for quite some time, and that his wife has unofficially taken over the Boston Cosa Nostra Family for the time being. Since she is here rather than her husband, it means he's not getting any better.

"I'm sorry to see that Don Leone is still not feeling well," I say as I take a seat across from her while Filip comes to stand behind me.

Nera nods in greeting. "He's recuperating."

"So, what can I help you with, Mrs. Leone?" I ask and lean back, spreading my right arm over the back of a neighboring chair. "I was rather surprised to get your message."

"A little birdie told me you've recently engaged in a new business venture. I have a proposition for you—a mutually beneficial affiliation."

One of my eyebrows shoots up. Word travels fast in our circles, but still, it's concerning that she got wind of such information so soon. "I thought you're getting your guns from Endri Dushku?"

"Yes. But I'm looking to make new alliances." Her blood-red lips pull into a smile.

"Endri and I have an understanding. We don't step on each others' toes. I'll think about your offer and let you know my decision."

Nera Leone rises from her seat. "Thank you. It was nice meeting you, Mr. Popov."

I follow her with my eyes as she leaves the diner, her two men trailing close behind. They get inside the cars and pull onto the road, raising a cloud of dust from the loose gravel around the potholes marring the lot.

"Boston faction has been working with Dushku for years," Filip says. "Why the change of heart so suddenly?"

"No idea."

Across the street, movement within a derelict motel

attracts my attention. A man in a black coat steps out from the farthest room on the ground level. He meets my gaze and holds it for a moment. As I reach inside my jacket for the gun in my shoulder holster, the man breaks our eye contact and turns, heading around the building. His steps are sure and steady, so I get a good look at his long jet-black hair, twisted into a thick braid, and a black rectangular case hanging over his left shoulder.

"Is that what I think it is?" Filip asks next to me.

"Yes. The guy is casually strolling around carrying a sniper rifle on his back. And I'm pretty sure he had us in his crosshairs the entire time we were meeting. That room he just left is directly across from the diner; the window has a clear line of sight to the table I was sitting at."

"You think he's one of Nera's goons?"

A black sports car pulls out from behind the motel, then heads the same way as the Italians.

"I'm not sure," I say. "But I have a feeling that if we had given off the slightest indication of harming that woman, we'd both be lying on the ground. With holes through our heads."

Filip and I get in our respective vehicles, turning in the opposite direction than Leone's brigade.

We're half an hour from the house when my phone goes off on the dashboard. My gaze snaps to the screen showing Relja's name. The phone rings twice, then stops. A signal for me—something is wrong at the club.

Fuck. I hit the gas pedal. A look at the rearview mirror confirms that Filip is accelerating as well, his phone pressed to his ear and probably getting all the details from one of our men.

Fifteen minutes later, my phone starts to ring and vibrate again, and this time, it keeps going, setting off a clusterfuck of panic in my head.

The house is under attack.

Sienna

The lights go out.

Did a fuse blow? I move my notebook away and climb off the bed, feeling my way to the balcony door.

The outdoor lights are off as well, and none of the other windows are lit. The grounds around the house are shrouded in absolute darkness, except for the two specks of light beyond the trees at the main gate. What the fuck?

The bedroom door bursts open, making me jump and swivel around.

"Get back from the window." Adam's voice booms from the doorway.

A faint yellow glow of the emergency lights from small recessed fixtures low on the walls just barely illuminates the space behind him as it falls onto the hallway floor.

"Adam? What's going on?"

"We're under attack." He ushers Tara inside my room. I haven't even noticed her standing behind him. "Lock your-selves inside the bathroom. When it's over, someone will come get you."

A loud metal bang erupts outside. The next moment, the radio in Adam's hand cracks, then Relja's voice fills the room.

"They've breached the gate."

"No time," Adam barks and takes a flashlight off his belt before placing it in Tara's hand. "Bathroom. Now. Both of you."

"Tara? Where's Drago?" I choke as she pushes me toward the en suite, leading the way with the small flashlight.

"He's still not back from a meeting. Come on."

The roar of engines from several approaching cars pene-trates the walls. Other than the earlier bang, which I assume was a vehicle ramming the gate, there are no other sounds. No gunfire. No one is shouting. The house is silent. If the mansion is under attack, wouldn't there be yelling and the hustle of all the people who are currently inside? Why is it so eerily quiet?

"I don't hear anything," I say as we stumble inside the bathroom. "What the fuck is going on, Tara?

"The Romanians decided to pay us a visit." She reaches behind her back and takes out a gun. Placing the end of the flashlight between her teeth, she releases the magazine to check it, then snaps it back. "One of the guys on guard down the road reported multiple vehicles heading toward the compound. They just broke through the gate, so we're waiting for them to get here."

"Did they cut the power?" I ask, my eyes fixed on the gun in her hand.

"Nope," she mumbles around the flashlight. "We did."

"What? Why?"

"Standard protocol." She throws me her phone. "You can watch if you want."

"You have a *protocol* for an assault?" Shaking my head, I take a seat on the closed toilet lid and stare at the screen showing a dark, grainy video. It's certainly a feed from the security camera, but I can't figure out which one. A second later, headlights enter the screen, approaching fast, the glow illuminating the front driveway.

"They can't drive in the dark with no lights on." Tara snickers. "They're sitting ducks now. We can see them, but they can't see us."

"Why hasn't anyone tried to stop them?" I choke out, watching as four black vans stop on the gravel some distance from the house.

"Shooting at moving vehicles is a bitch." She shoos me to the side, taking half of the toilet seat. "Any moment now."

I don't have time to ask her what she means, because a sudden flash fills the screen, lighting the front yard like it's midday.

The men in black clothes, who only moments before poured out of the vans, are now ducking every which way, blinded by the massive floodlights aimed at them. The thirty or so gunmen, each armed with an automatic rifle, momentarily turn into a mindless, murdering horde.

Gunfire explodes into the night.

About a dozen end up sprawled on the ground before the rest scatter around the lawn, shooting at the house.

"Drago is going to be pissed," Tara mumbles over the sound of gunfire outside.

"Because of the attack?"

"Because he wasn't here." She snickers. "I'll make sure—Fuck!"

She cuts off, staring at the phone, as two more vehicles pull up to the outer limit of light bathing the driveway.

"Fuck. Fuck. Fuck!" Tara barks out and swipes her gun off the bathroom vanity. "Stay here. I'm going downstairs."

"What?" I grab her forearm.

"There are only eighteen people here. Relja sent the rest as a backup to Naos when Misha called half an hour ago. It seems like the attack there must have been a distraction. We're stretched too thin, even with the advantage of being fortified inside."

"I'm coming with you," I say.

"Not happening."

"But—"

"You told me you could never shoot at anyone, Sienna." She fixes me with an unwavering stare. "You can't help. Stay put."

With those words, Tara dashes out, closing the bathroom door in her wake.

I take in the gloomy interior around me, the glow of the small flashlight the only source of light. The cacophony outside is still raging, but it seems more controlled now than before.

Rather than a string of machine gun fire, the shots now are individual, with stretches of time in between. Precise. The attackers have regained their bearings and stopped the aimless assault.

I grip the edge of the vanity so hard my knuckles hurt. The echo of shots might be the same as at the shooting range, but it's different knowing that many of the bullets will hit flesh, not cardboard targets. Wounding, maybe even killing Drago's people. His family. But they don't feel like just my husband's family anymore. They feel like mine, too. Fighting off the men who are attacking their home. My home, now. And I'm hiding in a fucking bathroom.

I pick up the flashlight from the counter before dashing into the bedroom. The balcony door is ajar, and the noise outside is deafening. I'm still standing close to the bathroom threshold when a stray bullet hits the balcony railing, sending shards of stone flying in every direction. My eyes fall on my nightstand. The gun Drago gave me is tucked inside the drawer.

My mild-tempered, quiet sister killed the man who kidnapped and violated her. Asya, who never even raised her voice at anyone, pressed the gun to that bastard's forehead and pulled the trigger. I don't have the guts to do that. Would never be able to do anything like it no matter the circumstances, but going downstairs without a gun is stupid. I rush across the room and grab the Glock from the bedside table.

It's worse than I thought. Much worse. I stop midway down the stairs and gape at the scene in the hall below.

Heading downstairs, for some reason, I imagined Drago's men crouching next to the windows and only popping out to return fire from time to time. The entire action movie scene played out in my head. The good guys took quick glances at the enemy, sent a few bullets their way, then pulled back to a covered position. Safe behind thick walls. Unhurt.

I couldn't have been more wrong.

The floodlights are spilling through the broken windows and the wide-open front door, creating dark voids and threatening shadows. Just over the threshold, a body of a man I don't recognize is sprawled on the floor, his vacant eyes staring at the ceiling. Blood pools on the tiles around him, spreading toward another body lying close by. A shaky breath leaves my lungs as I realize that I don't know either of them. Must be the attackers.

Adam is hunching under the window to the left of the entrance, gun in his hand poised to shoot at any moment. Blood is oozing from the gash on his shoulder, saturating his torn, white T-shirt. He pays it no mind as he suddenly straightens, sending a hail of bullets through the broken pane. The instant he drops back down, a storm of gunfire erupts outside. Glass shards, wood splinters, and drywall fragments rain around him.

On the other side of the door, two of Drago's men are returning fire. Another, Relja, is collapsed on the floor with his back against a wall. He's pressing his hand on the wound in his thigh as blood seeps between his fingers. Through the open doors leading to the grand dining room, I notice several other men holding positions by the windows. Some are shooting while others are reloading their guns. Most are bleeding, whether from bullets or shattered glass, but they keep fighting.

I grip my gun harder, but I can't make myself move. It's as if my feet are glued to the wooden stair beneath me, and I've lost all control of my lower limbs. My chest is rising and falling in quick succession, the sound of my short breaths mixing with the erratic beating of my heart. The thunderous pounding seems somehow louder than all the noise around me. At least Drago isn't here. He would have been out there, somewhere in the middle of this shitstorm, and I would have fucking lost my mind worrying about him.

Tara bursts through the kitchen door on the far side of the dining room and, keeping low to the ground, rushes into the foyer. She squats next to Relja and tucks her gun into the back of her pants. With quick and sure movements, she grabs him under his arms, heaving him away from the wall. Relja yells at her, but the gunfire is too loud for me to make out what he's saying. Tara ignores his outburst and starts dragging him away, but barely manages to move him. He's too heavy.

The sensation returns to my feet. I take one step forward, and then I'm running down the stairs. On my left, something shatters. The crash is loud, and there is a sharp sting as the shards hit my legs. Probably the remnants of one of the enormous floor vases Keva keeps along the walls. The porcelain fragments crunch under my soles as I hurry toward Tara, who is now gripping Relja's forearm, trying to pull him across the floor.

"Sienna! What the fuck are you doing here?" she snaps when I reach them.

"Helping my family." Imitating Tara, I stick the gun into the waistband of my turquoise leggings and grab Relja's other arm. "To the kitchen?"

Tara blinks at me, then quickly nods.

By the time we get Relja to the kitchen, he's lost consciousness and a lot of blood. The situation here doesn't seem any better than in the dining room. Three men are by the windows that face the front yard, firing at the assailants. Across the room, Jovan is crouching by the open door to the backyard, gun in hand, and aiming at the absolute darkness on this side of the mansion. I don't get a chance to contemplate what he's doing because a low growling sound outside is followed by an ear-splitting scream.

"Zeus got him," Jovan says, then lifts a two-way radio to his mouth.

I miss what he says when I notice Keva kneeling between the kitchen island and the countertop cabinets, finishing wrapping a kitchen towel around a guy's biceps. She sees us coming and crawls toward us.

"Get behind the island!" she orders. "Now! Both of you!"

"Hurry." Tara pulls on Relja's arm again. "The island is bulletproof."

Someone actually makes armored kitchen cabinetry? I shake my head.

Keva presses her palm over the wound in Relja's thigh while we drag him the last few feet to a safer spot. Another round of gunfire explodes, bullets hitting appliances and cupboards above us. Something on the counter wobbles and then crashes to the floor.

"If that's my favorite coffee machine, I'm going to gut someone," Keva mutters as she reaches for a drawer and takes out a tablecloth. She tears a long stripe and ties it tightly around Relja's leg. "This one needs a hospital as soon as possible."

"We can't take him to a hospital with a gunshot wound!" Tara chokes out. "Drago is going to kill you."

"Filip called fifteen minutes ago. Her don"—Keva nods toward me as she checks Relja's pulse—"said we can take the wounded to Cosa Nostra's clinic if needed."

"Don Ajello?" I ask, dumbfounded, at the same time as Tara yelps, "How the fuck did he know?"

"Beats me." Keva shakes her head. "That man knows everything."

Things seem to be calming down, because now there's only an occasional shot that disturbs the night. The sound of labored footsteps reaches me, and I peek around the kitchen island to see Beli carrying one of the guys over his shoulder.

"Upper chest," he barks as he lowers the man next to Relja. "No exit wound. I'll pull the van to the back door, and we'll get them both in."

"There are still gunmen outside!" Keva exclaims.

Beli pulls a shotgun from his back and cocks it. "Concerned about my well-being, sweet pea?"

My jaw hits the floor. *Sweet pea*? I thought Keva and Beli hated each other. When I look at Tara, she just rolls her eyes and mouths, "*Don't ask.*"

Keva flips him a bird, then focuses on the new casualty. I help her remove the guy's shirt, all the while thanking the heavens for that meeting my husband went to. This could have been him. Knowing that Drago wasn't caught up in this attack is the only thing that kept me from losing my shit the last half an hour.

"Oh, and the boss is back," Beli says on his way out.

My hands still on the wounded man's shirt while a sinking feeling forms in the pit of my stomach.

Chapter
Twenty-Two

Drago

I STEP OUT FROM THE COVER OF A TREE AND AIM MY GUN at the man crouching by the fountain. The bullet hits him in the back of his head, blood spraying the white marble. I'm going to annihilate every motherfucker who dared to attack my home and family.

My eyes jump to the last window on the top floor. The lights are out, just as in every other part of the house. Sienna is probably freaking out, but Adam said he left Tara with her. That knowledge helps subdue my anxiety somewhat. I almost lost it when I received that second signal from Relja and narrowly avoided crashing into a semi when I floored the gas pedal.

Even outnumbered, my men have done a good job fighting off Bogdan's guys. Most of the attackers are dead, their bodies littering the lawn and paved surface around the abandoned vans. A few are still alive, trying to keep themselves hidden and waiting for an opportunity to flee. Well, not happening. I've already ordered to have the gate secured, and Filip is there with three of our guys, ready to finish off anyone who tries to escape.

Deep growling sounds on my right as I head to the mansion. I glance in that direction and find Perun and Zeus tearing
at a man wearing tactical clothing. There is enough light to see
matching satin bows around my dogs' necks. Orange today.

A smile breaks across my lips. It means my wife dressed
the dogs after I left. She likes to coordinate their bows with
what she wears. My sparkling little bundle of joy, who's so
much more than anyone sees at first glance. Jesus fuck, I'm a
goner for that woman.

The rumbling of a vehicle makes me look back toward
the mansion. Beli is parking a van next to the kitchen door.
Adam exits the house, holding one of my guys in a fireman's
lift. Iliya and Jovan follow, supporting Relja between them. I
grit my teeth. Fucking Salvatore Ajello. I can't stand that man,
especially knowing he made Sienna spy for him. I wish I could
have told him to shove his offer to have my men treated at his
hospital, but unfortunately, we both knew there was no way I
would refuse. And I'm certain he's going to find a way to cash
in his favor. With interest, no doubt.

Beli jumps into the driver's seat and pulls away, maneu-
vering between the Romanians' vehicles and the dead attackers, and heads for the compound gate. Getting rid of all the
bodies and the vans is going to be a pain in the ass.

Their guns at the ready, Adam and Jovan approach the
carnage, the bulk of it amassed before the front doors, checking out the dead. Iliya, meanwhile, heads toward the back of
the house.

"Did you find Bogdan?" I ask as I approach.

Adam shakes his head. "I got a glimpse of him earlier, so
he was here for sure. Jovan is checking out the backyard. I'll
call the gate and see if maybe they got him."

"I want everyone on alert until his body is found."

The gunfire has ceased, and it looks like we're finally done
rounding up Bogdan's men, thank fuck, but I'm not calling it

finished until I see the motherfucker's corpse with my own eyes.

With one last glance at the bodies lining the driveway, I head toward the garage to check if some of the bastards are hiding there, but out of the corner of my eye, I catch a reflection of shimmering turquoise blue. My head snaps to the side, zeroing in on the figure standing in the kitchen doorway. The power has been restored inside the house, so I can clearly see my wife, in her mermaid leggings, staring at me. A relieved sigh leaves my lips upon seeing her unharmed and well. The next moment, however, I'm filled with rage. Was she there the whole fucking time, while bullets rained all around?

"What the fuck, Sienna!" I roar, cutting a path across the lawn and rushing toward her. I'm going to kill whoever is responsible for allowing her downstairs. "Get back inside. Now!"

She just keeps staring at me while a tear slides down her cheek. The look in her eyes, as they bore into mine, is of utter relief, and my rage dissipates immediately. She was worried about me.

"I said, get back inside!" I continue shouting, but she just smiles. What am I going to do with her? No one is allowed to ignore my direct order, but when it's her, I don't really mind. Damn it.

I'm only a few steps away when Sienna's eyes dart to the side, somewhere behind me. The smile disappears off her face, and is replaced with sheer terror.

It's not a conscious move. There is no rational thought, only pure instinct, as I turn on my heel, shielding my wife and facing whatever danger lies ahead. My gun is primed, the metal warm in my palm as I raise my hand, ready to neutralize the threat.

But I'm too slow.

A gunshot pierces the air.

Sienna

There are moments that you know will haunt you forever, even if you live a thousand years. Those moments fundamentally shake your existence, changing the trajectory of your life. The new journey before you is one you never saw coming. One you couldn't plan for. A path you've never seen. Whether karma or destiny, those moments are rarely of your own choosing.

Faced with one such moment, you know nothing will ever be the same. It becomes a nexus, a pinpoint in time where everything is thought of as "before" and "after."

I've already had two such instances in my life. When Arturo told us that our parents had died was the first. The second was when I found out my sister was gone, her fate unknown.

With every fiber of my being, I hoped never to encounter another such moment again.

When I saw a man step out of the garage, his gun raised and pointed at me, I froze. Even my lungs contracted, unable to draw in air, and all I could do was stare. The only part of me still capable of movement was my heart. It raced at triple its normal speed, pounding upon my ribcage.

Then, Drago's huge frame materialized before me. Instead of the gun, my eyes locked on my husband's broad back.

Bang!

My hand flies to my chest because, for an instant, I'm certain my heart ceased beating, pierced by a bullet at close range. Drago tenses in front of me. The gun slips from his hand and drops to the half-frozen grass at his feet.

Bang!

A scream builds inside me as I watch my husband fall to his

knees and slowly start listing forward. The moment stretches, and time stops.

Over the top of Drago's head, I see the man by the garage throw away his gun and reach into his jacket. Air rushes into my lungs, and with it, absolute calm.

Without thinking, I grip the Glock at my back. I forgot I even had it when the gunman's sights were aimed at me. Although, at that time, I'm not sure I would have taken it out had I recalled. All doubt is gone now.

The attacker is pulling another weapon from his jacket, swinging the barrel to finish Drago off. His choice. And I make mine.

My hand is steady as I lift my gun, and my breaths are even. I'm scarcely aware of the shouts coming from the driveway, growing louder, getting nearer. In a split second, I aim at the guy's head and, without a trace of hesitation, pull the trigger.

Bang!

The man jerks backward. A big red hole appears where his left eye had been.

I did that.

I killed him.

I've taken a life. And I don't regret it.

The gun falls from my hand, and then I'm running. To Drago, lying on his side on the cold, dead lawn.

"Baby." A strangled whisper leaves my lips as I drop down to the grass next to him and carefully roll him to his back.

The front of his shirt is saturated with blood. I grab the sides and tear it open, then press my palms over the two bleeding wounds on his upper chest. Despite my efforts in applying the pressure, the red liquid keeps seeping between my fingers.

There is a touch on my face as Drago's bloody hand cups my cheek. My gaze snaps up, my eyes lock with his.

"I thought you faint at the sight of blood," he says, his voice barely a whisper.

Shouts and the sound of running feet are getting closer, but I can't look away from him.

"Don't you dare die on me, Drago," I choke out while tears run down my cheeks. "Don't you fucking dare."

Hands grab me from behind, pulling me away. Iliya drops down next to Drago, pressing his bundled coat over the wounds on my husband's torso. He's blocking my view, and I can't see Drago's eyes. I snarl, kicking my legs, trying to get free. I need to have my eyes on his! For some reason, I'm convinced that for as long as I can hold his gaze, I'll be able to keep him alive.

A car pulls up beside us, and then Filip and Jovan are lifting Drago and laying him on the back seat. I scream. Howl. And bare my teeth. Strong arms hold me back, keeping me in place. A man's voice says something about me giving them room. I sink my teeth into his forearm, and a metallic taste fills my mouth.

"Jesus!" someone yells. "Let her go, Adam. She can ride in the back with him."

The moment I'm free, I rush toward the vehicle and climb inside. I kneel on the floor of the back seat and press my palms over Drago's hands while he's holding Iliya's coat to his upper body. My God, there's so much blood.

"Look at me!" I cry as the car lurches forward.

I'm not sure if he heard me, but his eyelids flutter open, and his green gaze meets mine.

"Good." I nod. "We're going to a hospital where they'll patch you up. And you're going to keep your eyes open the entire way there."

Drago moves his gaze to the top of my head, his eyes crease in the corners. "I should have known."

"Known what?"

"Orange bow. Like the dogs." He laughs, then breaks out in a cough, wheezing as he struggles for breath.

I press my lips together as a half laugh, half sob threatens to burst out of me. "I knew you'd love it."

My voice breaks, and I swallow hard, struggling to keep my composure and my balance. Whoever is behind the wheel seems to be driving like a maniac. I feel every bump, every curve in the road, the side of my head hitting the back of the passenger seat with every shift.

"I love every single thing about you, my glittery little spy." He turns his hand, entwining his fingers with mine.

"Even my chicken jacket?"

"Especially"—he takes a shallow breath—"especially your chicken jacket, *mila moya*."

I can't hold the tears at bay anymore, so I let them fall. "I love you, Drago."

A faint smile pulls at his lips. "I know."

His hand trails along my arm to my neck, pulling me down to whisper next to my ear. "I fell in love with you the moment I saw you in that dreadful gold onesie."

I close my eyes and press my lips to his. "Please, don't leave me."

The car screeches to an abrupt halt. The doors fly open, and people in medical scrubs lift Drago, putting him on a gurney. By the time I scramble out of the car, they are already bursting through the sliding doors of the hospital.

My eyes are glued on their retreating backs as I run, run after them and my husband. I'm not letting him out of my sight.

My blood-covered palms press to the glass as I stare at the doctors and nurses gathered around the operating table. One of the medical staff insisted on me staying in the waiting room, but I told her I'd kill anyone who tries to keep me away from my husband. She must have believed me because shortly after I was escorted to this small observation lounge. That was hours ago.

"He's going to be fine," a female voice says next to me.

"You don't know that," I croak, not bothering to look at the person who's spoken.

"Trust me. My mother-in-law has more experience with gunshot wounds than the entire emergency department of a New York City hospital." She taps her nail on the glass window. "She's the classy lady who's currently elbows-deep inside your husband's chest. Ilaria."

I steal a quick glance at the woman by my side. Milene Ajello. The don's wife.

"Last week, I saw her digging out a bullet from Pietro's thigh with her bare hands," she continues. "Sometimes, I really fucking hate this life, you know?"

"But you still married our don," I say, back to keeping my vigil over what's happening in the operating room.

"Yeah, well, he kinda threatened to start a war if I didn't." Milene's tone is serious, but in the reflection of the glass, I see her lips curl into a smile. "If I wasn't mad as hell at him at the time, I might have thought it was romantic."

I find it hard to imagine Salvatore Ajello being considered romantic. It's akin to calling a guillotine adorable.

"Does it ever get easier? Being scared all the time? Worrying that something bad will happen?" I ask.

"No. Not really." She wraps her fingers around my forearm and squeezes lightly. "It's how it is when you're in love with a dangerous man."

We both stare into the OR. They must be wrapping up. The frantic pace and urgency that enveloped the room when the surgery began has eased, and I decide it's a good sign.

"Would you like me to find you a change of clothes?" Another squeeze to my arm. "You're covered in blood."

"I'll ask Jovan to get me something," I say, keeping my gaze glued on Drago. With so many medical personnel around him, I can only catch a glimpse of his arm and legs.

Milene leaves, her footfalls echoing through the hallway as they recede. Inside the OR, the don's mother steps away from the operating table and takes off her blue surgical gown and gloves, throwing the garments into the trash can. She pulls down her mask next while addressing a nurse at her side.

When Ilaria looks up, our gazes connect through the window. My handprints mar the otherwise spotless glass. My husband's blood. So so much of it.

As Ilaria exits the room, heading in my direction, the panic I've been keeping under tight control swells. I take a step back and attempt to calm my heart rate as she opens the door of the observation lounge.

I hold my breath.

"He'll live."

My lungs expand as I inhale. The first real breath I've taken in the last four hours. Ilaria is saying something else—details of what was done during the surgery and the expectations for the recovery process—but I barely hear it as only two words are running on repeat through my brain.

He'll live.

 Drago

I FUCKING HATE HOSPITALS.

The smell alone brings up the worst of my memories. Glancing down at my side, my eyes fall on Sienna's sleeping form. When I woke up, she was in the bed next to me, her face snuggled into my neck while she held my upper arm in a viselike grip. She didn't even stir when the doctor came in earlier, rambling about my wounds. I cut the woman off the minute she started speaking and told her to return when my wife was awake. I don't care if she's Ajello's mother, no one gets to wake up my Sienna.

I reach across and brush back the few tangled strands falling over Sienna's face. I was a hundred percent sure I wasn't going to make it, but the idea of leaving her was unacceptable. So I clung to life by sheer will alone. If she hadn't been in that car with me, imploring me with her eyes to keep fighting, I probably would have been a goner before we arrived at the hospital.

The door to the room opens, and Adam steps inside. I press my finger to my lips, signaling for him to be quiet.

"Everyone pulled through," he says, but since I can't hear

anything, he's likely mouthing the words. "Relja has a nicked artery, but he's going to be fine."

I nod and switch my focus to the clear imprint of teeth on his forearm. "Did Bogdan's men resort to biting when they ran out of bullets?" I whisper.

"Um, that was your wife." He shifts his weight from one leg to another. "I tried to keep her back while the guys were loading you into the car."

Raising an eyebrow, I glance down at the angelic face tucked into my side. Little hellion.

"Bogdan?" I ask.

"Dead. Sienna shot him in the eye. I swear, if I hadn't seen it myself, I wouldn't have believed it."

Yes, my sparkling wife is capable of so much, we've just scratched the surface. I can't wait to spend a lifetime getting to know each of her graces.

"Tara and Keva are outside. Can I tell them to come in?" he asks.

"Nope. Tell them I'm fine and to drop by in an hour or so."

When Adam leaves the room, I look back at my sleeping wife. She's starting to stir awake.

"I heard you started biting my men." I lift my hand and stroke the line of her tiny nose. "Do I need to limit your playing time with my dogs, Sienna? They may be a bad influence on you."

Her lips quiver, and she squeezes her eyes shut. When she opens them again, tears are brimming her dark-brown depths.

"Watch my mouth very closely, Drago," she chokes out. "So you don't miss anything."

"All right."

"I had to keep my hands pressed over your maimed chest so you wouldn't bleed out. Can you imagine how it feels to watch the love of your life dying in front of your eyes? Monitoring your every breath, wondering if it's going to be your last? If you weren't connected to a damn machine tracking your heartbeat right now, I would punch you in the face," she bites out while tears stream down her cheeks. "If you ever dare to pull this kind of shit again, I'm going to kill you."

I smile and tilt her chin up to place a kiss on her lips. "I must say, when I imagined the moment you'll finally confess that you love me, it didn't include death threats."

"It most certainly does." Her fingers stroke my hair. "I love you. But you already knew that."

I lean forward and nibble her lower lip. "Yes. I see you, my Sienna. I always have. Why was it so hard for you to say it?"

A small sigh escapes her, and when her eyes meet mine, they seem so sad.

"I've had this silly conviction that if I never acknowledge my feelings for you, you would be safe from harm," she says. "People I love often get hurt because of me."

"What are you talking about?"

"My parents. Asya."

"Your parents died when you were a child. There's no way you could have been responsible for their deaths. I *know* because I've been dealing with your brother for many years and looked into his background. *Mila*, your parents got caught in the crossfire and fell victim to the ambitions of a greedy man. The old Don of New York did shit all to protect his people. What happened to your parents and to your sister is not your fault. We already talked about that, baby."

A tear rolls down her cheek. "You almost died for me. You put yourself between me and—"

"No." I press my finger over her mouth. "That was my doing. I started this whole mess with Bogdan, and I'm responsible for the consequences of it all. You had nothing to do with that. Do you understand?"

"Then, can you please stop provoking people? I don't think I can go through this again, because every time I close my eyes,

I see you covered in blood." Her lips quiver. "I was so scared, Drago. I've never been so terrified in my entire life."

"I'll try my best." I trail my hand down her front and hook my finger on the waistband of her lime-green leggings. "But first, we need to wipe those images from your mind and replace them with something else."

Sienna's eyes flare. "You can't be serious."

"Do you want me in pain? Because from the moment I woke up with you snuggled into my side, my cock has been as hard as a fucking steel rod."

Her eyes travel down my exposed chest, past the bandages wrapped around my upper torso and my abs, and stop on the massive bulge in my boxer briefs.

"You'll have to be on top this time," I add.

Sienna pulls her bottom lip between her teeth, and the sight almost makes me snap. "I don't think it's a good idea, Drago."

"I said"—I take her chin between my thumb and finger and tilt her head to face me—"get. On. My cock." I put a bit more pressure into my hold. "Now, Sienna."

Her eyes never leave mine as she slides off her leggings and the orange panties that match her bow, then pulls my boxer briefs over my hips and thighs, exposing my throbbing cock. She throws one leg over my hips and, bracing her hands on the edges of the bed on either side of me, poises her core right over my hard length.

"This is beyond reckless," she mumbles. "What if you tear your stitches?"

Moving my hand to her pussy, I press my thumb over her clit, massaging it in slow, tiny circles. I don't fucking care about the damn stitches. I don't care about anything other than having my dick inside my wife. After everything that happened, the need to be joined in the most carnal way is impossible to ignore. Wetness coats my fingers, but I keep teasing her, watching her suck in a shaky breath.

"Say my name," I urge and pinch her clit.

"Drago," she moans, but I don't catch the full sound of it.

"Louder."

Her hair is falling over her face as she glares down at me. "We're at a hospital!"

"I said"—I pinch her clit again, harder this time—"louder."

"Drago!"

I let the sound wash over me, then slip my finger from her pussy and grab her waist, pulling her down. The mix of pain and pleasure hits me as she welcomes my length inside her inner walls. I feel the strain in my muscles and the pull of stitches on my skin, but I ignore the ache and sting and focus on the sight of my wife panting above me. So beautiful. And mine.

My cock isn't even halfway in her, and already her pussy spasms around it. She supports most of her slight weight on her arms. The little sparkly minx is being careful, trying to make it easier for me. Not happening.

Holding her waist, I lift her and then slam her down, impaling her. A groan rumbles inside my chest once I'm fully sheathed inside her sweet warmth.

"Drago!" Sienna gasps and tries to rise, but I keep her in place, marveling at the feel of being within her.

"Don't you dare get off my cock," I bark. "Now ride me, or I swear to God, I'll rip out these fucking tubes and pin you under me."

Sienna shakes her head and leans forward, leveling her face with mine. "You're a masochist, my love."

"I guess I am." I slam into her from below and one of the stitches gives away.

My name leaves Sienna's lips, a scream, probably, since I catch a part of it. I watch her as she rolls her hips, each move bringing me closer to the brink.

The door to the room suddenly flies open, and a nurse rushes inside. Yeah, it was definitely a scream. The woman's eyes bulge at the sight of us, her hand flying to her mouth in shock.

"Out!" I snarl. "Now!"

The nurse crosses herself and, turning on her heel, high-tails it out of the room.

"Drago," Sienna pants as she rides my cock. "Did someone just walk in on us?"

"Of course not, *mila moya*." I move my hand to her pussy and press my thumb on her clit. "Now, come for me, my sparkling star."

Sienna throws her head back, her body shaking as her muscles spasm.

"That's my girl," I groan and explode into her, all the while feeling a few more stitches break.

CHAPTER
Twenty-four

 Sienna

Two months later

"**S**EAT BELT FIRST, SIENNA."

Trying my best to keep my face serious, I strap myself in and place my hands on the wheel.

"You turn on the ignition here." Drago points to the button on the right side of the dash, then moves his hand to the shift lever. "We're in park now. You need to press the brake and gear into drive."

My resolve slips, and I feel my lips tilt upward. While I'm not a super proficient driver, I know very well how to start a car.

When I asked Drago to teach me to drive all those months ago, we weren't on speaking terms, and I was just looking for a way to spend some time alone with him. After everything that happened since then, it completely slipped my mind, until today.

Drago has been so stressed lately, going around with a scowl on his face, trying to catch up on all the work after spending weeks recuperating from being shot. So, after lunch, I decided it was time to do something fun and asked him to finally give me that driving lesson. And I conveniently withheld the fact that Arturo taught both me and Asya to drive when we were sixteen.

"Make sure you check the rearview and side mirrors before you pull out," he continues.

"Oh, I already checked my makeup. I'm good."

Drago narrows his eyes at me. "To make sure no one is behind or beside you, Sienna. Not to reapply your lipstick."

"Oh, sure." I chuckle. "How about we wash the windshield first? Where's that thingy that sprays water?"

"The windshield is fine as it is. Put your right foot on the gas ped—" He looks down at my feet. "Jesus Christ, Sienna."

"What?" I ask when his eyes meet mine, an incredulous look on his face. "You told me to put on comfy footwear."

"You're not learning to drive in four-inch heels."

"Why? These are my favorite boots. Super comfy. See?" I turn on the ignition, shift, and step hard on the gas. The car lurches forward.

"*Jebote*!" Drago roars and grabs the steering wheel. "Stop! Now!"

I ease off the gas and apply the brake, stopping just a foot from Beli's flower bed. "That went well, didn't it?"

Drago's eyes wrinkle at the corners as he watches me. His lips are pressed tightly together, as though he's barely containing a burst of laughter.

"Yes, it was fine, baby. Shift in reverse and back up a bit." He lays his hand over mine on the shifter and guides it into gear, then moves his palm to my leg. "Press the gas lightly."

"Okay." I drive to the starting point, but, on purpose, stop later than I should. The back of the car ends up inside a juniper shrub.

Drago cringes. "That's good." Quietly, he mumbles in Serbian, "*Keva ce glavu da mi otkine.*"

"Why would Keva rip your head off?"

"The car is hers."

"Why are we using Keva's car?"

"All the other cars are manual. Automatic transmission is easier for beginners," he says in a serious tone. "Let's try again, but slowly this time."

"How slow?"

He takes my chin between his fingers and brushes his lips on mine. "Slow enough so we don't kill anyone."

"All right." I smile and press the gas pedal just a tiny bit.

The car moves forward at a snail's pace, and Drago nods his approval. "Good. Now, just a little faster and try turning around at the end of the driveway."

We're moving at not even ten miles per hour, and he keeps his left hand on the wheel, surveying the driveway as if expecting me to swerve to the side at any moment and crash into the hedge of evergreens. I find it really hard to keep my composure, seeing him so focused on the task.

"It's okay, Drago." I smile and glide my hand over his on the steering wheel. "You can let go. I know how to drive."

"Of course you do." He nods toward the windshield. "Eyes on the road."

Sighing, I step on the gas.

"Sienna. Slow down, baby."

I keep a moderate speed for the next fifty yards, then circle the landscaped island in the driveway at the front of the house, twice, and then proceed to neatly park the car beside the garage.

"How was that?" I smirk. "Looks like I'm a fast learner."

Drago watches me through narrowed eyes, then grabs my chin again. "Who taught you to drive? Was it one of my men? I want a name."

"My brother taught me. Years ago." I tilt my head down and nip his thumb. "You needed to relax a bit. You work too much."

"And this is your idea of relaxation?" The tone of his voice is serious, but his lips curl upward.

I lean forward and nudge his nose with mine. "You had fun. Admit it."

"I quite enjoy your antics." He brushes the back of his hand down my cheek. "But I have a better idea for 'fun' and 'relaxation,' Sienna."

"Does it include riding with me?"

"It definitely includes riding." He pushes his seat back, then grabs my waist, helping me scramble over the center console and into his lap.

I'm reaching for Drago's zipper when I notice Filip coming up behind the car. "Crap. Filip is on his way."

"Just ignore him and he'll go away." Drago caresses my thigh, pulling my skirt up while nibbling on my lower lip.

Filip walks up to the passenger door and knocks on the window, then looks in and snaps his head to the side.

"Drago?" I pant as his hand slides between my legs, his fingers brushing my pussy over my wet panties, "I don't think he's leaving."

"Jesus fuck," Drago lowers the window and gives Filip a menacing glare. "What is it now?"

"You told me to let you know the moment I heard anything about the situation in Boston," the second-in-command mumbles. "Maybe I should come back later. You two seem . . . busy."

The warmth of a blush creeps into my cheeks, and I bury my face in Drago's neck.

 Drago

"Your skills of deduction are top-notch," I snap. Can't I get twenty damn minutes with my wife? "What happened in Boston?"

"Don Leone passed away," Filip says, his gaze pointedly focused on the roof of the car. I think we're making him uncomfortable. Good.

"He's been sick for years, so it was expected. Who's taking over the Family?" I pull Sienna's panties to the side and stroke her soaked pussy with the tip of my finger.

"Nera Leone."

"A woman officially running a Cosa Nostra Family?" My eyebrows draw together. "That'll be a first."

Sienna's warm breath fans my neck, and she shudders when I slide my finger inside her.

"Well, she won't be for long," Filip continues. "One of our informants just sent word. Someone put a hit out on her."

Figures. I would bet it's someone from her own Family. "What's the bounty?"

"Two million. And the Sicilians already took the job."

"Shit. When?"

"Yesterday." He shifts his weight from one foot to the other while his eyes wander everywhere except inside the car. "Should we let Nera know? So she can increase her security or whatever?"

"The Sicilians have a twenty-four-hour turnaround time. If they took the job yesterday, she's already dead." I slip another finger into my wife's pussy, enjoying the way her body trembles. "And if that's all you had to tell me, you better get lost, or you'll be dead, too."

"Got it." Filip turns on his heel and strides back to the house.

Repositioning my hold, I pinch Sienna's clit, then press on it with my thumb. Her grip on me tightens, her teeth sinking into the skin on my neck as she comes all over my hand.

"That was fast." I bury my nose in her hair to inhale her scent, nearly getting my eye poked with the decorative flower haircomb set at the top of her head. "Will you please stop buying hazardous hair accessories?"

Sienna giggles into my neck and wriggles her butt, grinding over my aching cock. I glide my palms over her sweet ass and grab the edge of her panties, tearing them up.

"Yellow?" I ask as I pull the lacy fabric from under her.

"Yes," she says while fumbling with the zipper on my jeans. "Your favorite color."

The moment my cock is free, I grab her ass cheeks and slam her down onto my throbbing dick. Sienna sucks in a breath and, cupping my face with her palms, touches her forehead to mine.

Most of the soft sounds she makes are lost to me, and I hate being robbed of the opportunity to hear her little moans and gasps as she rides me. But I can still feel her breath mixing with mine. The tips of her fingers as they stroke my face. The shivers that pass through her body. Every single thing she does makes my soul glow.

"Yellow isn't my favorite color," I mumble into her lips as I assault them with vigor. "You are, *mila moya*."

CHAPTER
Twenty five

Sienna

One week later

"**W**HAT'S SO IMPORTANT THAT YOU CAN'T stop looking at your phone?" I ask as Drago lowers his cell to the table for the tenth time in the last hour. "A business emergency?"

"Yeah." He nods and, nonchalantly, reaches for his coffee.

I narrow my eyes at him. "Mm-hmm . . . If there is an emergency, why are we still sitting in a restaurant, having a second cup of coffee after spending the whole morning buying me shoes?"

"Now you're complaining because I bought you shoes?"

"You insisted we come to the mall at seven, Drago."

I tried explaining to him that no mall opens before nine, but he wouldn't listen. The man basically carried me out of the house, stuffed me into his car, and left the grounds at breakneck speed as if someone was chasing him.

"Maybe I just wanted to enjoy a lazy morning with my wife." He shrugs.

"You're the worst workaholic there is. I'm amazed you'd

even know the meaning of 'lazy morning.'" I take a quick look at Drago's watch. Half past eleven. "And it's almost noon."

Drago's phone vibrates with an incoming message. He glances at the screen, then takes out his wallet and drops a few bills on the table. "We're heading back."

"So, you're not gonna tell me what's going on?"

"Nope."

I sigh and rise to straighten my dress. It's cute and orange, and has a wide lavender belt that matches the shade of the pretty open-toe boots Drago bought for me. "You're worrying me. Are you sure everything is—"

Drago's arm wraps around my waist, making me squeal in surprise as he lifts me. His eyes bore into mine as he holds me pressed to his chest while my legs dangle above the ground.

"Everything is fine, Sienna. But we need to hurry."

"Why?" I lightly nip his lower lip.

"You'll see."

I try persuading him to tell me what is happening as he carries me outside and across the parking lot, but he doesn't utter a word. His lips remain sealed during our drive as well, curled slightly into a self-satisfied, barely there smile.

"What's with the cars?" I ask when he turns onto the road that leads toward the mansion. Vehicles are parked on each side, and there are dozens of them. "Hey, that's Arturo's."

My husband just keeps driving as if he doesn't notice the myriad of cars that stretch all the way to the gate and beyond.

"Drago!"

"Yes, *mila*?"

"What's going on? What are all those cars doing here?"

"Sorry, baby. I didn't catch that," he says as we pull up to the compound entrance.

The gate starts sliding to the side, revealing a tunnel made of great flower arches that line the driveway to the mansion. I stare open-mouthed as we pass through, taking in the multitude of colorful flowers—big pink and red roses, lilies, daffodils, and many more, weaved into the branches of greenery that make up the structures and tied with wide silk ribbons.

Between the arches, I catch glimpses of two enormous white tents, one on each side of the lawn. The panels of the tents are rolled up, exposing long tables covered in bright-yellow tablecloths and flower arrangements. Elegantly dressed people are milling all around—inside the tents and over the grassy grounds—enjoying drinks and appetizers while waiters rush among them. There must be at least five hundred people, maybe more.

"Drago?" I choke out.

As the car comes to a stop at the end of the archway tunnel, just before the landscaped driveway island with a fountain in the middle of it, music suddenly blasts from somewhere to the left of us. Still in shock, my eyes find Drago, who's sitting with his arms crossed over the steering wheel, watching me with an amused smirk on his face.

"You said you'd like us to crash another *svadba*," he says. "So, here we are."

"But . . . but whose *svadba* is this?"

Drago leans forward and places his palm on my cheek. "It's ours, baby."

I swallow, trying to keep my composure. And I thought I couldn't love this man more than I already do. My lips are trembling so badly, I can hardly speak. "Why?"

"Because I know you wanted one." He slams his mouth to mine, then mumbles into my lips. "But no dancing on the table, Sienna."

I just smile. What kind of *svadba* would it be if the bride didn't dance on the table?

The thought leaves me as I once again get lost in my

husband. His taste, his scent, the feel of his palm as it slides to my nape, pulling me closer. I'm drowning in absolute bliss when a shrill, angry yell explodes to the right of us. I jerk back from the kiss and look through the open window, searching for the source.

A group of people gathered around something just outside one of the tents. I recognize Relja and a few others of Drago's men within the crowd, as well as Don Ajello and his wife who are standing a bit to the side.

"What the actual fuck," Drago mumbles and exits the car. I also dash out and trot after him, wondering what the hell is going on.

"You slimy Italian bastard!" Tara's shout comes from somewhere within the circle of onlookers. "How dare you come here after attacking my brother!"

"You should get professional help for your anger issues, lady," Arturo replies in an even tone.

"Oh, yeah? I'll give you a professional."

Several people take a hurried step back, exposing my sister-in-law in the middle of the crowd as she reaches for a platter of canapes on the nearby buffet table.

"Tara! Don't," I yell as I follow Drago at a run across the lawn.

I'm not sure if she hasn't heard me or simply decided to ignore my warning, because she launches the huge round serving tray toward my brother as if it's an oversized frisbee. Dozens of bite-sized hors d'oeuvres fly off the silver projectile, hitting the bodies and faces of people gathered around the scene while a makeshift weapon slices the air toward my brother's head. Arturo ducks at the last moment, and the platter ends up in the rose bushes behind him.

"Goddamned crazy woman!" he roars and lunges toward Tara who's already reaching for something else to throw. "Were you raised in a fucking jungle?"

Everyone around seems to be frozen in place, simply gawking at the commotion unfolding before their eyes. Even the music has died down, and I spot the band members leaving the raised platform stage and creeping closer to have a better look.

"Tara!" Drago hollers, closing in on her.

An evil smirk breaks across Tara's lips as she grabs an enormous jug filled with punch off the table. In an incredibly elegant move, my sister-in-law turns on her heel, the sides of her long pale-blue wrap dress flutter with the spin and reveal her long legs clad in lacy stockings that are held up by a set of garters in the same azure shade. Pink liquid splashes all over my brother's face and chest. Pieces of lemon cling to the lapels of his jacket and shirtfront.

Too late, but Drago finally reaches his sister. He throws her over his shoulder as she drops the glass jug and screams for him to put her down. Ignoring her outbursts, my husband proceeds to carry Tara toward the house. Meanwhile, I come up to Arturo, stopping before him. His hands are fisted at his sides, and he's fuming. I can almost imagine steam rising off his dampened clothes and skin.

"That nutcase needs to be locked away in a fucking asylum," he growls through his teeth.

I bite at my bottom lip to avoid bursting into a laugh and reach to swipe a lemon slice from his shoulder. "She's just a little protective. You're overstating."

"Overstating?" Arturo snaps as he passes his palm down the front of his designer-cut jacket that's dripping punch into a puddle at his feet. "Believe me, I'm not. Dear God, I pity the man who chooses to get married to that banshee."

I sigh. Family gatherings and holidays are definitely going to be interesting.

Milene

Several days later, New York.
Salvatore Ajello's penthouse

I take a sip of my lemonade, watching my husband over the rim of my glass. The TV is on, but he's been absently massaging my feet for the past ten minutes, not really paying any attention to the game. He's plotting, and based on the smug look on his face, it's nothing good.

"What are you up to, Salvatore?"

He tilts his head to the side, then lifts my foot to his mouth and drops a kiss on the tips of my toes. "Why do you ask?"

"You had that same look on your face when you decided to marry Arturo's sister off, planting her into the Serbian organization to spy for you."

"It was a clever plan." He nods and moves his hands to my other foot. "Too bad it hadn't worked out like I expected."

I barely contain the laugh that's threatening to burst out of me. He was so mad when Sienna kept feeding him random nonsense during her check-ins. Broken fridge and truck's carburetor issues my ass! "Yeah. Arturo is still pissed at you about that."

"He is. He's also become extremely brooding these past few months. Snapping at his subordinates at littlest of provocations."

"Maybe he's just lonely and doesn't know how to deal with it." I shrug.

"You think?"

"Definitely." I nod. "He's been taking care of his sisters for so long, and now, with both of them married, he doesn't know what to do with himself. Maybe you should arrange a marriage for him, too."

"That makes sense."

"What?" I nearly choke on my drink. "I was kidding."

"It would need to be someone who can handle him and all the shit he's been through. Not a meek Cosa Nostra princess who would look at him as if he's some kind of God. Arturo requires a challenge. Someone who won't dance to his tune."

"Jesus fuck. Can we just forget I said anything?" I shake my head.

My husband narrows his eyes at me. "I haven't forgotten a single word you've said to me from the moment we met, cara."

Yes. He has a memory of a damn elephant. "You can make an exception in this one instance."

"No. It's a brilliant idea. And I think I have a perfect woman in mind. They'll make a magnificent match." A corner of his lips curves upward. "Unless they kill each other in the process."

epilogue

Drago

Several years later

I CROSS MY ARMS OVER MY CHEST AND REGARD THE line of women standing in front of me, their backs to the garage wall.

"I thought we had an agreement, but it seems I was wrong," I say. "So, who was it this time?"

No one speaks. Their hands are clasped in front of them, all four looking guilty as hell. I take a step forward, coming to stand in front of my wife. She's wearing a blue silk jumpsuit, with silver hearts merrily spanning the material, and sky-high heeled sandals that match the glittery shapes.

"Sienna? Was it you?"

"Of course not, baby." She gives me one of her bright grins. "You know I would never."

Giving a nod, I move to stand in front of my eldest daughter. She's dressed in a matching jumpsuit to her mother's, but hers is green. "I didn't expect this from you, Alexandra."

"It wasn't me, Daddy. I swear!"

"Mm-hmm…" I move down the line to my middle daughter. She's gripping the hem of her frilly gold skirt, trying to keep her face serious, but it's as plain as day that she's barely containing her laughter. "We had a serious talk after you sprinkled the glitter dust all over the food in the fridge, and we established that some things are not meant for play."

She presses her small hands over her mouth, giggling. "But I didn't do it, Daddy!"

I shake my head. Having three daughters is a handful. Having daughters who are all a carbon copy of my wife certainly makes life unpredictable. And exciting. I reach out and adjust the decorative flower holding up Irina's ponytail, then turn and crouch in front of my youngest girl.

"Did you paint Daddy's bike tires pink, Dina baby?"

She bites at her lower lip. "Yup."

"And do you remember how we talked about that it's dangerous to go into the garage alone?"

"But I wasn't alone." She pouts. "Mommy was with me the whole time."

"Oh, she was, was she?" I throw a look at my wife who's pretending to be engrossed in her silver-painted nails. "So, Mommy helped you?"

"No. I did it all by myself. Your bike is all black, and I wanted to make it pretty." Her head bobbles with absolute certainty of her statement.

"Daddy uses the bike for work, Dina."

"I know." She smiles, looking all proud of herself. "Now you have the prettiest bike in the world! You can take it to your meeting and show your friends."

I imagine the looks on my men's faces when I arrive at an interrogation session on a bike sporting pink tires and sigh. At least, this time, there's no glitter on it.

"And your helmet will now match," she adds.

"My helmet?"

"Yes. Irina and Alexandra helped me put small butterfly stickers on it. They are pretty pink, too!"

Jesus Christ. "But no glitter?"

"That's only for the girls, Daddy." She scrunches her nose in disapproval. "Can we go to the kitchen now? Keva is making apple pie, and she promised she'd let us taste the filling."

"Then you should hurry, before Relja eats everything."

I watch my daughters run to the back door of the house, followed by three dogs wearing huge colorful bows around their necks, then straighten and face my wife.

"It wasn't you, hmm?" I wrap my hand around her waist and lift her against me, crushing her to my chest.

"It's only watercolor paint." She smiles. "It'll wash away."

"And the stickers?"

"That one was all girls. I'll try to peel them off with the nail polish remover."

"Just leave the blasted things." I dip my head and press my lips to hers. "How long will that pie keep them occupied?"

"Ten minutes tops. The apple filling is already done."

"Is it?" I smile.

Keeping Sienna pressed to my body, I reach for my phone with my free hand and dial Relja.

"Go to the kitchen," I bark. "Take the pie filling Keva had made and dump it in the trash. When she comes after you, just let her know she needs to prepare a new one and have the girls help her from start to finish."

Relja's hysteric babbling comes from the other side, but I just cut the connection and slip the phone into my back pocket.

"Keva is going to kill you both." Sienna snorts.

"Then I need to make sure our impending deaths aren't for nothing." I carry my wife inside the garage and hit the button to close the sliding bay doors.

I wonder if her panties match her shoes and the nail polish today.

The End

Dear Reader,

Thanks so much for reading Drago and Sienna's story! I hope you'll consider leaving a review, letting the other readers know what you thought of *Silent Lies*. Even if it's just one short sentence, it makes a huge difference. Reviews help authors find new readers, and help other readers find new books to love!

Here is the link to *Silent Lies Amazon page*
(scan the qr code)

For book extras (family trees, bonus scenes, and book art) visit by website:
www.neva-altaj.com

For blurb reveals and latest news (like free book days):
subscribe to my newsletter (just scan the code below).
No spam, I promise!

To connect with other Perfectly Imperfect readers
join my **FB ReaderGroup "Neva Altaj's Perfectly Imperfect Readers"** where you can share your thoughts, guess the MCs in the following books or just talk books in general.

Next in the series

The next book in the series is **Darkest Sins,** which follows Kai and Nera :D. It's a grumpy-sunshine, opposites attract, age-gap story with a stalker hero :D.

Nera
In a night of blood and death,
Fate brought us together.
I thought I was saving a life of an innocent man,
A man I'd never see again.
I was wrong.

A slight shift in air.
A glint of silver eyes in the darkness.
I may not see him, but I know he's there.
My angel of death,
Lurking in the shadows,
Watching over me.
Protecting me,
Before disappearing into thin air,
Until we meet again.

A man who took a bullet for me,
But he won't touch me,
Love me,
Or even share his name.

Kai

Darkness. Pain. Blood.
It's all I ever knew.
An empty shell of a human being,
No heart. No soul. No dreams.
Surrounded by death,
I was a dead man walking.

But then, the light shined through my darkness,
Breathing life into my lifeless soul.
My fearless tiger cub,
My only reason to keep living.

Every time I have to leave her in the light,
My black heart breaks and bleeds,
As I retreat to the shadows,
Where I belong.

I cannot change the past,
Cannot take back what I have done.
My darkest sin.

Here is the link to *Darkest Sins Amazon page*
(scan the qr code)

ABOUT THE author

Neva Altaj writes steamy contemporary mafia romance about damaged antiheroes and strong heroines who fall for them. She has a soft spot for crazy jealous, possessive alphas who are willing to burn the world to the ground for their woman. Her stories are full of heat and unexpected turns, and a happily ever after is guaranteed every time.

Neva loves to hear from her readers,
so feel free to reach out:

Website: www.neva-altaj.com
Facebook: www.facebook.com/neva.altaj
TikTok: www.tiktok.com/@author_neva_altaj
Instagram: www.instagram.com/neva_altaj
Amazon Author Page: www.amazon.com/Neva-Altaj
Goodreads: www.goodreads.com/Neva_Altaj

Made in the USA
Monee, IL
03 January 2024